WILD FIRE

Acclaim for Radclyffe's Fiction

Finders Keepers "is a delightful slow-burn, enemies-to-lovers romance…It also has puppies—six adorable, bright eyed, floppy eared, soft and cuddly puppies. I admit it. I'm an absolute sucker for sweet, furry baby animals. Add them to a romantic couple in a story, and I'm hooked."—*Rainbow Reflections*

Only This Summer "is an absolute must-read for anyone who enjoys a well-written lesbian romance novel…A law enforcement officer with a penchant for trouble meets a doctor who is desperate to get away and find some modicum of peace…What I've found is typical in Radclyffe's storytelling is the depth and complexity of the characters. They are richly drawn and fully realized, making it easy to invest in their journeys and root for their happy endings." —*station12reads*

"Radclyffe writes fantastic books. They are easy to read, well-paced, with relatable and realistic characters. I find [the *PMC Hospital Romance*] series particularly fun to read because Radclyffe was a practicing surgeon before turning full time to writing, so the medical storyline reads so well. Her stories tend to be a slow burn with lots of flirting and tension building and a spicy, well-written, realistic payoff at the end…I really enjoyed that the 'rivalry' [in *Perfect Rivalry*] was more of an ambitious respect for another—so, not enemies to lovers but more cranky to inseparable."—*rubiareads*

"After seven books [in the *Rivers Community Romance* series] about the lives and loves in this small town, I do admit that I am starting to wonder if there may be some pheromone that lures unsuspecting, brilliant, handsome/gorgeous, brooding/plucky lesbians into town where they get sucked into the Rivers hospital community…All that [in *Pathway to Love*] with smoldering chemistry between the mains as well as lots of action in the ER/OR and the bedroom. But, hey… these are Radclyffe novels. And I get sucked into each and every one of them."—*MEC for TBR Reviews*

"Medical drama, gossipy lesbian romance, and angsty backstory all get equal time in [*Unrivaled*], Radclyffe's fifth PMC Hospital Romance…[F]ans of small community dynamics and workplace romance without ethical complications will find this hits the spot." —*Publishers Weekly*

Praise for Julie Cannon

Shut Up and Kiss Me

"A feel good, tingly romance."—*Best Lesfic Reviews*

"Fast-paced, sexy, and fun with a bit of an insta-love plot (a trope I love!) I thoroughly enjoyed this read."—*JK's Blog*

"Great story, and I will definitely read this author again!"—*Janice Best, Librarian (Albion District Library)*

Wishing On a Dream—Lambda Literary Award Finalist

"[The main characters] are well-rounded, flawed and with backstories that fascinated me. Their relationship grows slowly and with bumps along the way but it is never boring. At times it is sweet, tender, and emotional, at other times downright hot. I love how Julie Cannon chose to tell it from each point of view in the first person. It gave greater insight into the characters and drew me into the story more. A really enjoyable read."—*Kitty Kat's Book Review Blog*

"This book pulls you in from the moment you pick it up. Keirsten and Tobin are very different, but from the moment they get together, the heat and sexual tension are there. Together they must work through their fears in order to have a magical relationship."—*RT Book Reviews*

Smoke and Fire

"Cannon skillfully draws out the honest emotion and growing chemistry between her heroines, a slow burn that feels like constant foreplay leading to a spectacular climax. Though Brady is almost too good to be true, she's the perfect match for Nicole. Every scene they share leaps off the page, making this a sweet, hot, memorable read."—*Publishers Weekly*

"This book is more than a romance. It is uplifting in a very down-to-earth way and inspires hope through hard-won battles where neither woman is prepared to give up."—*Rainbow Book Reviews*

By Radclyffe

Innocent Hearts

Promising Hearts

Love's Melody Lost

Love's Tender Warriors

Tomorrow's Promise

Love's Masquerade

shadowland

Turn Back Time

When Dreams Tremble

The Lonely Hearts Club

Secrets in the Stone

Desire by Starlight

Homestead

The Color of Love

Secret Hearts

Only This Summer

Fire in the Sky

Wild Fire

First Responders Novels

The Honor Series

The Justice Series

Midnight Hunters (writing as L.L. Raand)

PMC Hospitals Romances

Provincetown Tales

Rivers Community Romances

By Julie Cannon

Come and Get Me

Heart 2 Heart

Heartland

Uncharted Passage

Just Business

Power Play

Descent

Breakers Passion

I Remember

Rescue Me

Because of You

Smoke and Fire

Countdown

Capsized

Wishing on a Dream

Take Me There

The Boss of Her

Fore Play

Shut Up and Kiss Me

The Last First Kiss

Summer Lovin'

My Secret Valentine

Fire in the Sky

Wild Fire

Visit us at www.boldstrokesbooks.com

WILD FIRE

by

RADCLY*f*FE AND
JULIE CANNON

2024

WILD FIRE

ISBN 13: 978-1-63679-727-4

THIS TRADE PAPERBACK ORIGINAL IS PUBLISHED BY
BOLD STROKES BOOKS, INC.
P.O. BOX 249
VALLEY FALLS, NY 12185

FIRST EDITION: OCTOBER 2024

CREDITS
EDITOR: STACIA SEAMAN
PRODUCTION DESIGN: STACIA SEAMAN
COVER DESIGN BY TAMMY SEIDICK

Acknowledgments

Writing never gets "old," nor does the pride and pleasure of knowing that someone, somewhere, is enjoying what I've written. So thanks to all for reading and/or listening. Thanks also to Julie Cannon—collaborator extraordinaire Stacia Seaman for exquisite editing, Paula Tighe for the first read and insightful input, and Sandy Lowe for the ideas, inspiration, and expertise.

—Radclyffe

My thanks to Rad and all of the wonderful women at Bold Strokes Books that made this book, and every book, as good as it can possibly be. And thank you to the readers who make the solitary work of writing our stories a pleasure.

—Julie Cannon

PROLOGUE

The only sound was her own breath rasping through the soot-coated fabric of the neck gator covering her mouth, an eerie cocoon of silence surrounding her that had the hair on her sweat-coated neck and arms standing up. Riley peered right and left, checking on her crew. Her stomach clenched. The shadowy silhouettes of the firefighters who had fanned out to either side as they cut and cleared the line downhill from the advancing front were barely discernible smudges in the smoke haze now. The sky had long since disappeared, the forest canopy obscured by roiling clouds of ash.

She mentally visualized the map of the terrain and the position of the fire's last known direction. If the wind had shifted, the front might have veered down the south side of the mountain range—away from their location. That might account for the sudden silence. Another look overhead. The blanket of smoke hung motionless, no sign of headwinds strong enough to divert the front.

Her spine tingled and every nerve ending burned with tension. Something was...not right.

Her crew. Her call. Her ass in a sling if she was wrong.

She tugged the radio from the shoulder of her Nomex jacket, already keyed and open to the channel of her six-member crew.

"Ranger crew 2-8, evacua—"

The roar of a freight train barreling down the mountainside on a wave of searing heat struck her like a tornado and tore the words from her throat. Deafened, momentarily disoriented in the blackout, she shouted into her radio, "Blow-up! Evacuate or cover. Mayday. Mayday."

The flames, like the exhalation of an ancient fire-breathing beast, rose above the forest, topping the tree line, igniting the world surrounding her. Her fire-retardant gear grew so hot her skin burned beneath the protective layers. Air so scorching her lungs burned.

No time, no escape.

Riley shouted as if they would somehow hear her over the thunderous roar. "Deploy your shelter. Now!" She kept calling out, desperate to reach them. "Get together, on your stomachs. Get your tent under your feet and over your heads. Wrap up in a cocoon."

"Is everybody good?"

"Is everybody good?"

"Talk to me!"

When she couldn't wait any longer for a response, she ripped her fire shield free and deployed the tent, crawling beneath it as the ground around her crackled and singed. With her last gasps of breathable air, she prayed for the first time in her life.

Please save my crew.

CHAPTER ONE

Is it true?" Elizabeth Sutton said by way of greeting when Olivia answered her phone.

Olivia Martinez closed her eyes on the Manhattan nightscape outside her high-rise condo and sank into the plush cushions of her cream wool bouclé sofa. So much for hoping she'd have some time to process. News traveled fast—all the way to the ass-end of the universe, apparently. "Would it work if I said I didn't want to talk about it?"

"Would it work if I got on a plane and showed up to kick your butt?"

Olivia smiled wryly at the image on her phone of her former boss and best friend. Elizabeth's tanned, makeup-free skin glowed, her blond hair caught back in a messy ponytail, her azure eyes sparkling. Obviously, married life agreed with her. "Who told you—not my mother—please tell me not my mother."

"Ah, no. Was it that bad?"

"I've had worse—but I can't remember when."

She still hadn't really recovered from *that* conversation, or the look of incredulity and, worse, barely concealed disappointment on her parents' faces at dinner earlier that night. Canceling the weekly dinner hadn't been an option. Her mother always spent the entire afternoon every Sunday after church making her signature dish and Olivia's favorite of *pepian de indio*—cutting up chicken, adding spices to the tomatoes, tomatillos, and other vegetables, and simmering the sauce for hours.

Olivia *had* to go to dinner, and keeping the news from them wasn't an option. Plus, she *so* sucked at lying to her parents.

"So," she'd begun not too elegantly, scooping another helping of spicy sauce and chicken onto her plate, "I've quit my job."

Her father, seated at the head of the table as he always was in a white shirt and impeccably pressed trousers—Sunday attire—very carefully put down his fork and stared at her from beneath dark brows out of even darker eyes filled with instant concern. "Why? We didn't like how you traveled all over the world for months at a time so Elizabeth could build new resorts, but we thought you were happy there."

That hadn't been easy to explain.

Her father had been teaching at the same college for almost thirty years. He'd begun as a janitor despite having been a college teacher in Guatemala, had completed his equivalency certification requirements at night in the States, and now was a tenured professor in the engineering department. His loyalty to his family, friends, and the college was unswerving. Her mother had waited until Olivia was in middle school to begin teaching English as a second language and had gotten her social work degree simultaneously. Steadfastness, dependability, and adherence to tradition defined her parents.

So…no way was she telling them *all* the details. Not about the almost instant harassment she'd endured when she'd returned to the Manhattan offices of Sutton Properties after spending seven months in Wickenburg, Arizona. Seven months as Elizabeth's exec and right hand, go-to, all-around gal Friday while Elizabeth headed the project to turn a dude ranch into the newest property in the ever-expanding portfolio of Sutton Resorts. Seven months when she'd secretly counted down the days until she could leave the hot, dry, venomous-creature-infested desert and return home.

Home to Manhattan. Where she had lived since she was four years old, where she had a small handful of close friends with whom she enjoyed all the city had to offer, and where her parents were. From her first memories, her immigrant parents had been her staunchest supporters—teaching her as a child that she could do anything and be anything she desired. Even moving their small family from Texas to Manhattan, where they could provide her with the education and social options to succeed. She loved sharing her life with them, despite the constant, unspoken, yet in-her-face pressure to get married and have babies. At thirty-six, she was at the point in her life where she couldn't see spending more than a few dates with anyone, let alone the forever connection of a child.

She'd come home from Arizona, but everything at Sutton had changed without Elizabeth. A new job description, a new boss, and a whole lot of resentment that she'd retained many of her connections to those in management even after having been assigned to a remote outpost for the better part of a year. Those connections hadn't helped her put a stop to the verbal abuse or the rumors her new boss had spread about her, but when he'd put his hands on her, she'd had enough. Her parents didn't need to know the ugly details of that—she'd handled it, as they'd taught her to do. After the obligatory fact-gathering by HR, the matter was closed with a twelve-page settlement agreement and a very high six-figure amount, contingent upon her resignation. As if she'd want to work there any longer.

She'd carefully concentrated on her meal and stuck to the truth—most of it. "It was just time to move on. It wasn't the same, not working for Elizabeth."

Her mother shot her father a glance—that silent communication Olivia recognized as her mother letting her father know she wasn't happy about the turn of events. She'd seen it before when they'd been trying to understand why their daughter would trade living in an upscale condo in Manhattan, the city that never sleeps, for a small town in Arizona that rolled up its sidewalks at night and barely rated a mark on a map.

"What now, then?" he asked.

Excellent question—and one she needed some time to consider. That's what she'd been hoping to do when she'd finally escaped her parents after convincing them she'd be fine. Not to worry.

"I know it wasn't your father who told you I left," Olivia said to Elizabeth. Two weeks before the grand opening of the reimagined Red Sky Ranch and Resort, Elizabeth had had a major falling-out with her father. Jonas Sutton was a magnate in the high-end resort and spa industry with thirty-two first-class properties around the world. He was also a first-class son of a bitch. When he'd threatened to shut down the project, Elizabeth outmaneuvered him, for which he was likely never going to forgive her. But now the Red Sky Ranch and Resort was hers.

Elizabeth laughed—a low, smoky sound that Olivia realized she'd missed terribly in the months she'd been back. "We are not speaking. It was Marilyn. She thought I should know—and I should. *You* should have told me. What happened?"

Olivia told her what she hadn't told her parents—only realizing as she did how much she needed to share the story and let it be done. To wash the anger, the pain, and the loss away.

"That little prick," Elizabeth seethed when she'd finished. "Did you hire a lawyer? I hope to hell you put his puny little balls in a vise."

Olivia laughed, and God, it felt good. "I didn't need to resort to threats or much of anything—there were texts. And I have to say, more than one person ready to verify my story. No one in HR or higher up wanted a mess on their hands. The settlement was fair, so—"

"Bullshit—there's no way to make that fair."

Elizabeth's anger warmed her. She could always count on Elizabeth.

"Okay—you're right. But I could at least leave without worrying about how I'd eat. And I know the amount stung." She still felt a little whisper of pleasure knowing she'd won. Even if she had no idea what the hell she'd do next.

"As it should have." Elizabeth took a breath. "So—what now?"

The question of the day.

"I'm considering my options."

"What would they be exactly?"

Olivia laughed again. "God, I've missed you."

"I've missed you, too. It's hell trying to get through all the paperwork without you."

"Mm, I'm sure Kelsey is helping," Olivia said softly. She and Elizabeth had been friends since middle school, when she'd discovered Elizabeth couldn't understand their reading assignments. Her parents had taught her that helping others was part of being a good person, and she'd taken it upon herself to help Elizabeth. Elizabeth had the ability to remember everything she heard, and Olivia had spent hours reading their assignments out loud. As for college, Elizabeth's parents would accept nothing less than the college of *their* choice. Elizabeth wouldn't go without her, and Olivia had been fortunate to get a partial gymnastics scholarship. Her parents had worked hard to provide her with the rest. When Olivia had asked her to come work for her at Sutton Properties, Olivia didn't hesitate. As Elizabeth's admin, she briefed Elizabeth on project details and anticipated what information Elizabeth would need before every meeting. The exorbitant amount of money Elizabeth paid her notwithstanding, Elizabeth was her best friend, and she loved her job. Of course, all that changed when Elizabeth left Sutton Properties and Mr. Grab Ass became Olivia's boss.

"Kelsey is a lifesaver," Elizabeth said, "but she's got a full plate handling the trail hands, the outdoor guest events, and the livestock."

"You need a good personal assistant."

"Who I need is *you*," Elizabeth said. "Come back. You know there's a job here for you. And I've got an offer you can't refuse."

Elizabeth had asked Olivia to stay and manage the resort once already, but Wickenburg was not her idea of a place she would ever choose to live. Sixty miles northwest of Phoenix, the town had a population of around seventy-five hundred, another thousand or so scattered around in various farms and ranches, and more multilegged—or slithering—desert inhabitants than residents. Olivia had grown fond of the staff at the ranch and had met others in town she enjoyed—a quick image of one such resident with wind-tousled, light brown hair and piercing green eyes flashed through her mind—and she shook her head at the distraction. Reality check here. Remote desert life, far from the excitement and cultural energy of the city—and from her parents—was not for her.

"The last time you said something like that to me," Olivia said, "I ended up in the desert in the middle of the summer for what felt like forever."

"Hey, it was only seven months, and you had the time of your life."

"If you call being covered in dirt, chased by dust devils, and finding desert creatures in my shoes the time of my life, you need to get out of the sun. Your memory is affected. Why do they call them dust devils anyway? More like a mini tornado in the middle of nowhere."

"Being a bit dramatic there, Olivia? It couldn't have been more than a little whirlwind." Elizabeth's smile contradicted her words. "Besides, tornados come out of the sky. Dust devils come up from the ground. Thus the name dust devils."

"Tomato, *tomato*," Olivia replied, with an exaggerated English accent for the second *tomato*. "Anyway, now that you've heard the story from me—and not that I don't love seeing your smiling face and hearing all about your hot sex life with your new wife—tonight is just not a good time. My parents were a bit shell-shocked about the job thing, so they neglected to hound me again about having grandkids, but they should be back to that soon. As to the hot sex I'm *not* having, I'm in a bit of a dry spell and don't want to think about it. I have to *have* sex first to be able to pop out kids, and neither one of those is happening anytime soon."

"You need to come work for me," Elizabeth repeated.

"What I need is a good orgasm or ten by someone other than myself." Olivia groaned, reminding herself to add batteries to her Amazon order.

"Anyway," Elizabeth went on as if Olivia hadn't already said no in a dozen inventive ways, "as I was saying, I *need* you to come work for me. It's not like you have a job lined up, plus you'll be bored to tears in a week—at most."

"I am not moving to Wickenburg. I can't think of six good reasons to do that, let alone one—okay—two, after seeing you. I really do miss you." Like a part of her. They'd been each other's confidante, ally, support system, and on occasion, conscience for twenty years.

"I miss you, too," Elizabeth said softly. "I love Kelsey more than I ever thought possible, but part of me is lost without you. You've always been my person."

"Damn it," Olivia whispered, tears thickening her throat. "Why couldn't you have fallen in love with someone in New York City?"

"Because we don't get to choose love? It chooses us, I think." Elizabeth took an audible breath. "Besides, I can think of a few reasons for you to come back—in addition to the many challenges and the excitement of running this place *and* working with me on a few more projects I have in mind, there's a certain hunky item I seem to remember you dancing with more than once at my wedding, for starters."

Olivia's stomach gave a little hitch. Riley Mitchell of the green eyes and buff body. Six months ago when she'd returned to Wickenburg for Elizabeth's wedding, she and Riley had spent most of their time together during the four days she'd been there, helping with wedding details and rehearsing their parts. Riley had stood with Kelsey at the service, as Olivia had with Elizabeth. In the months since she'd been back in the city, she'd thought of the energy between them when they'd danced more than once, especially on her infrequent dates when heat had been distinctly absent.

"Who said anything about moving?" Elizabeth asked when Olivia didn't take the bait and mention Riley.

Olivia wasn't going there. Riley was delicious to look at and sexy in the extreme, but she was not dating material. Besides being Elizabeth's wife Kelsey's best friend—and therefore not someone to get involved with, as Olivia had seen how tangled those situations could get—*extreme* personified Riley Mitchell. From the little Olivia had seen of Riley, she played hard and liked life on the edge. The compete opposite of Olivia.

"Working for you is not a telecommuting position," Olivia said.

"Am I that high maintenance?"

"You said it, not me." Elizabeth would know she wasn't referring to her dyslexia—helping Elizabeth navigate the volumes of paperwork and prospectuses involved in the projects Elizabeth headed was just part of Olivia's job. What had challenged her had been Elizabeth's relentless drive to succeed—not just succeed, but to do more, be better than anyone else in her position. That had often meant dragging Olivia halfway around the world for weeks and months on end in high-profile, high-pressure situations. Not her natural comfort zone, but she had to admit, often exciting.

"Like you're not a pain in my ass," Elizabeth shot back.

"Then why do you want me back? Does your ass need kicking?"

When Elizabeth laughed, Olivia realized again just how homesick she was. Not for a place. For her friend.

"Because the Red Sky Resort is expanding," Elizabeth said in a tone she rarely used, solemn and deadly serious, "and I can't do it without you. Come out, work, and see what happens."

CHAPTER TWO

Jesus, Riley, ease up." Kelsey Brunel wiped a tanned, muscular arm over her sweat-covered forehead. Her dark, always unruly hair stuck out in all directions, and her damp T-shirt clung to her solid frame. "It's racquetball, not World War Three. You're killing me."

Riley Mitchell readied her next serve. Kelsey might be her best friend, but a game was a game—why play if you don't plan on winning. She'd learned that lesson early in life from growing up in a house full of men. Brothers who showed her no mercy in sports, in games, hell, even in competing for the best grades in school. They'd taught her with a few bruises, a little mockery, and a lot of example that if she was going to do something, she'd better be the best at it. "Married life is making you soft."

Riley fired the serve at the front wall and Kelsey lunged to return it as it shot back across the service line.

"Nah," Kelsey gasped as they rallied, "but the regular sex…might mellow…you out. You should…try it."

"Who wants mellow?" Riley said, aiming for the side wall and a low bounce off the front. Kelsey missed the return shot, and Riley grinned. "Just for that comment, though, I'm going to show you no mercy."

"You're already cleaning my clock. I've seen no mercy," Kelsey said.

Riley served out the set, and they headed to the locker room.

"I'm really glad Elizabeth added the courts," Riley said after stowing her gear in her locker.

"You mean after she built an indoor sports facility?" Kelsey shook her head. "I argued against it at first—who wants to be inside when you can be out riding the trails or hiking in the most beautiful countryside in the world?"

Riley laughed. "City people, for one. Besides, the indoor courts are perfect when it's too hot outside for the guests to play tennis. And seeing as how I'm your best friend, I get to play for free."

Kelsey chuckled as she pulled on a dry navy-blue polo with the ranch's crest on the chest. "Well, I have to admit, she was right. About this, the indoor pool, and the golf course—and hell, just about everything. The ranch hasn't lost anything—it's just grown better."

"Can I tell her you said that?"

Kelsey just smiled. Riley recognized the look. Married *did* look good on Kelsey. Not anything she wanted for herself, but some people wanted that kind of responsibility. That commitment. She preferred her relationships to be a lot less complicated.

"Speaking of changes," Kelsey said, "Elizabeth's starting a new project. And cooking up ideas for more."

"Oh yeah? What's she going to do?"

"Stay for dinner tonight, and she'll likely talk your ear off about it."

"You know I never turn down a home-cooked meal, especially when it's here."

"Must be because you're either eating at the firehouse, in one of the restaurants in town, or out of a box," Kelsey said.

Riley couldn't argue. Why cook for one? Even if she wanted to, she was so rarely home she'd never get to eat the leftovers. "Let me grab a shower."

"I want to check with the fitness trainers and see how the schedule looks," Kelsey said. "I'll be in the front office."

"Five minutes," Riley said.

The shower took her three. Living most of the time in a fire station or bunking in the field with other firefighters had taught her to be quick with personal matters. She hadn't planned on staying around after her sets with Kelsey and hadn't bothered to bring a change of clothes, but her uniform was clean enough. She pulled on the dark pants and long-sleeve navy-blue T-shirt with the WFD logo sewn on the left chest and sat to lace up her regulation black jump boots.

She joined Kelsey and walked out into a wave of desert air, warmer than usual for February. The sports complex, as the hand-painted wooden sign beside the crushed stone walkway indicated, stood at one end of a meandering half-circle of buildings spread out over three acres of rolling land dotted with cacti, mesquite trees, and clumps of brittlebush and other low-growing plants. The ranch house and main office stood at the center of the semicircle, with the horse barns and corrals off to one side and the guest casitas on the other. The new buildings of red stone and natural wood kept the rustic sensibility of the original dude ranch. Past the recreation facilities, the winding path led to the guest casitas. Kelsey and Elizabeth had remodeled one of the more secluded ones to give them privacy and some distance from the guests after they married.

Elizabeth greeted them as they walked inside to the rich aroma of spices and peppers. "Perfect timing. Dinner is just about ready."

Riley's mouth actually watered. "Smells great. How the hell do you have time to cook?"

Elizabeth smiled and brushed a strand of honey-blond hair from her cheek. "I *helped*."

At Riley's raised brow, Elizabeth laughed. "I warmed up the tortillas just now. Charmaine sent down the rest of dinner from the main kitchen a few minutes ago. We're getting her chef's special along with the guests tonight. I just opened a bottle of wine, but there's cold beer if you want it."

"Thanks," Riley said. "Beer works."

"I'll get it," Kelsey said and kissed Elizabeth swiftly as she passed.

The change in Kelsey still caught Riley off guard now and then. Until Elizabeth, Kelsey had been pretty much a loner—like her. Not a player, maybe, but never serious about a woman either. And always carrying a shadow of pain in her eyes. Kelsey and Elizabeth had met almost two years before and married six months earlier in a simple ceremony at the ranch. The shadows in Kelsey's eyes were gone now, replaced by a light that damn near blinded. Riley was glad for her. Not that marriage and forever were anything she chased after for herself or even believed possible.

"Did you win?" Elizabeth murmured.

Riley grinned. "It was close."

Elizabeth linked her arm through Riley's, the casual contact strange but…nice. "Spoken like a true friend. Come sit down and relax."

Riley followed Elizabeth to a table big enough to seat six in an alcove adjoining the well-equipped kitchen. The view overlooked the undeveloped rolling land crisscrossed with horseback trails that gradually rose to the foothills at the base of the Black Hills mountains.

When Kelsey brought in the food, Riley only half contributed to the casual conversation as she ate, comfortable knowing her friends were used to her silences. When she'd sated the first wave of hunger, she said, "This is great, as usual. I'll have to stop by and ask Charmaine to marry me."

Kelsey laughed. "Get in line."

"You eat like it's your last supper," Elizabeth said teasingly.

"For me it might be," Riley said automatically and instantly regretted it when Kelsey and Elizabeth stared. The easy banter they'd shared over dinner disappeared in a cloud of tension so thick Riley could see it. In a tone she hoped was light enough to convince her friends she hadn't been serious, even if she had been, she added, "What? It might be the last good meal I have for a long time. I live and eat at a firehouse, remember?"

Some things she didn't discuss, even with friends. Especially not friends who couldn't know the risks that came with her job—no one could who wasn't on the job. So explaining that she was mentally and tactically prepared for death was not only impossible, it was unkind to even try. Hell, why burden the people she cared about? She'd known the odds of being seriously injured or even losing her life when she'd signed on, and certainly had that made clear in training and on the job. So she lived every day as if it might be her last and didn't give the future much thought. Her personal life and finances were not complicated, and she'd completed all the necessary arrangements and paperwork should any of a dozen unforeseen events happen during a callout. No one knew better than her how quickly situations changed in an active burn.

"So, ah," Riley said, hoping to defuse the tension, "Kelsey mentioned you had some new projects cooking."

Elizabeth's eyes gleamed. "A couple."

Kelsey laughed.

"What's first?" Riley reached for her beer—her first and only, since she was driving. "Planning a concert arena?"

"Arena yes—but not for people," Elizabeth said. "Or I should say, not just people. We're expanding the stables and building an indoor riding arena. Along with a jump course—eventually."

Riley glanced at Kelsey, whose expression was hard to read. Riley would have expected Kelsey to be against anything that diminished the rustic appeal of the ranch. A dude ranch was about the *outdoor* experience. Trail rides, overnight camping, hikes, nature walks. "Sounds…uh, interesting."

Elizabeth laughed. "We already give lessons with the trail rides, and an indoor ring will let us expand that part of the ranch experience for some guests who are more comfortable trying something new in a familiar setting. That's just for starters."

"I'll bet." The idea made sense, but then Elizabeth's ideas usually did. "When do you start?"

"As soon as the new project manager gets here."

Riley frowned. "You're bringing in someone from the outside?"

"Not exactly," Elizabeth said slowly, her gaze intent. "Olivia is going to head the project."

"Olivia?" Shocked, Riley tightened her grip on the Hop Knot can. Worried she might crush it, she slowly relaxed her fingers and gently set it down. She didn't bother asking *Olivia who?* There could only be one Olivia—the Olivia who had spent seven months in Wickenburg over two years ago and one brief, four-day stopover months later that Riley still hadn't forgotten. The five-foot-tall, wavy-dark-haired, gorgeous Olivia Martinez of the quick wit and sparkling deep brown eyes who laughed easily and would go to battle to protect Elizabeth.

"She's coming back?" Riley asked.

"Mm-hmm." Elizabeth refilled her wine glass and gestured to Kelsey. "Babe?"

"I'm good," Kelsey said, watching Riley.

"Why?" Riley said.

Elizabeth tilted her head. "Why what?"

"Why is she coming?" Riley was pretty sure she was speaking English, but Elizabeth looked at her as if she wasn't.

"She's going to manage this place—thank God," Elizabeth said. "We need her."

"I thought she hated it here and couldn't wait to leave?" She'd known from pretty much the start that Olivia would be leaving as soon as she could, and since Olivia hadn't indicated any interest in women, Riley'd kept everything on the friendly level. Still, she thought of her. Olivia was hard to forget. Since Riley hadn't expected to see her again, she hadn't tried to forget her. She'd never met anyone who'd captivated her from their first encounter—and not just because she was beautiful, smart, and sexy. Olivia exuded energy and…steel. Like she'd face any obstacle without fear. Riley envied her that.

"What can I say?" Elizabeth asked playfully and shrugged. "I have outstanding powers of persuasion."

Kelsey leaned over and kissed her wife. "That I can definitely attest to."

"Some things are just meant to be." Elizabeth smiled. "Besides, she didn't really hate it here. She's just not a small-town girl, so the... pace...took some getting used to."

"I would've said the same thing about you," Kelsey said.

Elizabeth took Kelsey's hand and kissed her palm. "True, but I found a reason to stay that was far more exciting than Manhattan. Olivia will be fine. When she commits to something, she's all in. In a few weeks, she'll be too busy to miss the city."

"Good that everything is working out, then." Riley drained her beer and pushed her chair back. "I've got an early shift. I ought to get on."

Kelsey stood. "I'll walk you out."

"Thanks for dinner," Riley said to Elizabeth.

"Make it sooner next time," Elizabeth called.

The sun had set, and moonlight flooded the hills with silver as Riley stepped out onto the wide plank porch, Kelsey at her heels.

"I know the way," Riley muttered.

"You okay?" Kelsey asked.

"Why wouldn't I be?" Riley strode along the stone path toward the small lot by the stables where she'd left her truck. She'd worked a grassfire the day before, had only a couple hours' sleep, and then spent the morning inspecting the site for a new construction at the fairgrounds for the county. Tired maybe. That's all the heavy feeling in her body and the weariness tugging at her was about.

"I kinda thought you looked a little unhappy about Olivia coming back."

"Why would I be?"

"I dunno," Kelsey said. "That's why I'm asking, considering you've got a little thing for her."

Riley stopped and shot her a look. "What the fuck? I don't have a thing for her. I hardly know her."

Kelsey huffed. "That's bullshit. You've talked with her a dozen times out here when she worked with Elizabeth, and—"

"That was work." Riley started walking. "I don't mix work with women."

"And," Kelsey said, keeping pace, "you spent the day on the boat with her, had dinner with her—"

"That was a group thing. Let up," Riley griped.

"*And* then a fair amount of time dancing with her at the wedding reception. *Not* a group thing. Besides, I know the look."

Riley pulled her keys from her pocket, unlocked her truck, and tossed her gym bag onto the front bench seat. "There is no *look*. I'm not looking for anything more than simple and easy. That is not Olivia Martinez."

"True." Kelsey laughed. "If you say so."

"I say so." Riley slid into the truck and looked out. "Let me know when you want to get your ass kicked on the court again."

Kelsey shot up a finger as Riley pulled away. She sighed as she drove off the ranch and headed home on the empty two-lane that wound through the desert. Kelsey wasn't entirely wrong. She wouldn't call how she felt about Olivia *a thing*. A thing usually involved wanting to get a woman into bed—to share some up close and personal time, naked. To scratch the itch—to discover what it was about that particular woman that heated her up and made her hungry.

Sure, she wouldn't say no if Olivia suddenly appeared naked in her room. Who but a corpse would say no to a woman with Olivia's body, her face, her smile? Not that Olivia had ever given any hint she was interested in going there. And that was probably—definitely—for the best. Olivia was too complicated to be a thing. She wasn't someone to bed for a week or month and then laugh and say thanks when the heat died down. Olivia would leave her scorched and simmering like a fire smothered for air, just waiting to explode. Fuck, no. Absolutely not a thing.

Sure, seeing her when she'd been in town for the wedding had been…good. Different than the times they'd been together before. Olivia had been more relaxed than when she'd been neck deep in the takeover of the ranch, and Riley had looked forward to just hanging out with her—discussing the wedding, grabbing lunch together, talking a little about how they spent their days. Maybe there'd been a little something new percolating between them that was different than when Olivia had first arrived. Maybe their eyes held a little longer when they looked at each other, and maybe her pulse *had* raced a little when she first saw her every day. And yeah, all right, she had a hard time concentrating at the rehearsal dinner with Olivia sitting beside her and smelling so damn fresh and delicious. She sure wouldn't forget the way Olivia felt when they danced any time soon either—like Olivia intended to melt right into her body as they pressed together.

But forget her she had—mostly. Olivia had left, as Riley always knew she would. Hell, she'd dropped her off at the airport, hadn't she?

The day after Elizabeth and Kelsey left for their honeymoon, she'd driven Olivia to the airport, expecting that to be the last time she saw her. Oh, Olivia might visit now and then—after all, she was Elizabeth's BFF—but that would only be for a few days. Not enough time for a vacation fling. And where TF had that thought come from anyhow—as if Olivia had even shown any interest. Talk about getting way ahead of what was in front of you.

Saying goodbye had been a lot harder than she'd expected, though. The ache in her chest and smiling like this being the last time she ever saw her didn't hurt had been tough. Luckily, she'd had years of hiding what hurt.

She'd hefted Olivia's suitcases from the truck as a redcap waited to pile the luggage onto a cart, saying as she set them on the curb, "Hope you have a good trip."

Olivia's touch on her arm drew her gaze up, their eyes met, and she froze. Couldn't look away. Olivia was a good eight inches shorter, but as Riley straightened, Olivia had no trouble stretching up until their eyes were level. Riley froze. She could've sworn Olivia intended to kiss her right there on the departure curb.

Olivia's arms came around her shoulders, and she hugged her. Olivia's breath whispered across her neck, soft and warm. "Take care of yourself, Riley."

Ambushed by the flush of heat that spread through her, Riley had struggled for words. Olivia kissed her cheek, turned to the redcap standing a few feet away, and disappeared with him into the crowded terminal. Riley had stood staring until the blare of a horn jerked her back to reality. She'd jumped into her truck and pulled out into the crawl of vehicles in front of the terminal.

She'd driven home on autopilot, wondering what the hell had just happened. She caught sight of her face in the visor mirror and touched the remnants of Olivia's lipstick adorning her cheek.

Like Olivia, the faint mark was long gone, but Riley could still see it in her memory.

CHAPTER THREE

Olivia stared out the window as the plane began its descent into Phoenix. Everything she knew about the city came from her go-to research source, Google. The city sprawled in the center of the Salt River Basin, the Sonoran Desert defining its southern margins and rings of towering mountain ranges with equally colorful names rising in the distance. Despite having lived in Wickenburg for the better part of the year, she still saw the desert as an alien landscape, the absence of green the most striking bit of disharmony. Even though she lived in a steel and concrete jungle, she frequently escaped into the eight-hundred-plus acres of Central Park to stroll beneath leafy green trees amidst flowering bushes, myriad flowering plants, and numerous ponds home to birds and turtles. She never failed to feel lighter after a brief time lost in her wanderings. Here, the flora and fauna were foreign and, to her mind, often dangerous. She wouldn't call herself an animal lover, having been raised without pets due to her parents' busy work schedules and her gymnastics training schedule, but she liked them. Cats and dogs and bunnies. Not so much things that slithered and crawled and howled at night.

On her first sighting, she'd thought the strangeness of everything—the land, the climate, the inhabitants—only temporary, that her stay was only temporary. And as much as she had complained about the heat and the dust and the dangers of desert living, she'd secretly had to admit there was beauty, too. Sunrises so exquisite she'd lose her breath taking in the bursts of flaming orange, red, and gold over the purple ridged mountains, bathing the land in fire. And on those rare occurrences when it rained, life bloomed everywhere, cacti bursting with flowers as if they had been hiding their beauty until just the right moment. And even some of the animals she found unexpectedly interesting, especially the amusing, ubiquitous long-eared jackrabbits and the majestic big-horned sheep she'd seen from a distance when Kelsey and Elizabeth had talked her into a trail hike. But she drew the line at things without legs. Not interesting, amusing, or anything she needed to see ever again.

The plane dropped through the cloud cover and the city jumped into view, that bit at least familiar. This time, though, her expectations were distinctly different. Before she'd been a visitor. Now she wasn't sure what she was. An itinerant worker, a *locum tenen*, filling in until Elizabeth found someone full-time? That suited her. She could put this hasty and not altogether rational move out here into the mental box she could live with. One job, just like before, with a beginning and an end. Of course, this time she didn't have anything to return to, at least as far as jobs were concerned, and that made this beginning filled with trepidation.

She took a deep breath. Well, she was here, and she'd have a job to do, and she wouldn't be alone. She had friends, or at least acquaintances. She liked and admired Kelsey, respected the hard-working staff and trail hands who'd chosen a difficult, often dangerous life for the freedom it gave them. She'd always been a loner, in her deepest reaches. She had Elizabeth, the one person in her life other than her parents who had always been there. The one person she trusted more than any other. Other than Elizabeth, no one really knew her.

And then there was Riley, whom she had distinctly avoided thinking about as she'd tidied up her affairs the last few weeks, leasing her condo yet again, spending as much time as she could with her parents, and packing away much of her wardrobe. Riley didn't fit neatly into her category of friend or acquaintance. She'd spent more time with Riley than anyone other than Kelsey and Elizabeth during the months she'd been there, but she didn't exactly have *friend* feelings for her. She didn't think of her other friends with the same twist of anticipation she often did when she knew she'd be seeing Riley, and she certainly didn't dance with her other friends in the same way. Her skin heated at the memory. She couldn't even blame too much champagne for dissolving the barriers she usually kept firmly in place. She'd only had one glass. She had no explanation for the way she'd relaxed into Riley's arms as they'd danced, or for the way that Riley's hand spread firmly over her lower back had left her breathless. No explanation she cared to look at too closely, at least.

As soon as the wheels touched down, she put all thoughts of Riley and dancing out of her mind. She hurried through the arrival area, found a porter, and pointed out her luggage. Once again she followed a stranger pushing a cart with all her worldly goods and stepped out into the bright sun. She blinked and fumbled on her sunglasses. No one with any sense spent any time outside in this climate if they could help it, and certainly not without sunglasses. She'd never understand why anyone stepped out of air-conditioned spaces—something hard to come by on a dude ranch—unless they had to. Unfortunately, considering the work she was about to do, she wouldn't be able to avoid it. Something else not to think too hard about.

"Olivia!"

Hearing the familiar voice, Olivia's nerves instantly settled. She spun around into the crushing arms of her best friend. She took a few seconds just to enjoy the rush of relief and joy before prying herself out of Elizabeth's grasp. "Hey, it's only been a few months since you saw me. Turn me loose, I can't breathe."

"It's been forever, and I can't help it if I've missed you."

Elizabeth still gripped her shoulders with a smile Olivia suspected mirrored her own. Elizabeth practically glowed, looking relaxed and... happy. Olivia had seen Elizabeth in every situation from tense to celebratory, especially when a big project came to a successful end, but she'd never seen her look quite like this. Elizabeth's newfound life and love with Kelsey had changed her. Olivia acknowledged the twinge of envy—who wouldn't have just a hint of jealousy at seeing something so special—and quickly put it aside. Growing up, she'd dreamed of finding that kind of love—the love she saw in her family—but as time passed and she never felt that special connection, the dream gave way to the reality of her life. A life she enjoyed and accepted.

"We're in Lot E just across the way," Elizabeth said, handing a ticket to the parking valet, and after a mercifully short wait, Olivia settled into the front seat of Elizabeth's SUV.

Her flight had landed mid-morning, local time, and traffic around the airport and on the interstate was light. Twenty minutes later they turned off the highway onto a much smaller feeder road that would take them to the Red Sky.

The view out the window abruptly changed once they were beyond the sprawling city limits. Only an occasional vehicle passed them headed for the metropolis. Flowers bloomed in vivid blues, yellows, and apricot along the road, and patches of bright green dotted the red-brown desert sands. White flowers topped the arms of majestic saguaro cacti as they traveled the two-lane road, passing signs for places aptly named Vulture Mine, Calamity Wash, and Dead Horse Trail.

"It sure looks a lot prettier than the first time we came," Olivia said.

"We got here in the beginning of summer," Elizabeth said. "All the spring flowers and blooms were on their way out. We're just heading into spring now, an absolutely beautiful time of the year in the desert."

"You really don't miss Manhattan, do you," Olivia said softly.

"I don't," Elizabeth said after a moment. "I don't miss the crowds, and the rush, and the pressure to win everything, everywhere, all the time. I don't miss my father subtly reminding me that his love was conditional while he favored the ass-kissing, walking penises he surrounded himself with." Elizabeth laughed and shook her head. "I can't believe I still care, damn it, but not as much anymore." She glanced at Olivia. "I miss you every single day, but you're all I miss."

"They *are* a bunch of penises with feet," Olivia said, making Elizabeth laugh, but she fought a wave of sadness, too. She'd never actually envisioned a future without Elizabeth—seeing them working and sharing adventures for years to come. Oh, she'd imagined shadowy *others* in the picture—lovers and friends, but she'd never foreseen one of them uprooting, leaving Sutton, leaving everything they knew behind. No, she couldn't do that. Even if she had left Sutton and was now rootless, too. Her chest tightened. Manhattan was home, and home was everything.

As they passed signs for Lake Pleasant, she remembered the lazy afternoon she'd spent out on the lake with Elizabeth. Kelsey and Riley had joined them, and she'd had her first Jet Ski ride, her arms around Riley as they flew from crest to crest, the cool spray drenching them both.

"Did you and Kelsey have a chance to get out on the lake last summer?"

"A time or two—the ongoing renovations at the ranch kept us pretty busy all last year."

"I hope you had a chance to repeat your tryst out on the boat," Olivia said, teasing a little.

"Tryst?" Elizabeth asked, not even pretending to not know what Olivia was referring to. "You still favor those Regency romances, don't you."

"Yes, when I have time." Olivia laughed. "How about tête-à-tête? Work better for you?"

"That sounds like a parlor game. I remember every time Kelsey and I *tryst*, as you call it." Elizabeth flushed. "The boat might come to mind, since you asked."

"I'm glad."

Elizabeth looked her way, then back at the road. "About what?"

"That you're happy."

"I am. I never thought I'd find someone I'd even think of spending the rest of my life with, and certainly not in the middle of the desert."

A tingle of longing skittered through Olivia, surprising her. A forever person for *her* had not featured in her shadow future.

"What about you? Seeing anyone special?" Elizabeth asked, surprising her again. As close as they were, one thing they never discussed was Olivia's intimate life—as in sex life. She didn't offer, and Elizabeth didn't ask.

"No, no one special." Actually, that would be simply no one. No one interested her, and at this point in her life, she wasn't interested in going through the motions of trying to find a spark.

"I bet Eddie and Consuelo aren't real happy about that."

"That's putting it mildly. Good God, they act like it's the nineteen-thirties and a woman is not complete without a husband and a brood of kids."

"Did they say that?"

"No, but I can feel it. They left Guatemala and most of their family so their children, i.e., me, could have a better life. They've never said as much, but I know that's what they want for me—a better life that includes children. That clock is ticking louder and louder every day. When I broke off my engagement to Brian, I thought my dad was going to have a stroke and my mom disown me."

"It's not that bad," Elizabeth said. "They've always supported you professionally."

"You're right. They've always accepted what I've decided to do in the end." Olivia sighed. "But I know they *think* I'd be happier with a traditional life, like they have. It did take some convincing for them to accept that Brian did not make me happy. They thought it was just cold feet on my part." She shuddered. "The thought of *Brian's* cold feet in bed every night was not something I looked forward to."

"They just want what's best for you." Elizabeth paused. "I suppose I'm just projecting because no one in my family ever cared what was best for me. I'm sorry you're getting pressured."

"No, you're right. They love me, and I love them for it, but our ideas are different. Really," Olivia said, "can you see me with spit-up on my shoulder? Besides, the whole childbirthing thing is a little terrifying."

Elizabeth stifled a chuckle. "I'm sure plenty of women feel the same way, but the species does go on."

"Yeah," Olivia mumbled, "and it can just go on without my help."

Thankfully, Elizabeth gave the whole topic of parents and babies a rest. As they approached Wickenburg, signs of civilization returned—first scattered ranch houses set far back from the road at the end of single-track dirt-packed lanes, inevitably with corrals filled with horses, then a convenience store with two gas pumps out front, and finally the network of paved streets signaling the outskirts of town.

"What happened to the Farmer's Daughter?" Olivia sked when they passed a blackened lot where the dairy bar and restaurant had been. "I loved their ice cream!"

"You love all ice cream," Elizabeth said. "It burned down since you were here last. Everyone in the county is hoping they rebuild."

"Oh, that sucks. I hope they do. They have to have insurance, right?"

Elizabeth shrugged. "Should have. I guess the insurance company is waiting on the fire investigation report."

"Oh," Olivia said, her pulse oddly jumping. "Right. I guess Riley would be doing that."

"I'm sure she's involved," Elizabeth said absently, slowing for a trio of kids biking in the road. "She's the county fire inspector, plus she was one of the fire department first responders."

Riley rarely talked about her work—at least she hadn't to Olivia when they'd spent time together during her last visit. Neither of them had actually gone into anything very personal, sticking to safe subjects like the changes at the Red Sky and the million and one details about the upcoming wedding.

"How is she doing, besides working hard?" Olivia hoped her question sounded casual. For some reason, what should have been a natural question to ask about a shared acquaintance seemed terribly revealing, as if she was admitting to something she'd wanted to keep secret.

"Oh, Riley is Riley," Elizabeth said, turning off on the new bypass the town had approved to help traffic flow out to the Red Sky. "She works hard, plays hard." Elizabeth glanced over. "You didn't keep in touch? I thought you two were getting friendly."

Plays hard. What did that mean? A girlfriend—or several? And what if that was true? Hardly her business.

"We texted a little after I got home this last time." She'd gotten a few butterflies of anticipation each time a text appeared, which was silly now that she remembered. "But you know how that goes—we're both busy. We just sort of drifted."

"Well, you can catch up soon. She ought to be at the ranch when we get there."

"Oh," Olivia said, her heart pounding again. "That's…nice."

Elizabeth scoffed. "You don't have to pretend you're not interested with me, you know. I've never breathed a word, not even to Kelsey."

Little steel shutters clanged down, setting her defenses securely in place, and Olivia asked, considerably cooler now, "Interested?"

"Listen," Elizabeth said, turning in beneath the twenty-foot-high, arched gate announcing the Red Sky Ranch and Resort, "I know we don't discuss the minutiae of your sex life, but I do have eyes. And I seem to remember you describing her as H-O-T the first time you saw her and making some remark about her throwing you over her shoulder if you ever needed rescuing."

"And I remember saying that in jest *and* that I was simply observing she was attractive."

"One of God's finer specimens," Elizabeth muttered.

Olivia groaned. "How could I forget that you never forget anything you've heard."

Elizabeth's near-total recall of auditory input was what allowed her to be so successful despite her difficulties reading. If Olivia read her a ten-page proposal summary, Elizabeth could recall every word months later.

"You have to admit, you like her. You spent most of your free time with her the last time you visited."

Olivia could count on one hand, as all she needed was one finger, the number of times she'd shared the details of her sex life with Elizabeth—not because she didn't trust her, but because nothing about her very occasional one-nighters on a business trip bore repeating, which was a sad statement in itself. She *had* told her about the one time in college when her hormones had gotten the better of her brain and she'd jumped into bed with Sadie MacIntyre in her dorm room. Her parents had shown up unexpectedly and nearly walked in on them naked and…well. Trying to explain why she didn't more actively pursue relationships with women led down the twisted path of parental and religious conflicts. Not something she really wanted to get into when there was no good reason to. She was fine with the physical outlets she had. She just didn't care to relive them in the bright light of day.

"I can *like* someone without being *interested*," Olivia said.

"Yes, you can." Elizabeth pulled into the small lot for staff beside the main house and turned to look at Olivia. "But if you *were* interested, there's nothing wrong with that."

Olivia completely disagreed, especially where Riley was concerned, for an easy half dozen reasons. "I'm really glad to see you, even if you are a major pain in my butt."

"I love you, too," Elizabeth said as several of the staff came down the path with a luggage cart. "Let's get you settled and go find us some hot cowhands."

Olivia could only laugh. Elizabeth knew her better than that. And so did she. Hot cowhands of any gender were not on her to-do list.

Chapter Four

"Ouch, damn it." Riley yanked off her work glove and stuck her thumb in her mouth. "That hurts."

"If you keep missing the nail with that hammer, you might actually manage to break your finger," Kelsey said.

"It's fine," Riley muttered. Ordinarily she liked working outside, no matter the project, and she'd promised Kelsey a week before that she'd help her build a shed behind the barn to store the overflow horse tack. After the night she'd had, she probably should have canceled, but pride and friendship wouldn't let her. "Just clumsy."

Kelsey raised a brow. "Since when? You're always dead on with a hammer. Did you take another extra shift again?"

"Nope," Riley said. "And before you ask, no, I did not go to the bar. I fell asleep in front of the TV and didn't sleep very well."

All true, except the reason for her restless night had been more due to the therapy session than the night on the sofa. That usually happened after an hour with Dr. Townes. She'd complained once that the department-mandated quarterly counseling sessions were supposed to help prevent anxiety but were more like riding a roller coaster in the dark. Destination unknown.

Dr. Townes had merely nodded with a sympathetic smile and said, "That sometimes happens. Your brain is still sorting out the feelings that might have come up during our talks. As time goes on, and you resolve some of those concerns, you'll have less carryover."

Unlike many of her fellow firefighters, Riley didn't mind the sessions that the department required for all the first responders. The brass believed that getting in front of any potential psychological issues was far more effective than dealing with them once they arose, and Riley had more reason than most to agree. The nightmares that sometimes followed kicked her ass, though. Last night had been one of those nights. For some odd reason, she never had the nightmares when she slept at the fire station, and like everyone else working twenty-four hours on, she managed to get enough sleep between calls to function. If she ever sensed she wasn't a hundred percent, she'd relieve herself of duty. No way would she be anything but totally prepared, both mentally and physically, for her job. Lives depended on her. Her chest tightened, and she quieted her mind, shutting down the memories, a technique she'd been working on with Dr. Townes. "I'm good. Let's get this sucker done so we can eat. You promised me lunch, remember?"

"Okay. Just don't want you to damage any of your love tools." Kelsey wiggled her fingers and moved her eyebrows up and down.

Riley snorted. "I haven't thought of that since I was fifteen—and I'd rather keep it that way."

"How are things keeping, anyway?" Kelsey said, lifting another board into place for Riley to nail in. "Since I'm not around to help you out, are you managing to find your own company?"

Riley placed a nail and drove it home with one swift strike. She pulled another nail from her tool pouch and set it beside the first. "I've been managing to find my own company for twelve years or so. I just let you come along to give you pointers."

Kelsey laughed. "Right. So, anyone new?"

"Nope," Riley said in a tone she hoped shut down that topic. Kelsey's comment immediately brought Olivia to mind. Ever since she'd learned Olivia was coming back to the Red Sky, she'd been thinking about her. Her feelings about seeing Olivia again were all over the place. Part excitement, part frustration. She knew better than to contemplate getting something on with a straight woman, which she figured Olivia was. Most people were, right? Olivia hadn't sent any kind of signal she was interested in anything physical, and Riley was experienced enough to know. Sure, she could push a little—try a little more pointed flirtation and a little seduction—but that wasn't really her thing. She didn't want to seduce anyone. She wanted a woman to desire her as much as she desired them, even if it was just for a night.

"I can still get away for a night, you know, help you out," Kelsey said.

Kelsey was joking and Riley knew it. "Thanks, but I can get what I need when I need it."

"Good enough." Kelsey set her hammer on a stack of plywood and gestured toward the path down from the main building. "Speaking of getting what you need, look who's here."

Riley carefully finished nailing the section she was working on. She rose just a little unsteadily before turning to look. Olivia and Elizabeth skirted the paddock, heading in their direction. Olivia wore a loose, long-sleeved light tan shirt tucked into wide-legged flowing trousers a shade darker and another pair of those ridiculous-for-the-desert sandals that still looked sexy despite being useless. Her gleaming, jet-black hair was sleeked back and tied at the back with an orange and green scarf affair. A few wisps of hair had gotten loose and floated against her neck. She had a long, lethally beautiful neck. Riley couldn't see her eyes beneath her designer shades, but she didn't need to. She remembered the exact mahogany color and the small flecks of gold around her irises. Riley swallowed and winced. Her throat was just dry from being out in the damn sun for hours, that was all.

"I thought you said she was due next week," Riley croaked.

"Did I forget to mention she got all the arrangements done early and decided to come out?" Kelsey said, her focus riveted to Elizabeth.

Exasperated and struggling to keep some kind of cool when her insides were a jangle of anticipation, Riley muttered, "Yeah, you forget that little detail."

Kelsey didn't reply, if she'd even registered their conversation, but stepped forward and wrapped Olivia in an exuberant hug.

"You look great. How was your trip?"

Olivia laughed, her arms slipping easily around Kelsey's shoulders as she returned the hug. "The best part just happened. Hi, yourself."

Riley watched their effortless connection, unwelcome butterflies skittering around her insides. She could have sworn her cheek tingled in the spot Olivia had kissed her that one and only time. Olivia removed her shades and turned her way with a warm smile, her eyes sparkling. Riley should probably say something, but her throat was still dry, her mind blank.

"Hi," Olivia said, searching Riley's face.

Her voice was as smooth and sexy as Riley remembered, too.

"Hey, there." Riley cringed. For someone known to have a pretty good game, she was coming off like a loser now. She tried again. "You look terrific."

Olivia tilted her head, a bit of a question in her eyes. "Thanks."

"I thought you weren't coming until next week." Riley wanted to throttle herself. What a way to make a woman feel welcome. "Sorry, that didn't come out right. Great to see you again."

"You, too." Olivia regarded her tentatively.

What? Why was she suddenly acting like she'd never seen a beautiful, sexy, knock her breath out woman before? Maybe because she hadn't—not like Olivia.

Kelsey nudged her, and Riley's brain started working. She took a step closer and opened her arms. "Welcome back."

With a brief look of relief, Olivia met her halfway and hugged her.

Olivia *felt* even more amazing than Riley remembered, Olivia's body meeting hers with soft warmth in all the right places. A perfect fit. Olivia's hands drifted lazily up and down Riley's back, squeezing her tighter. She smelled amazing, too, a subtle blend of vanilla and spice. Riley inhaled, closing her eyes for a second, stunned at the calm that enveloped her. When Olivia tensed, she stepped back, releasing her. "Sorry. I'm sweaty and probably smell worse than the horses."

"I like the way you smell." Olivia frowned, one hand trailing down Riley's arm. "You've lost weight, though. On purpose?"

"Ah—yeah, I guess. I mean, I've been busy." Self-conscious, Riley blurted, "If I'd known you were coming, I would've cleaned up."

"No need. You're fine the way you are."

Riley had a hard time looking away from Olivia's intense gaze. She had plenty of practice flirting. But was that what was happening? Or was it just wishful thinking?

Kelsey cleared her throat. "What do you say we take this reunion up to the house, have a drink and some lunch?"

"Great idea," Olivia said, waiting for Riley to join her as Kelsey and Elizabeth started back.

"It's good to see you," Riley said, instantly realizing she'd already said that. Hurrying on, she added, "I was surprised when Elizabeth said you were coming out to work on one of her projects."

"Me, too," Olivia said.

Riley relaxed as the tension twisting her brain and her vocal cords broke. "So how did you manage it? Some kind of leave of absence or something?"

"No, I quit Sutton."

Riley blinked. "Wow, I don't remember you saying anything about that when you were here last."

"It was…sudden." Olivia shrugged, an expression passing over her face Riley couldn't quite decipher.

Sadness? Or maybe just exhaustion after a long flight.

"Are you glad about the move?"

Olivia smiled, a smile Riley had a feeling took some effort. "Yes. It wasn't the same without Elizabeth there, and life is too short to do something you hate."

"I didn't realize you didn't like that job. I guess we never talked about it."

"Oh, it wasn't all bad. Everything changes, right?"

Riley grimaced. "Probably so. Anyhow, I know Elizabeth is psyched you decided to come back. I was surprised you said yes." Damn, it, she'd already said that, too. "Sorry. I'm just…I didn't expect to see you again. So soon. Today."

"I understand. I'm still a little surprised myself," Olivia said quietly. "But you've probably noticed, Elizabeth is very persuasive. Besides, I do have friends here, other than her, I mean. I hope I have friends here."

Olivia's gaze searched hers, and Riley said the first thing that came into her head. "You do. Me, for one. I was…sorry…when you left before. Why didn't you stay?"

"My life was…is…in Manhattan. And at the time, so was my job."

"Now what? Long term, I mean."

"I don't know," Olivia said. "I'm using this time to figure out what I want to do for the rest of my life."

"Here is a pretty good place for that," Riley said, adding hastily when Olivia shot her another questioning look, "to do that. Figure things out, I mean."

Olivia held Riley's gaze a moment longer. "Yes, I think you're right. This might turn out to be exactly what I need for a lot of reasons."

Riley wasn't exactly certain what they were talking about any longer, but she felt herself sliding ever deeper into quicksand. As was her habit, she decided to retreat. "Listen, you might think I smell good, but I'm not so sure about that. I'm going to grab a quick shower at the gym. I'll be over in ten minutes."

"Sure," Olivia said, "but I meant what I said earlier. You're fine. In fact, I like the way you smell." She blushed. "But I should see if Elizabeth needs any help."

Olivia turned and hurried away before Riley could make another half-assed statement. *Very smooth, Mitchell, very smooth.* With a shake of her head, she jogged off toward the gym, hoping she could get through lunch without embarrassing herself any more than she already had.

She couldn't help grinning to herself, though. Olivia liked the way she smelled.

CHAPTER FIVE

A flood of memories washed over Olivia as she made her way through the main floor of the guesthouse. Not much had changed since her last visit. Gleaming hardwood floors showed years of scuff marks from countless pairs of boots. The pillows on the sturdy, dark leather furniture had been changed, and one of the large recliners that flanked a matching loveseat was new. Another half dozen appropriately Southwestern-styled sofas and chairs sat in groups for comfortable socializing. A large vase of spring flowers sat atop the mantel of the massive fireplace that dominated one wall, the large river stones climbing from the hearth to the tall ceiling. Olivia remembered sitting in front of the fireplace with Riley the day before Elizabeth and Kelsey's wedding, both of them weary from rehearsals and making a run to town for champagne at the last minute when the delivery arrived with wine coolers instead. They'd joked about that, Riley suggesting beer would have been so much simpler if only Elizabeth wouldn't have had a coronary. Olivia smiled to herself, recalling how easy it had been spending time with Riley. And wondering why their reunion just now had been so awkward.

Marie, the daughter of the main chef and head housekeeper, came through the double swinging doors from the kitchen at the far end of the adjoining dining room, saw her, and hurried toward her with a small squeal of excitement. "Olivia! It's so good to see you again."

Olivia pulled her into a quick hug. "You look wonderful. How is your mother?"

Marie laughed. "Busier than ever, and she loves it. Do you need anything?"

"No, I'm sure you're busy. Is Elizabeth here?"

"In the kitchen."

Olivia pushed through the doors into the enormous kitchen and slowed, realizing after catching a snippet of conversation that she had unwittingly walked into the middle of a standoff between Charmaine and Elizabeth.

"I'm not too busy to take care of guests," Charmaine said, hands on her hips and blue eyes snapping. In a lot of ways, she reminded Olivia of her mother, unassuming physically but formidable in every other way. Kind, warm, and a will of steel.

"And you have plenty of guests to take care of," Elizabeth, another woman with an indomitable will, said with a nevertheless affectionate tone. "Since I didn't give you any notice that we'd want lunch, I can just as easily pull out something from last night's din—"

Charmaine looked aghast. "I'll not have you serving leftovers to guests."

"I'm not sure Riley or I can be categorized as guests," Olivia said with a laugh.

Charmaine spun in her direction, her face instantly lighting up with a smile that touched Olivia all the way through. "You're here already. Oh my goodness, come here."

Charmaine opened her arms, and without thinking, Olivia stepped into them. Her mother always smelled of sandalwood and something that reminded Olivia of sunshine. Charmaine carried the slightest scent of fresh flour and nutmeg. Olivia hadn't realized how much she missed the physical contact, but living alone and only occasionally having the energy or desire to go in search of a physical encounter, she often went a long time without simple intimacy other than the habitual kiss on the cheek from her mother. She lingered a few seconds before stepping back.

"I'm so glad to see you," Olivia said.

"I hope you're here to stay this time," Charmaine said.

"Well, I..." Olivia glanced at Elizabeth. "I guess we'll see how this new project goes."

Charmaine waved a hand. "With you two in charge, can't help but be a success. Go outside now, enjoy the sunshine, and take that one with you." She pointed at Elizabeth with a frown. "Leftovers, indeed. I'll have Marco bring out some iced tea in a moment. Go now, both of you, and let me work."

Olivia murmured to Elizabeth as they dutifully headed for the rear verandah, "I thought you were the boss?"

"Shut up." Elizabeth laughed. "Believe me, I do not want her job. The guests care more about food than anything else."

Riley, her hair damp, sat beside Kelsey at a round table with a hand-painted tile top beneath a pergola covered with twining vines that offered shade and relief from the relentless glare of the sun. An Olympic-sized pool with more tables, umbrellas, and loungers stretched along the back border of the verandah. Olivia settled across from Riley at the table already set for four. Riley had changed into a simple red polo with a Wickenburg Fire Department emblem on the chest, and she looked great in it, her shoulders and upper arms stretching the fabric just enough to show the definition of muscles beneath. The long-sleeved shirt, Riley's preference, covered most of the scars Olivia knew marked her forearms.

She raised her gaze to find Riley watching her, and her face grew hot. She needed to get a grip. First, she'd been nearly flirting with her after being back five minutes, and now she was ogling her. She did not flirt, and she did not ogle.

Riley grinned.

The arrival of Marco, a longtime member of the house staff, with a tray laden with a huge pitcher of sun tea, a dish of freshly cut lemons, and a tray of appetizers that reminded Olivia it was well past her lunch time saved her from further embarrassing staring.

"Charmaine said lunch will be ready in fifteen minutes," Marco said. "If anyone prefers a mimosa or wine, I'll bring it right out."

"Not me," Riley said as the others also declined. "I've got a shift tonight."

"I thought you were on days the rest of the month," Kelsey said, slipping several bite-sized canapés onto her plate. "The new captain working you overtime already?"

"Nah. I'm taking a few half-shifts for Rodriguez. His wife is due any day, and she doesn't like him being away for twenty-four hours."

"New captain?" Olivia said, sipping the sweet tea. Finally a nice safe conversational topic that didn't center on her abrupt move or her not so subtle interest in Riley.

"Riley's friend Hadley," Elizabeth said. "Riley somehow talked a very well-qualified, experienced candidate to up and leave the big city for Wickenburg."

Olivia glanced at Riley. "You didn't want the job?"

"Nope," Riley said, avoiding Olivia's gaze. "Desks and paperwork are not my thing."

Something about the way Riley said it made Olivia think there was more to the reason than she was saying, but she was stuck on the *friend Hadley* part. Hadley he or Hadley she? They must be pretty close if Riley could get them to move from the city—any city—to nowhere-on-the-map Wickenburg. Close like she was with Elizabeth, or close like intimate-close? A pang of what she refused to call jealousy stabbed her. Not jealous—why would she be? Just curious. She couldn't think of a subtle way to probe for more info, but Elizabeth would know. She'd subtly grill her later.

"What city?" Olivia asked casually.

"Phoenix," Riley said.

That qualified as a big city. And was near enough to Wickenburg that Riley could have met the mystery captain somewhere…somehow… in a more than friendly way.

"That seems like a big change," Olivia said.

"I suppose. She left a Monday through Friday, nine to five schedule to go back to shiftwork and callouts." Riley shrugged. "Some people just want a change." She looked directly at Olivia for the first time since the topic arose. "Right?"

"Of course." Olivia smiled. No need to telegraph all her private thoughts every time Riley simply looked at her.

"Since we're discussing the department," Riley said, "I need volunteers for this coming weekend."

Kelsey groaned. "Not roadside cleanup already."

Olivia pictured traipsing along in the boiling sun with a big black garbage bag and a pointy stick collecting trash. Horrified, she immediately started searching for an excuse.

Riley laughed, a deep melodious sound that brought back images of them bouncing over the waves on the Jet Ski, her arms wrapped around Riley's firm midsection, her front literally plastered to Riley's back. The intimate sensation came back along with the memory, and she carefully did *not* look at Riley.

"That's not until next month," Riley said. "This is the pancake breakfast benefit to raise money for the summer school programs."

"Eating pancakes?" Olivia asked, looking around the table.

Riley grinned. "You have your choice of jobs—serving, cleanup, kitchen help."

Olivia glanced at Elizabeth, waiting for Elizabeth to decline.

"It's fun," her traitorous best friend said. "I'm for serving."

"I'll take cleanup," Kelsey said.

Olivia surrendered gracefully. "I guess that means I've got kitchen duty, but I have to warn you I have no skill. My mother cooks—I eat. Or I order out."

"No problem," Riley said. "Hadley and I are cooking. We'll show you the ropes."

"Great."

Hadley again. Wonderful.

Marco emerged from the house pushing a cart laden with silver domed plates, and the topic of Hadley shifted to casual chatter about the ranch, guests, and inevitably, weather. As the meal wound down, Kelsey checked her watch and looked at Riley.

"Do you have another hour or so of hammering in you?"

"Yep." Riley pushed back her chair. "I'm good if you are."

Kelsey kissed Elizabeth quickly. "I'll see you later."

Riley paused. "Welcome back, by the way."

"Thanks," Olivia said.

Elizabeth watched them go before turning to Olivia. "Do you need some downtime?"

"I could use a few minutes to unpack, shower…adjust."

"You okay?"

"I'm fine." Olivia sighed. "Everything…everyone…is familiar. I feel like I've come home, in a weird way, and that's a little confusing."

"Maybe home is about people and not places," Elizabeth said quietly.

"That's very Zen. You've changed."

Elizabeth regarded her quizzically. "Have I?"

"Mm. I know damn well you got me out here because you've got projects—plural—in the making. That's the old you. The new you has slowed down to human speed."

Elizabeth laughed. "Let's see if you still think that in a week."

"And then there's this pancake thing," Olivia said. "First it was a rodeo, then we ended up at a hoedown. Who are you again?"

"I'll never be considered one of the locals, but I do live here now." Elizabeth shrugged. "Besides, you'll have fun. You already know Riley, and Hadley is great."

Olivia pounced at the opening. "Hadley—he or she?"

"She. I've only met her once, right after she arrived. Riley was giving her a tour of the area, and they stopped out here and had drinks. Hadley's nice and has that *I fight fires for a living* buff body like Riley's that I admit I'd be all over if I wasn't wildly in love with Kelsey."

A tour. Sounded…friendly. Olivia sighed. Might as well ask. "They must be pretty close if Riley got her to move out here. Are they a thing?"

"No. I gathered they go way back—baby firefighters together before Hadley left for big city, bright lights." Elizabeth paused. "I didn't get any vibes from the two of them, but Riley's pretty private about that sort of thing. Kelsey wouldn't tell me if they were together if Riley didn't want it known. Kelsey has never even told me how Riley got those burns."

"No, I think that must be Riley's story to tell."

Olivia realized she would like very much to know that story, and a great many other things about Riley, including just how close she and her new captain really were. She wasn't used to being preoccupied with a woman—or anyone, for that matter. She was single for a reason, one of them being she found safety in distance. She had already made one enormous change by coming out here with no long-term plans. She did not need something or someone else adding to the chaos of her life.

She stood and placed her glass and plate on the nearby serving cart. "I'll see you in an hour, and you can tell what I'm really doing out here."

"Give me two—I've got a list of calls I need to return," Elizabeth said as they walked inside. "If you're really sure you don't want more time to relax, I'll be in my office."

"I'm fine," Olivia said. "Work is exactly what I need."

CHAPTER SIX

The suite one of the staff took her to was the same one in the main guesthouse she'd stayed in during her last visit. The walk up the wide wooden staircase to the second floor felt as familiar as everything else about the ranch—as if she hadn't been gone for going on two years. Elizabeth hadn't changed much in the sitting area, keeping the Santa Fe–style furnishings while adding a new multicolored woven rug and a little more color with the throw pillows on the butter-soft brown leather couch. A fireplace holding stacked logs dominated one wall with two oversized fabric chairs and a square wooden coffee adorned with a vase of fresh flowers centered on it. A king-sized bed, dresser, and nightstands completed the adjacent bedroom and en suite. As with the great room downstairs, every window offered a sweeping view of some part of the ranch and the jaw-dropping vistas beyond—they were in the middle of twenty thousand acres of undeveloped land, most of which belonged to Elizabeth and Kelsey. The idea boggled.

Olivia's shower took all of fifteen minutes, and after another twenty spent arranging her cosmetics in the bathroom, plugging in her electronics, and unpacking her clothes, she was done. She spent another half hour on a call to her parents, assuring them the accommodations had all the modern amenities, and no, she was not staying in a camper as she had done the first time she'd lived on the ranch. Trying to convince them that an air-conditioned trailer the size of a small home had been anything but rustic had been a lost cause. Some battles just weren't worth the energy.

Tasks completed and too restless to sleep, she grabbed a pale pink, wide-brimmed linen hat and headed outside.

As she wandered down the crushed stone path from the main

guesthouse toward the cluster of individual casitas, she surveyed the changes in the six months since she'd last visited. Off to the right, another barn with adjacent paddocks had been added, here and there several signs pointing out walking trails—these bearing welcoming names like Sunrise Vista and Flowering Cactus rather than Dead Gulch, Calamity, and Vulture—and a new pickleball court. Elizabeth had been busy. Olivia turned in at the path heading toward the new rec center, which had been only partly completed when she was last there.

She halted as Riley walked toward her carrying a gym bag in one hand. Riley looked relaxed, which was unusual, now that she thought of it, and, well, great. Riley moved like she enjoyed being in her body, her stride confident and strong. Everything about her radiated energy, as if she was prepared at any moment to leap into action. Olivia supposed she was. Maybe that was what had drawn her attention from the first— how different Riley was from her. *She* never acted without thought—a lot of thought. She wouldn't call herself a woman of action, but she found it attractive. Very attractive.

"Hey," Riley said. "Nice hat."

Olivia laughed, knowing without a doubt Riley had never worn anything remotely like it in her life. "Thanks. All done with the…what were you two building, anyhow?"

"A shed for extra tack and the like."

"Doesn't Elizabeth have a crew for that kind of thing?" She automatically turned around and walked beside Riley before hesitating. "Sorry. Do you mind company?"

"Not when it's you," Riley said. "And this was just a little job— the construction crew has bigger things to work on."

"So you're off to work now?"

"In an hour or so."

"Until tomorrow morning?"

Riley shook her head. "I'm working an extra twelve, so not until the next morning."

"That's right, you said that. Are all the shifts that long? Twelve hours?"

"Actually, they're twenty-four."

Olivia gaped. "In a row? When do you sleep?"

Riley laughed. "Yes—in a row. And we sleep when we're not working."

"Define working. That is not entirely clear to a civilian, you know." Olivia's knowledge of what firefighters actually did beyond putting out fires with large hoses and water was essentially nil. Of course she knew the work was dangerous. She'd been a child during 9/11, but she knew of the aftermath and the huge toll taken on the first responders, especially the firefighters. The pictures in her head of the men and women running *into* flaming buildings verged on terrifying, and the scars she'd seen on Riley's arms didn't help. She didn't want to think of Riley—someone she knew and…liked…very much—being injured in the line of duty.

"Probably seventy percent of our callouts are for medical emergencies or accidents. The rest are fire related—in town and wildfires."

"I saw the Farmer's Daughter had burned when we drove in," Olivia said. "I'll miss that place. Are there a lot of fires in town?"

"Some in town. Some out in the desert."

"Really? In the desert?"

"It depends on the season," Riley said easily, as if she'd given the information many times. "When it's dry and hot, we'll see fires from lightning strikes in the foothills and the desert. And of course, there are always fires from careless campers and other people."

"I can't imagine there's much in the desert to burn," Olivia said.

Riley shook her head. "There's a lot out there—scrub and trees, even the cactuses. And at higher elevations, evergreens and such."

"So back to the first question—when do you sleep? And eat?"

Riley smiled. "You get very good at sleeping whenever you can between calls. We cook and eat on a regular schedule, and there's always extra food around in case we're out on a call and miss mealtime."

"You're telling me you mostly live where you work," Olivia said lightly.

"Keeps me out of trouble."

"Oh? Do you often get into trouble?"

Riley gave her a slow sexy smile. "Depends on how you define it."

Olivia knew she was treading on dangerous ground but couldn't seem to stop. "I imagine it involves trouble of a pleasurable nature."

Riley laughed. "You have an interesting imagination."

"So I've been told." Olivia halted where the path joined the small gravel lot that held half a dozen pickup trucks. "I hope you have a quiet shift. I should get to work myself. Elizabeth got me out here to do a job, not wander around flirting with the locals."

"Is that what you've been doing?"

"Fortunately not very effectively. Sorry about that." Olivia raised and lowered both hands. "Must be jet lag. I don't usually embarrass myself or anyone else."

"I never said you weren't effective. And I'm not embarrassed."

"Thank you for saying that. I should go."

"Olivia?"

Olivia's stomach flip-flopped at the tender way Riley said her name, and she backed up a step, very much afraid she'd do something she'd regret even more than a little flirting. An image of kissing Riley came to mind.

"I hope you tell me what you consider *pleasurable* trouble sometime," Riley said before adding, "I'll see you."

Olivia turned and hurried up the path toward sanity as the sound of a truck starting up and gravel popping beneath tires signaled Riley driving away.

Flirting with the locals?

Why had she just said that? Why was it whenever she was around Riley, whatever was in her head came out of her mouth? She would have closed her eyes and wished to be somewhere else if she hadn't been worried about stepping on some creature in the path.

She hurried through the main house to Elizabeth's office, which adjoined the dining room and had once been a lounge. The door was partially ajar, and she rapped on it as she pushed it open and walked inside. "Hi, it's…oops. Sorry!"

Elizabeth leaned against the front of her large walnut desk, firmly locked in Kelsey's arms.

"Hey—isn't there some rule against sex in the workplace?"

"It *would* have been sex if you'd been a few minutes later." Elizabeth rubbed her lipstick off Kelsey's lips.

"You two could get a room. There's only eighteen of them just upstairs."

"There's actually only twelve," Kelsey said, "and you gotta strike when the iron's hot."

"And it was definitely hot," Elizabeth added.

After another quick kiss, Kelsey said, "I'll see you at dinner."

"It's a date."

As Kelsey walked out, Olivia sat in one of the plush chairs facing Elizabeth's desk. "Sorry about that."

Elizabeth laughed, taking the adjacent chair. "Don't be. We weren't actually about to…" She tilted her head as if turning over a thought in her mind. "Well, maybe we were."

Olivia rolled her eyes. "Stop bragging." She pointed to the long worktable beside the seating area. An unfurled blueprint covered most of the surface, with several other rolls in a stack nearby and three thick file folders which she recognized all too well. The prospectuses—more like bibles—for every project. She'd studied dozens just like them and read aloud portions to Elizabeth over the years. Strangely, the sight of them gave her a little thrill. Every new project was a new adventure—one she'd missed since she'd been back at Sutton. "So tell me what we're doing here."

"First tell me if you're okay."

"What? Of course I am. You and I have flown thousands of miles in the last ten years or so—a cross-country trip isn't going to bother me."

"I wasn't talking about jet lag. I mean you personally. You seemed a little distracted at lunch. Is something wrong?"

Olivia was tempted, but what could she really say? That she wasn't herself, at least not whenever she was around Riley? That Riley had a strange effect on her, and whenever she thought of her, she entertained ideas she rarely imagined doing? Elizabeth knew her well, but she didn't know the details of her intimate experiences. Her fascination with Riley was just that—an attraction not the least bit based in reality. She'd spent time with her, yes. She liked her, yes. She thought she was hot—well, who wouldn't? But all of that was just biology, or chemistry, or hormonal—not anything she ever based her actions upon. Her brain ruled her behavior, not her body.

"I'm fine," Olivia said, "just really ready to get to work."

"All right then," Elizabeth said, her eyes glinting with that edge of excitement that never failed to pull Olivia in with her. "Big picture? We're starting an equestrian therapy program."

"A what? I know the words, but the picture is fuzzy."

"An equestrian therapy program," Elizabeth repeated. Like saying the same thing twice would explain it.

Olivia huffed. "Have you been in the sun so long that you've forgotten I'm from Manhattan? Do horses actually need therapy?"

Elizabeth laughed. "No, silly, the horses are central to the behavioral health therapy program. The clients might be affected by a wide range of conditions—trauma, ALS, autism, anxiety disorders—all the information is in the prospectus."

"Of course." Despite her sarcasm, Olivia was intrigued. "This is a million miles away from what Sutton pictured for this place when they sent us out here."

Elizabeth's gaze flared. "That's because our vision goes beyond the bottom line."

"*Your* vision," Olivia said softly.

"Not just mine—ours. Kelsey had input, and you will, too. That's why I need you here. I need you to see what I haven't. We have a conditional license, but the final approval is contingent on what you're here to help us build."

Olivia squeezed Elizabeth's arm. "I love you. And I'm in."

Elizabeth looked the tiniest bit relieved.

"Hey—did you ever for a second doubt me?" Olivia said.

"I know this isn't your favorite place or—"

"*You* are my favorite person. And there are plenty of things I like about this place."

"Name one besides Charmaine's cooking."

Olivia almost said Riley, but decided now was not the time to open a door she didn't want to walk through. "I never have to check the weather to see if I need an umbrella."

"Nice try." Elizabeth rose. "Come on—I've got some other ideas I want to run by you. Your copy of the ETP prospectus is labeled over there. You can take it with you."

"Pretty sure of me, weren't you," Olivia said, joining Elizabeth at the drafting table.

"I was prepared to beg."

"Ha—as if. Let's talk personnel first," Olivia said.

They spent the rest of the afternoon discussing managerial choices for the various arms of the equine therapy program as well as budget director, construction teams, general manager, and the dozens of other people they'd need to hire or train.

"When we get this off the ground," Elizabeth said at last, "you'll be the project manager."

"Me? That's your job. I'm the majordomo, remember?"

"Not anymore. I have plenty to do with my part of running this place and consulting."

"Aha." Olivia pointed a finger. "So you've done it. Your father will have apoplexy over you competing with him."

Elizabeth shrugged. "Different league." She grinned. "For now."

Considering the dozens of international projects Elizabeth had overseen, Olivia had no doubt she'd soon be bidding on the same development projects as Sutton Properties. "All right. As the project manager, I'm calling it a day. My stomach is on East Coast time and I'm starving. Are you still eating dinner every night with the guests?"

Elizabeth took her responsibility of owning the Red Sky seriously, and personally interfacing with the guests was part of that.

"Most nights—on occasion we claim a night for ourselves. Tonight we'll be in the dining room." Elizabeth added casually as they walked toward the door, "Riley joins us a few times a week when she's free."

"That's nice," Olivia said, ignoring the flutter in her middle. "I'm sure that's a welcome change from firehouse food."

No reason to ask Elizabeth exactly *when* Riley might be joining them—none at all.

CHAPTER SEVEN

A *re you still working,* Elizabeth texted.
　　In the middle of finalizing the schedule for Phase One, Olivia ignored the text. She'd spent the last two days reviewing the prospectus for the equestrian center, the accompanying budget, the initial construction bids, and a plethora of other details that needed to be finalized before they could begin. She welcomed the work. Work kept her mind on the real and the solid and not on the fleeting images that popped up into her head out of nowhere—Riley's shocked expression the day she'd arrived and how Riley'd been fumbling for something to say. So un-Riley-like and adorable, not that she'd ever actually say that to her out loud. She remembered just how good it had felt to hug her, too—and damn it, she did not need the distraction.

　　Luckily, she had a hideout. Like Kelsey's ranch hands who lived on the ranch in their own bunkhouse, more than half of Elizabeth's on-site crew lived and worked out of the permanent trailers arrayed behind the stables out of sight of the guests. The rest of the crews traveled back and forth daily from town. As project manager, Olivia had her own trailer, large enough for meetings and comfortable enough for her to sleep in if she worked late into the night, which she expected to be doing regularly.

Dinner in ten minutes

　　Elizabeth always tracked her down. Olivia considered the consequences and took the safe route. She closed the document and texted, *On my way.*

　　She hurried up the path to the main house, checked the time, and detoured to the powder room to check her makeup. Two minutes was all she needed. She pulled open the door and ran right into Riley. Full body collision.

"Whoa," Riley said, grabbing her around the waist as she stumbled.

"God," Olivia gasped, "sorry. Are you hurt?"

Riley shook her head, her hands still on Olivia's hips. "No. You?"

Olivia edged back, and Riley released her. They'd been close enough she could still smell her cologne, a fresh sharp scent that reminded her of brisk early morning air. Riley's hair was a little wet, as if she'd just run her damp fingers through it. "I'm fine. What are you doing here?"

"In the bathroom?"

"No!" Olivia saw the grin and scowled. "Ha ha. Here. Didn't you just finish a shift this morning? Shouldn't you be sleeping?"

"You know my schedule?" Riley asked quietly, her gaze intense.

Olivia flushed. "Well, you did tell me just the other day you'd be working two nights, and…I remembered."

"I slept some when I got home this morning. Is it a problem that I'm here?"

"What? Of course not. You just surprised me. Look, I'm sorry. I have to go."

Riley chuckled and stepped out of the path to the powder room.

Olivia added hastily, "Not *that* way—I have to go to dinner. Elizabeth's waiting."

"We have five minutes," Riley said. "I'll wait for you."

"Oh. You're on your way to dinner, too." Of course—Riley was practically part of the family. Why all of a sudden had her brain stopped working? "Never mind—let's just go."

"Don't you need to…" Riley tilted her had toward the powder room.

Olivia decided screaming would only make the ridiculous situation more absurd. "No. It was a makeup check."

"Really?" Riley's gaze slowly traveled over her face, bringing heat to her skin. "You already look great."

"It will have to do," Olivia muttered, turning to go.

Riley hurried to keep pace. "Understatement."

Olivia slowed. "Thank you. You still smell nice, by the way." When Riley blushed, Olivia laughed and grasped her arm. "Hurry up, or we'll face the wrath of the Great Sutton."

"Can't have that," Riley said. "I'm looking forward to dinner."

"Me, too," Olivia said.

Much more than she was just a few minutes before.

❖

Dinner was undoubtedly delicious. Charmaine could probably head a kitchen in a five-star hotel, but Riley didn't taste much of anything. She was too busy trying not to look at Olivia, which was next to impossible considering Olivia was sitting directly across from her. Olivia didn't seem very talkative and avoided looking directly at Riley. Riley tried to recall saying anything that might have upset her, but as usual, she wasn't on top of things whenever she bumped into Olivia. The last thing she'd expected when she stopped in the powder room to wash up was for Olivia to barge into her the minute she opened the door. Full court press, even. They'd only been in physical contact a few seconds, but that was long enough to register Olivia's chest against hers and the quick rush of breath as Olivia gasped in surprise. Then all she'd been thinking about was how good it was to see her, even if Olivia seemed in a big hurry to be anywhere else but where she was. All she could remember saying other than did she need to use the powder room...smooth as usual...was that she looked great. Maybe Olivia thought she was just handing her a line? That wasn't a line, since it was true.

"When are you going skydiving again, Riley?" Kelsey said.

Olivia's fork clattered on her plate. "Sorry." She leaned forward, her gaze on Riley, her expression midway between perplexed and... appalled?

"Skydiving?" Olivia said in the same way she might have said *freebasing.* Her tone sounded as if the rest of the sentence was *have you lost your mind?*

Riley shrugged. Olivia didn't approve, apparently. The subtle criticism stung, but she wasn't all that surprised. Olivia did not strike her as a risk taker—at least not in the physical arena. She ought to remember that.

Riley turned to Kelsey instead. "Next week, as a matter of fact. If Phyliss is available." She glanced at Olivia, trying to be polite. "She's the pilot."

Olivia said, "Why do you do it? It's so dangerous."

"It isn't really," Riley said. "No more than any sport—if you know your limits."

"Sport?" Olivia grimaced. "You don't see people dying from playing tennis."

Riley chose to ignore Olivia's unspoken rebuke. She'd heard it all before.

"How many jumps have you made?" Olivia asked, her voice sounding pinched.

"A couple dozen or so."

"A couple dozen?" Olivia shook her head. "I've always thought people who went in for these extreme activities were secretly taunting death. Or had a death wish themselves."

Riley heard Dr. Townes's calm, steady voice. "Do you ever wish for death?"

That had been at the beginning, when maybe she had. Or in her dreams still. The room dimmed, and sweat broke out on her back and chest. The pressure in her head built and sounds faded. Her breath grew short. As the room spun, Dr. Townes's voice returned. *You are here and now. What is today?*

February 26.

Name four things you see.

Fork, salt shaker, flowers on the table, clock on the wall.

What time is it?

Dinnertime.

Who do you see?

Olivia, Kelsey, Elizabeth.

Olivia. Olivia staring at her, confused, worried.

The darkness faded, and her world settled. Kelsey touched her arm.

"Riley?"

Riley cleared her throat and drank several swallows of her water. "Sorry, what was I saying?"

Her voice sounded a little strained, but not like it usually did after she teetered on the edge of the darkness. This was the shortest episode by far.

"Skydiving," Olivia said, her voice still a little harsh. "You were explaining why you jump *out* of a perfectly good airplane."

"I skydive because I love the way it feels to fly—to feel the cleanest air I've ever felt, to see the mountains and the desert the way they must have been before we humans started chipping away at them. Because for few seconds, everything in my world is beautiful."

Olivia frowned, a crease forming in her otherwise smooth forehead, her eyes still troubled. Angry? Or concerned? "And the risk?"

"I'm experienced. I've made plenty of jumps with smoke jumper crews."

She must have raised her voice in self-defense because a girl around eight seated at the far end of the family-style table piped up. "What's a smoke jumper?"

Grateful for the change in topic, Riley said, "Someone who jumps out of a plane to fight a fire. It's usually a forest fire. The planes can get us into areas that the firefighters on the ground can't reach or haven't gotten to yet."

"Wow, that's cool," the young girl said, looking at Riley with awe. "I want to do that."

On steadier ground now, Riley mentally pulled up the talk she often gave when doing community outreach at schools. "You need a lot of special training, so it's important to work hard in school first," Riley added, glancing at her parents. "You want to be sure you're really ready so your mom and dad don't worry about you every day."

The girl's mother smoothed her wild curls and shot Riley an appreciative look, saying, "If you decide you don't want to be a jockey, we can take you by the local firehouse when we get home, okay? I bet we can find someone to tell you all about it. But school comes first."

The girl nodded and grinned.

The mother mouthed *Thank you* and Riley said, "No problem. Enjoy your stay at the ranch."

"Are you still doing that? Smoke jumping?" Olivia asked, as if their conversation had never been interrupted. She'd stopped eating and was so focused on Riley it made her nervous. Nervous and weirdly calm at the same time. Her life, her choices.

"Not recently." Riley skirted the essential details. "I started when I was nineteen. I'm still certified to jump but based here full-time now."

"Nineteen?" Olivia shook her head. "That seems so young to be doing something so risky."

"It was my job," Riley said flatly. "And what I was trained to do."

"More like a calling," Kelsey added quietly.

"Of course," Olivia said, her tone softer now, "I'm sure you're excellent at what you do."

Olivia picked up her wine glass and looked away.

Elizabeth broke the silence. "How's work on the center coming, Riley?"

"Getting there," Riley said. "The exterior walls are framed. We'll start setting in the windows and putting up the exterior sheeting on my next set of days off."

"What are you building?" Olivia asked.

"A house—well, more than a house. It's going to be a community center for at-risk kids in foster care or underprivileged homes. A place to come for counseling or tutoring or just group activity stuff. It's aimed to be a safe place for them to hang out."

"And you're helping to build it?"

"Help?" Kelsey shook her head. "She's donated the land to the town and is practically building it by herself."

"It's called the New Horizon Center," Elizabeth put in, "but pretty much everyone is already calling it Horizon House. Other than pouring the foundation, roughing in the electrical and plumbing, Riley's doing it with little help."

"Don't embarrass me," Riley said. "I do what I can when I can. It's no big deal."

Olivia sent Riley that intense stare again, the one that made her nerves jangle in a good way, mostly. "That's…admirable."

"It's as much for me as the kids," Riley said, trying to downplay the whole thing. "Working on it is the best therapy I've found." As soon as she said it, she tried to backtrack. "Keeps me out of trouble when I've got time to kill. Sometimes I forget I'm even there until the sun goes down, and I realize I'm hungry."

Olivia smiled at that, and Riley relaxed.

"That must explain why you're getting skinny," Olivia said.

"Hey," Riley said. "I am not skinny."

Kelsey laughed. "Lightweight, buddy."

The tension around the table dissipated, and after they'd finished dessert, Riley said, "I need to get along. I have day shift tomorrow." She stood. "See you all Sunday."

"We'll be there," Elizabeth said.

Olivia rose as well. "I have an early start, too. Budget meeting. 'Night, everyone."

As Olivia left the dining room with Riley, Olivia said quietly, "I'm sorry for the third degree over dinner. I was just…surprised."

"Surprised or horrified?"

Olivia sighed. "Actually, more knee-jerk terrified. To a person who always looks before they leap—figuratively and in reality—the idea of voluntarily doing death-defying things seems scary."

"You're here, aren't you?" Riley said. "That seems like a pretty big leap. From Sutton to the Red Sky."

Olivia laughed. "I suppose I do feel a little like I'm out on the edge of a cliff."

"You have plenty of people around who won't let you fall." Riley wanted to say she was one, but Olivia had made it pretty clear she didn't think much of her judgment. Why would she count on her for anything?

"I'm lucky," Olivia said. "At any rate, I apologize."

"Not necessary," Riley said. "I understand."

"Good night then," Olivia said, halting at the foot of the wide staircase to the second floor.

"See you Sunday." As Riley walked out into the night, she wished she didn't understand quite so well how little chance there was that she and Olivia would ever be more than friends.

CHAPTER EIGHT

Olivia closed the door to her room, mentally debating between a long, hot shower or a soak in the tub. The tub won out when she saw the complimentary bottle of wine on the table in front of the fireplace that had been there since the day she'd arrived. Merlot had never sounded so good.

She uncorked the bottle with the wine opener thoughtfully left with the bottle—because Elizabeth thought of everything—and poured herself a glass. If it needed to breathe, it had until she could get out of her clothes, fill the tub, and sink into the warmth. Five minutes later, she moaned as she slid into the lavender-scented water.

Usually she could clear her mind and think of nothing at all—one of the many benefits of years of yoga and meditation. Tonight, the peaceful relaxation escaped her. Her thoughts kept jumping back to dinner and the troubling conversation with Riley. And her own very out-of-character reactions. She'd known Riley's *job* was dangerous, but she hadn't imagined that Riley—or anyone, really—would voluntarily participate in something that could kill them. The image of Riley's body swirling through air and just falling still shook her. She'd overreacted in the moment and criticized Riley when it was none of her business. More than once, at that. Riley had been remarkably polite about it, even when she'd been visibly upset. For a moment, when a shadow passed over Riley's face and her eyes skated around the room as if she wasn't quite sure where she was, Olivia had expected her to get up and leave. Then Riley had focused on her, and the tension in her body and the disorientation in her gaze had disappeared. Another minute and she was herself again, calmly and patiently answering the child's questions about firefighting.

Olivia sighed and stepped out of the tub, reaching for one of the plush, sand-colored bath sheets from a stack conveniently placed nearby. Judgmental was not a word she associated with herself, but she'd been rattled by the thought of Riley being hurt. Of possibly being killed and not seeming to care.

She wrapped herself in the towel that draped her from chest to knee and kicked into fuzzy mules. As she started for the bedroom, her phone, which she'd left on the vanity, chimed with the distinctive FaceTime signal. Since she doubted it was Elizabeth, there was only one other person it could be. Holding the towel securely with an arm across her chest, she lifted the phone and, sure enough, saw her mother's face along with the request to answer icon. She debated for two brief seconds. If she declined the call, her mother would try again, possibly later that night. Her mother was a night owl, and even considering the time difference, Olivia didn't want to have to wake up to answer. She pushed accept and said, "Hi, Mama."

"Have you been swimming in the dark?" her mother said.

Olivia laughed and glanced in the mirror. Her hair was damp and disheveled, not something her mother was used to seeing. "No, I just got out of the tub."

"Oh. Well, I'll go, then. You should go to bed."

"No, no, it's not that late," Olivia said, moving through into her bedroom and propping the phone against the lamp on the dresser. "I'm going to move out of range for a moment and put on a robe. How are you? I'm sorry I haven't called. I've just been really busy since I arrived."

No way could she tell her parents that she had been completely distracted by seeing Riley again. Her parents understood how her work came first.

"It's okay, sweetie. We were just worried."

"I'm fine. You don't need to worry. I've been here before, and it's perfectly civilized." Olivia tried to reassure them that Wickenburg was not on the other side of the moon, but her parents would never be totally happy when she wasn't just a cab ride away. They'd had so many losses in their life, they were just the teeniest bit overprotective about her. Even though it was a minor pain in the ass at times, she accepted that they always would be. It was another tick mark on the "My parents love me" board. She loved them and understood. She'd always insisted on living her own life as she needed to, but she also let them express their worry when they needed to.

Her mother made a disbelieving sound.

"I'm fine," Olivia repeated. "Nothing happened the other times I've come here, and nothing will this time. Plus you know Elizabeth always sees to security wherever we travel, and this is her home now. I'm as safe here—safer—than in my condo."

Bringing Elizabeth into the conversation would help defuse their concerns. From the first time she'd brought Elizabeth home, her parents had treated her as their own. When Elizabeth came out as a lesbian to Olivia when they were fifteen and refused to hide it from Olivia's family, Olivia had been afraid that they would not let her see Elizabeth again. She'd been wrong. Knowing their strong religious convictions, though, she hadn't been naive enough to think her parents would be as accepting if it were her. An early lesson in keeping her private life so private became a way of life, even with her closest friends.

"We can't see you to be sure you're eating," her mother said.

Olivia smiled. "I'm eating. The head cook here is amazing. How are you both?"

"Oh, we're fine."

Something about the way her mother answered had Olivia's antennae quivering. Her mother was neither dramatic nor a complainer. A woman who had given up her home, all of her friends, her security, and her extended family to move to a new world, with no immediate support system, had to be able to see the world as it really was to have accomplished what her mother had. She'd raised a child, gotten an education, and worked full-time all her life.

If her mother was concerned, there could only be two reasons, Olivia or her father, and as far as she could tell, she hadn't done anything new to upset them in the last few weeks.

"How's Papa?" Olivia called as she opened the closet door, switched her towel for the robe, and carried the phone back to the bed. She propped herself against the pillows and balanced her phone again, this time on her knee.

"He's Papa," her mother said.

"Is he home?"

"No, not for another hour or so."

"He's working too hard, then," Olivia said.

Her mother gave that little shrug that said, "That's Papa."

"You sure nothing's wrong?"

Her mother forced a smile. "Can't I just be missing you?"

"Of course, and I miss you, too. Both of you."

"How long will you be gone this time?" her mother asked.

She couldn't very well say "I have no idea," which was true, and she had even less idea of what she really wanted to do when the project was over. "We're just getting started here. I'm not sure how long it's going to take."

"Pat Berubie's son said he can be out of your condo with one month's notice," her mother said, referring to one of her coworker's children who had sublet Olivia's place while she was gone. "So you don't have to delay coming home when you're finished."

"That's great," Olivia said. "I'll be sure to give him plenty of advance notice."

"He has a good job, you know," her mother said, far too casually, "and he's very good looking. A little young, but not such a bad thing in a man."

Olivia laughed. "Mama. He's twenty-three."

Her mother laughed too. "Like I said."

"All right, enough," Olivia said, not about to get into the sexual prowess of men at any age with her mother. She wished she didn't have to get into the subject of men at all and thought not for the first time that she needed to be more direct. But not over the phone, and not when something was clearly bothering her mother.

"How is Elizabeth?" her mother asked.

"Extremely happy, which is something I've never been able to say before, and extremely busy, which is nothing new at all."

"And her...ah..."

"Her wife? Kelsey is great."

"You'll send some new pictures, won't you, of everyone and the resort," her mother said, trying hard, Olivia knew, to be interested and involved in her life.

"I will, I promise."

"And you'll call us again soon and talk to your father about slowing down a little bit."

And there it was. "You think he'll listen to me when he doesn't listen to you?"

"Oh, he listens," her mother said with undeniable fondness, "and then he does what he wants. Somewhat like his daughter."

"Mama." Olivia laughed.

"He's not getting any younger," her mother said, "and he needs to rest more."

The subtext there was that her father, who all her life had had boundless energy, could not work the way he once could and refused to admit it. Her heart squeezed for a moment, and she thought of how much she loved them and how much they had sacrificed all their lives for her. "I promise I will call at least once a week if I don't hear from you first."

"And you'll tell me if there are any handsome young men at this ranch."

"I'll be far too busy to be thinking about that," Olivia said, an image of Riley popping unbidden into her mind. She was thinking about *someone* a great deal more than was normal for her. "I love you both. Tell Papa I said hello."

"I will. We love you, too. Talk again soon," her mother said.

When her screen went blank, Olivia closed her eyes. Her mother was worried about her father, which was nothing new really. Her father had always been a workaholic. On the other hand, her mother wasn't a worrier. She promised herself to call in the next few days and try to coax her father into taking her mother on a vacation. Their anniversary was coming up soon. He had plenty of seniority and could take some time off.

She shed her robe, set her alarm, and turned off the light. The moon was high and silvered the room, adding a touch of comfort. Turning on her side and pulling the pillow into her arms, she replayed the rest of the conversation.

When was she going to find a man she wanted?

Her parents were staunch Catholics, conservative in their views, and though her mother tried to embrace Elizabeth's marriage, the subject was difficult for her. Olivia had sidestepped the entire topic of marriage and children for a long time, partly to avoid asking herself hard questions and partly because she didn't want to distress her parents if she'd told them the truth. She'd never met a man or woman who'd interested her for anything more a casual affair. She'd never dated anyone more than a time or two, if that. She'd put that down to her nomadic lifestyle, following Elizabeth around the globe from project to project—five months here, seven months half a world away, with a stopover in Manhattan. Conveniently, that explanation also worked when her parents asked when she planned to settle down, and she didn't have to bring up the possibility of a relationship with a woman. On a scale of one to ten, with ten being a crushing disappointment, her falling for a woman would be at the top of the scale. No husband meant no kids to her parents' way of looking at the world.

So why had she immediately thought of Riley when her mother

brought up the subject that always crept into every conversation? Her life had taken a decidedly different turn in the last eighteen months, and maybe that was the explanation. Elizabeth had left Sutton, disrupting a relationship that had centered both their lives since they were children. Riley had caught her interest from the moment they'd met, that she could admit. Riley was funny and smart and unexpectedly compassionate. The work she was doing for the underprivileged children in the community proved that, as did her dedication to her work in the service of others. And being honest, Riley stirred up feelings that could not be ignored. She was sexy, and Olivia felt it. She'd left Arizona, but she'd never completely forgotten Riley.

Now she was back, and Riley still interested her. She hadn't prepared for the intensity of seeing her again, but she hadn't realized she needed to. Being around Riley again had awakened all those past feelings and impressions. She could imagine dating Riley, and that was new for her.

She didn't anticipate a relationship with Riley. Her stay here was time limited. They had little in common—Riley sought excitement and challenge, even when the risk could literally be deadly. *She* was grounded and cautious. Their lives were worlds apart on every level. Sex, on the other hand, now that was a possibility. She could admit that here in the dark, in the privacy of her own mind. But relationship or not, it was time she told her parents that the conventional kind of life they envisioned for her was not going to happen and why. They deserved her honesty, and so did she. When the time was right.

Riley drove down the last row of the RV park situated far enough outside town to be private but close enough to get to work easily. Her forty-three-foot, fifth-wheel toy hauler, complete with four slide outs, occupied the last lot of the end. The gleaming black and silver unit wasn't huge yet provided all the comfort she needed. The bedroom with adjacent bathroom, up three steps to the right of the front door, held a king-size bed with plenty of closets for her uniforms and a few casual clothes. The kitchen galley occupied the central area, with a media center that converted into a workstation to the left of the stove. A door on the opposite end led to the garage, used for storing toys. It could fit all types of all-terrain vehicles, but Riley used it to carry her motorcycle.

She flicked on the light over the small sink in the compact kitchen area, grabbed the canister where she kept the cat food, and walked out onto the tiny back patio to sit on the steps. The sky was the kind of black that only existed too far from major settled areas to be significantly contaminated by artificial light—deep and endless. Even the moonlight raced to earth as if trying to escape the pull of the dark surrounding it. Stars glinted razor-sharp. She tossed some cat food onto the concrete and waited. A few minutes later a long, sinuous shape emerged from the scrub at the edge of the cleared area and made her way over to the food.

"Hi, Artie," Riley said, watching the feral cat consume the crunchies. She wondered if feral was truly the right word when the cat made a nightly visit, although wild animals did do that, she supposed. The cat sat back and regarded her silently.

"Yeah, I know. You don't want to come inside, and I get that. Some things can't be tamed, right?"

The cat waited a moment more, stretched, and disappeared.

"Safe travels," Riley muttered and walked through to the bathroom. She twisted the shower handle to cold and stripped. Cold water, she'd discovered, drove the ghosts away and cleared her head.

What the hell had happened back there at the ranch? She'd never had an episode while she was at the ranch. The place calmed her. Her dreams, yeah, they haunted her still. But she'd had years to deal with that. Lots of therapy. She closed her eyes and raised her face to the icy water.

She couldn't blame Olivia for being critical, not for something so far out of her experience. Olivia couldn't be expected to understand why she did what she did. Olivia had been a little tough, yeah, and that was unexpected. And maybe coming from her, what felt like criticism had hit a little close to the bone. Why that should matter, she wasn't entirely sure. She cared what Olivia thought about her, and that was the problem maybe.

She stepped out of the shower, briskly toweled off, and rubbed the moisturizing cream that she got mailed from a specialty pharmacy in Colorado on her arms. The stuff was ghastly expensive but helped keep the scars from tightening up and causing her pain. She didn't care what it cost if it let her do her job. After pulling on a faded T-shirt and loose gym shorts, she went through to the kitchen, popped her second and last beer of the night, and sat down on the sofa to check her email.

The voicemail icon said she had a missed call. That must have come through while she was driving. Missing calls wasn't that uncommon. Cell service was pretty spotty in the stretch from the ranch toward town. But who? Then it hit her what day it was.

"Fuck," she muttered. How could she have forgotten? How could she have *let* herself forget? That couldn't really be the reason, could it, that she was so sensitive tonight? Was her unconscious mind still really that screwed up?

She almost didn't want to listen, and that made her a coward twice over. She tapped on the voicemail recording and saw the familiar face in her mind as the words tumbled out.

"Hi Riley, it's Ashley. I was just calling to see how you were doing."

The sadness in her quiet voice sent daggers into her chest.

"Luke was asking when you were coming over for dinner again. He really misses you. I know you're busy, but sometime soon, okay?"

There was a pause and Riley thought she heard sniffles. The knife plunged deeper.

"*I* miss you, too. Give me a call. We'd love to see you."

Another pause, this time longer, as if Ashley was trying to figure out what else to say. Or not to say. Their conversations hadn't always been this strained, but Riley no longer knew what to say either.

"It's Kevin's birthday tomorrow," Ashley finally said, her voice barely above a whisper.

The knife sank further and twisted. Riley knew that. It was something she'd never forget, along with his infectious laugh, and standing up with the rest of the crew at his wedding, or the way he talked incessantly about his wife and son, or the way he always thought he could beat her on the obstacle course and teased her about the women who practically fell at her feet.

Through the bedroom door, she could see the picture frame on the table by the television. Kev's smile was huge as he stood next to Riley when they'd graduated from the academy. They were so young and thought they were invincible. But that was then, and the cold slap of reality never failed to hurt.

"Okay, then," Ashley said, "I guess that's all. I hope you're doing okay. Please call…when you can."

The recording stopped, and Riley shut the phone. The pain never lessened. She'd learned to live with it, learned to function again. Trusted herself to do the job. But the memories of smoke and flames and the eerie silence never dimmed. Nor did the knowledge that it should have been her.

She needed some air. Back on the steps, she scanned the bushes and didn't see anything. Artie was off hunting, most likely. A minute passed and the cat appeared, as if she'd been watching. At least Riley thought she was a she.

"Sorry, friend, I didn't bring food out with me."

Slowly, Artie padded across the hardpacked earth, crossed the patio, and stopped a few inches from Riley's foot, staring up at her, the moonlight glinting yellow in her eyes. Slowly, Riley stretched out her hand and held it a few inches away from the cat's nose. Artie stood, butted her head against Riley's fingers, and then was gone as quickly as she'd come.

Maybe some things could be tamed. Maybe some sins could be forgiven. Maybe.

Sleep was a long time coming, and when it did, she dreamed of smoke and fire.

CHAPTER NINE

"Hey," Hadley said, walking into the kitchen at the firehouse. "What are you doing here? Weren't you off rotation until today?"

Riley glanced over her shoulder. "I slept here last night."

More correctly, she'd bunked at the station after a quick stop at her trailer to toss some crunchies out for Artie. She'd been tired after a couple of days fitting windows and nailing up Tyvek sheeting on the exterior walls at the center, but her mind had been racing too much for her to sleep. She hadn't called Ashley back, and she didn't know why not. She'd replayed the dinner conversation with Olivia and thought of a dozen ways she could have handled that better. And she fought the irritation that cropped up unexpectedly when she recalled Olivia's criticism. She wasn't usually sensitive about other people's opinion of her, but Olivia's mattered. A lot.

Riley nodded toward one of the big aluminum coffee urns on the counter. "Thought I'd better get an early start working on the brew. Our guys are gonna drink at least half of it as soon as they walk in, and we're going to need a lot for the breakfast."

"Going to help myself to some of that right now." Hadley drew the steaming coffee into a ceramic mug from the urn that Riley had just filled.

Hadley, as usual, looked parade ready in her navy-blue polo with the WFD emblem and captain's patch on the chest, pressed navy-blue cargo pants, and a shiny black belt and equally shiny black duty boots. Her medium-length red hair was neatly trimmed, and her green eyes bright and clear. The short-sleeved shirt showed off her toned arms, and the fit of her uniform spoke to her rigid workout regimen. She had a few pounds on Riley, all muscle.

"I understand Kelsey and Elizabeth got roped into working this morning," Hadley said. "Very nice job of recruiting."

Riley tensed. "Yeah, and another…friend. Olivia Martinez."

Hadley kicked back in the chair she'd pulled out from the long, wide oak table that filled the center of the kitchen eating area. "I don't think I know her. She out at the ranch? Are there any donuts left, do you know?"

"In the fridge."

"Who puts donuts in the refrigerator," Hadley muttered as she went over to the commercial-sized stainless steel refrigerator and poked around inside.

"People who don't want the mice to eat them." Riley set up the second urn. "Are you making the batter, Cap?"

"Sure, I can do that. We've got an hour, though, right? I thought I'd go for a run."

"Not wearing running gear."

"That's because I'll change into it when I get ready to go."

"So why didn't you just come in…" Riley shook her head. "Never mind. You're just a uniform kind of person."

"Habit," Hadley said. "You know what it's like coming up. Got to look the part to get the part."

"Yeah, not so much here. Maybe in the city. You're not riding a desk here, rank or not."

"That's part of the reason I'm here," Hadley said. "I want to work the line. I don't want to sit in meetings with the mayor and the city council or whatever talking about parade routes, budgets, and ceremonial events half my day."

"The guys appreciate a working captain," Riley said, starting to assemble the ingredients for the pancakes. They all referred to the crew as guys, gender nonspecific. Riley had known Hadley since they were recruits in the academy. They hadn't lost touch, even though they'd gone in different directions after they'd graduated. Hadley was a born boss, tough but fair, by the book but approachable, too. And most importantly, she never asked anyone to do anything she wouldn't do herself. The crews knew it, and that made for a happy firehouse.

"You could've had the job," Hadley said quietly.

Riley didn't look up from her task. "Didn't want it. Besides, you've got more experience."

Hadley snorted. "That's bullshit, and we both know it. We all started out together, remember?"

Sure, Riley remembered—her, Had, Kev…

"Burkhardt is retiring in June," Hadley went on, "and B Company will need a new lieutenant."

"You ought to let it go, Had," Riley said, getting down a bunch of mixing bowls. B Company was the first in line to deploy on forest ranger assist calls, including by air. She'd fought her last forest fire.

"We're going to need a lot of batter," Hadley said, backing off. "What about the bacon?"

"I saw a tray of stuff in the refrigerator."

"So you didn't tell me who Olivia was," Hadley said as she drained her coffee mug and carried it to the sink.

"She's a friend of Elizabeth's. And she's managing one of the big projects out at the ranch."

"It's a beautiful place. I got the sense from the rumor mill that a lot of folks weren't all that happy about the changes at first, but there's a lot of new business in town because of it."

"Elizabeth is smart, so is Kelsey," Riley said, dragging out a dozen boxes of eggs and piling them on the table next to a couple half gallons of milk. "Between them, they know how to cover all the bases. They're building an amazing place that will be good for the town, too."

"Yeah, well, you're doing something pretty amazing with that new community center. I wanted to talk to you about that."

Riley paused, looked over at her. "What about it?"

"I had a meeting with the mayor and a couple of the town council people last week about our budget." She shrugged and sighed. "Gotta be done. Anyhow. We've got a lot of discretionary funds and will have more after this benefit. I talked them into letting the fire department sponsor part of the center. It looks good for us tax-wise to make the donation. They'll want to run that by you when the time comes, since you'll be on the board."

"What? No. I'm not planning on anything like that," Riley said. She'd never intended to have a part in running the place. She wasn't knowledgeable enough, nor did she have the time. "The mayor or whoever needs to hire somebody. Somebody else."

"Well, how did you think it was going to work?" Hadley said, laughing. "You buy the place, you build the place, and you just give it away? It doesn't work that way. You'll have to be on the board, and having someone from the department involved looks good for us. Two birds, one stone."

"Can't you do it?" Riley said. "You're the captain."

"Nope. I've got enough meetings to go to. The town will need to hire someone in a supervisory capacity, and that takes money, too. Again, looks good for us from a tax point of view." Hadley leaned against the big table and sent Riley a look that said *You're not winning this one.* "Besides, once the WFD has an official role, the town can send a crew to help you get the place finished. Summer is a great time to get kids into the programs, so you want to get the place up and running ASAP."

"You've thought this out," Riley grumbled. A little pissed and grudgingly appreciative. Hadley was an organizer and damned persuasive, whether dealing with crews or politicians. Riley blew out a breath. "I didn't exactly think it would be so complicated."

"Maybe there was a time when this kind of thing wasn't, but it is now. Lots of rules and regulations. Especially where kids are concerned."

"Okay, okay, I get it. Fine, I'll go to the meetings or whatever."

"Excellent. I'll get on the mayor about getting some crews out there. She should have done that already. You'll still run the show." Hadley measured pancake mix into the first bowl.

"Thanks," Riley said, meaning it.

Hadley waved her off. "I've been here, what six—almost seven— weeks, and we haven't been out anywhere. I could use a little R&R. You ready for a trip to that bar you mentioned?"

"The Last Stop? Are you looking for a wingman?"

"I don't think I need one," Hadley said, grinning, "but really, just looking to unwind a little bit. Why, do you need one?"

Riley shook her head. She hadn't been to the bar in a month or so and hadn't hooked up with anyone in longer than that. "I wouldn't mind sharing a beer or two."

"Good. Soon then, huh? I'm going to go run," Hadley said. "All I've got to do is mix and pour when I get back."

"Sure. Have a good run." Riley glanced at the clock. Olivia would be there in less than an hour. The familiar buzz that started in her stomach whenever she anticipated seeing her kicked in.

She wouldn't mind sharing a drink with a friend, but she'd lost her edge where a casual night with a pleasant stranger was involved. Especially now, when the only woman she seemed to be thinking about was the one least likely to be spending the night with her.

❖

Elizabeth rapped on the trailer door and pushed it open. "Why are you working at six on a Sunday morning?"

"Because I would like to get this project off the ground before I'm ninety," Olivia said, sending a memo to the project managers about the upcoming week's schedule. "Why?"

"Because we need to leave so we can get to our proper workstations on time."

Olivia pushed a damp lock of hair off her cheek. The trailer was unexpectedly warm. It might be just coming into March, but it felt like summer was right around the corner to her. At least it wasn't sticky hot and smelling of city in the summer. "You're really going to make me do this?"

"I'm not making you do it," Elizabeth said, laughing. "That was Riley. You should've told her no if you didn't want to do it."

Feeling cranky, Olivia rose and pulled on her crossbody Coach bag, settling it beneath her arm. "I can't very well say no to helping some benefit for the fire department and orphans or whatever."

"Not exactly orphans, but that's true, you really can't," Elizabeth said, still smiling. "Kelsey is just checking something in the stable and will meet us at the car. Come on, it'll be fun, and the food will be worth it."

"*Fun* is a champagne brunch at eleven thirty in an air-conditioned restaurant."

"Yeah," Elizabeth said, walking with her toward her SUV. "We don't have any of those."

"Champagne brunches or air-conditioned restaurants?"

"Oh, we've mostly got air conditioning, except during the monsoon season."

"Please," Olivia said, "I don't really want to know."

"I think champagne brunch at the ranch is a good idea, now that you mention it, though," Elizabeth said.

"So do I." Olivia climbed into the back seat, and Elizabeth got behind the wheel. "Riley said Hadley was cooking with her. What's she like?"

"You'll like her. She's interesting and very good-looking." Elizabeth glanced over her shoulder. "And, you know, if you were so inclined, I think of the women-loving persuasion."

"I'm of no persuasion presently and not inclined in any direction," Olivia said. "Because I'm up to my ass in schedules and agendas and appointments."

Elizabeth turned and draped her arm over the seat to look back at Olivia. "How's it coming for real?"

Olivia settled back in the very comfortable leather bucket seat. "Actually, right now, things look very good. As soon as we get the site inspections done, we can break ground. Possibly as soon as the end of next week."

"It's a good thing we know the county fire inspector, if you remember," Elizabeth said, "and I'm sure the *fire inspector* will help push along some of the paperwork we need done if you ask her."

"Yes, aren't we lucky," Olivia said. Of course she'd been thinking about Riley being the country fire inspector. That's how they'd met the first time, after all. Some first encounters left an impression.

"You don't have a problem with her, do you?" Elizabeth asked, unusually serious.

Olivia straightened. "No, of course not. Why would you say that?"

"I got the feeling the other night at dinner that she annoyed you."

"I just—I don't know why I was so bothered by the whole skydiving thing. It just seemed so…irresponsible. But it's none of my business. I apologized."

Elizabeth's eyebrows rose. "You did?"

"I'm not usually that judgmental. I embarrassed myself. So, yes. I did."

"You are the least judgmental person I know, next to Kelsey. And Riley is like Kelsey—responsibility is her in her genes."

"Maybe where other people are concerned," Olivia said. "But she didn't seem too worried about herself."

"That's what makes her who she is."

"I know—and I have nothing but respect for her profession and everything she's doing for those kids. We just don't see the rest of the world the same way."

"Maybe you're more adventurous than you think. You're here, aren't you?"

Olivia laughed. Riley had said something similar. "Under duress. And I'm not here for adventure—I got enough of that the last ten years traveling around with you. All I want is to get my life back on track."

"Fair enough. Maybe the track will turn out to be different than what you expect. That's all I'm suggesting."

"I think I can steer my life in the direction I want it to go," Olivia said.

"Mm. So did I. Until I met Kelsey." Elizabeth turned around and started the SUV as Kelsey jumped into the passenger seat.

"Hope they're going to have some food for us when we get there," Kelsey said. "I'm starving. Morning, Olivia."

Elizabeth reached across and squeezed her hand. "Baby, you're always starving."

Kelsey, in an automatic gesture that somehow caused Olivia's heart to twist just a little, lifted Elizabeth's hand and kissed her knuckles. "Not anymore."

CHAPTER TEN

Elizabeth drove half a block past the firehouse and parked in the large lot just across the street. The community breakfast was due to start at seven, and at six thirty there were already quite a few cars in the lot with people inside chatting, looking at phones, and some apparently napping.

"I take it they're the early birds?" Olivia said.

"Oh yeah. They'll be lining up pretty soon," Kelsey said as they all piled out of the vehicle.

"I guess this kind of thing is popular," Olivia said as the three of them walked up the street to the Wickenburg Fire Department. The double garage doors stood open and the two big red engines stood in the bay, chrome and windows gleaming brightly in the early morning sun.

"All-you-can-eat for five dollars," Kelsey said.

"Really." Olivia shook her head. Five dollars in Manhattan would just about buy a bagel.

Kelsey led the way around the side of an L-shaped one-story building to a door on the side. Obviously, she'd been there plenty of times before. The door stood open, and when they walked in, a sandy-haired guy with broad shoulders and ruddy complexion saw them and grinned.

"Hey there, I see volunteers." He glanced at Olivia. "I remember you."

She remembered him, too. He'd been there when she and Elizabeth had come looking for Riley in need of advice. She searched her memory for his name. "Sven, right?"

His grin broadened. "I can see I made an impression."

Olivia laughed. Maybe all firefighters were genetically predisposed to be flirtatious and somehow inoffensive about it. Probably all as unserious about it as well. "It's good to see you again."

"We're supposed to be helping with setup," Elizabeth said. "And Olivia's got kitchen duty. Is Riley around?"

"I think she's in the big tent checking the steam tables. I'll take you two back there." He pointed over his shoulder. "Kitchen's back that way."

"Right, thanks," Olivia said. As Elizabeth and Kelsey followed Sven, she made her way through a lounge area populated with tables and chairs, a couple of sofas, the requisite giant TV, and a scattering of coffee tables. Double doors on the far end led into a brightly lit kitchen. She stopped just inside. A redhead about Riley's height, or perhaps a couple inches taller, stood at the stove in the familiar fire department uniform.

"Hello," Olivia said, "I think I'm supposed to be helping out back here?"

The woman flipped several pancakes on a large griddle and turned. Her eyes were the green of spring grass, a color that Olivia had often read about but rarely ever seen. Her complexion was lightly tanned, and when she smiled, the picture was altogether very attractive.

"I'm Hadley Archer. How are you at flipping?"

"Pancakes? I think I can probably handle that." Olivia walked forward with one hand extended. So this gorgeous woman was Hadley. The Hadley that Riley had convinced to leave her nice city job and answer the fire bells in Wickenburg. Wait, were there still fire bells? Were there *ever* fire bells? And why would anyone voluntarily do that without a very good reason? More money? Not likely here in this little town. Prestige—again, no. That left personal, didn't it. Rekindling old flames? Ha—bad pun. Stirring new ones? Olivia kept her *pleased to meet you* smile firmly in place and her imagination on hold. "I'm Olivia Martinez. Riley conscripted me for kitchen duty."

Hadley took her hand and shook it warmly. "Great. Watch these guys and go ahead and use the rest of the batter. I've got another bowl ready to go in just a minute."

"How many pancakes are we talking here?" Olivia asked, obediently taking the spatula.

"Last time I did one of these, we needed a few hundred. I'm thinking at least half that." Hadley shrugged. "It's my first time, so I could be way off."

Olivia could feel her brows climbing. "I think you're going to need a bigger griddle."

Hadley grinned. "My favorite movie."

"One of mine, too."

"What is?" Riley said as she walked in.

"*Jaws*," Olivia and Hadley said together.

Riley looked between the two of them. "Well, I can see you've appropriately bonded. There's a line forming outside, Had."

Hadley looked up at the big round clock on the wall. "That sounds about right." She set another double griddle on the eight-burner stove and turned on the flame. "We're just gearing up here for production. We should be fine."

Riley smiled at Olivia. "I can see you already have your assignment."

Olivia waved her spatula. "Official flipper."

Riley looked tired, although her eyes were clear, and she exuded her normal energy. She crossed over to Olivia, and Olivia detected her familiar crisp, mildly outdoorsy fragrance as she drew closer. She occasionally noticed when someone wore an attractive scent, but Riley's caught her attention every time. Made her want to move a little closer just to…

"Scooch over just a bit," Riley murmured. "I want to check the bacon in the oven."

"Oh, sorry," Olivia said hastily and stepped aside. Luckily she hadn't let the pancakes burn while she daydreamed of what? *Smelling* someone? One thing was certain—the desert climate was affecting her brain.

Riley and Hadley discussed how the preparations were going elsewhere, leaving Olivia alone with her pancakes. They all worked together for another twenty minutes, pouring, flipping, stacking with Riley carrying trays of food out to wherever they were going to be served.

"I understand that you've just recently moved here," Olivia said, as Hadley mixed another batch of batter.

"That's right," Hadley said, pouring the last of the pancake batter. "And you're working out at the ranch, right?"

"Yes."

"How are you liking that?"

"It's my second tour of duty," Olivia said, and Hadley laughed. A nice laugh, full and mellow.

From behind them, Riley added, "Olivia's a city girl, but she makes the best of it."

"Oh, I don't know," Olivia said lightly, "I think I've been appropriately inducted now. If you count the rodeo and the hoedown along with this, I'd say I've experienced most of the required activities."

"Oh, we've probably got some other excitement we can drum up before the summer's over. But that's a good start," Hadley said. "We've got the community birthday bash coming up pretty soon. You won't want to miss that."

"I can't wait," Olivia said.

Hadley laughed again, her gaze warm as she met Olivia's. "I'll make sure you get an invitation."

"I'll look for it." Elizabeth was right, Hadley was easy to be around, friendly and charming. And Riley's good friend. That was a relationship Olivia couldn't help wondering about. Exes? That was one she hadn't considered, and she didn't have any real reason to think that. Still, watching them together, kidding and talking about firehouse happenings, she could tell their connection was a long and easy one.

"Well, that about does it," Riley said after she returned from delivering the last tray of bacon. "I think it's time for us to start dishing out the food."

"I'm going to go greet some of the townspeople," Hadley said, "and leave keeping the steam tables full to you two for a while."

"No problem, we can handle it. Go do chief things," Riley said as Hadley washed her hands.

"That's part of the job I don't envy," Riley said after Hadley left them. "The politicking."

"She seems like she really enjoys it, and people can probably tell."

"You're right about that. Hadley is a people person, and that's why she's perfect for the job. And a helluva firefighter."

As they walked through the station and out into the large lot behind the building where a big, white tent that could've held a three-ring circus stood with a line of people already waiting to enter, Olivia said, "You've known each other a long time."

"Since we were recruits," Riley said.

"She's very nice."

Riley gave her a look. "She is."

Inside the tent, four tables stood end to end along the rear wall with a row of stainless steel steamer pans. The room was filled with rows of tables and chairs where people would eat family-style. Kelsey and Elizabeth were just unfolding the last of the chairs. Olivia saw them and waved.

"Might as well let them in," Riley called.

A young female firefighter opened the flaps on the front of the tent, and a rush of people moved toward the food line in a more or less orderly fashion. The next minutes passed by in a rush of conversation flowing from all directions that Olivia couldn't follow, for the most part people greeting Riley and other firefighters and talking with those in line about the news or the weather or some other town-related happenings. Olivia ignored the noise as food disappeared from the steamers at an amazing pace. As one tray would get nearly empty, she or Elizabeth or Kelsey or one of the firefighters would bring out another tray.

At one point Hadley appeared and scanned the food tables. "How we doing?"

"As long as there aren't another hundred people waiting outside, we should be all right," Riley said.

Hadley looked out over the jammed tables. "I think the bunch we've got could probably eat enough for another hundred people."

"It's barely seven thirty," Olivia said. "I can't believe it."

"Vultures," Riley said, and they all laughed.

By eight thirty, the room was still full of people lingering to talk and drink coffee. To Olivia's amazement, they somehow still had some food left over, and she realized she was starving.

As if Riley had read her mind, she said, "Care to join me for some pancakes?"

Olivia laughed. She was having fun, not something she had anticipated. "I'd love to. Thank you. Is bacon part of the invitation?"

"Absolutely."

Olivia piled food on her plate and followed Riley toward one of the nearly empty tables at the side of the room. They'd just reached the table when Riley went completely still, her plate still in her hand, as she stared across the room. For just a second, Olivia saw her pale before color flared back into her face. She looked where Riley was staring, and a young blonde with a young boy at her side threaded their through the tables in her direction. The blonde's attention was riveted on Riley.

"Ashley," Riley said in a voice just above a whisper. Riley had put her plate down and took a step away from Olivia. The blonde kept coming until she was stepping into Riley's arms. Riley held her as the blonde pressed her face to Riley's neck.

❖

For an instant, Riley's mind was blank, her body frozen. Ashley. Why was Ashley here? She could still hear her screaming how much she hated all of them—the firefighters who had let her husband die. She never wanted to see any of them again. She hadn't said it, but she'd meant *Riley.* Riley, who had let her husband die.

A tug on her leg and an excited young voice brought her back to the present.

"Riley—I mean—Firefighter Riley, can I see the fire truck?"

Ashley pulled away, wiping furiously at tears with one hand. "Sorry. I'm so sorry. He heard about the breakfast at school, and I had to bring him." She brushed a hand over the towhead's crop of sun-kissed hair. "Hey, Luke. We have to be patient, remember? Firefighter Riley is busy right now."

Riley bent down. "Just Riley is fine, Luke. How about some pancakes first thing?"

She barely recognized Luke. He was in school already? Could that really be possible? Luke had been a toddler when Kevin died. She'd seen Ashley frequently right after the tragedy, at the funeral, and later, helping her work through the details of Kevin's benefits and departmental family support and all the paperwork. Doing something, helping in some way, didn't relieve her guilt but kept at least some of it at bay. Then time had passed, and she'd returned to work, and they'd had less and less to say to each other. There'd been that one time she'd gotten together when Ashley had called her, and she'd taken Ashley and Luke for ice cream. Ashley had told him about his father, that he'd been a firefighter and that Riley was, too. Like most small kids, he was fascinated by the idea and had seen fire trucks during parades. He was still fascinated. Riley rose and took Ashley by the elbow, turning to introduce her to Olivia. She looked around and realized Olivia was gone.

"I'm sorry, I shouldn't have come," Ashley said. "He just wanted—"

"No," Riley said quickly. "It's fine. I'm glad you came. Some of the old crew are around here somewhere. They'd want to see you and say hi to Luke."

"I thought it would be harder," Ashley said quietly. "I thought it would make me sad or angry, but it doesn't, being here, where Kevin loved it so much. Seeing all of you, who he loved too."

Riley swallowed hard. She was glad things were easier for Ashley. She'd gotten used to living with the memories herself, and seeing Ashley and Luke, to her surprise, didn't make it worse. "Come on, let's go find Mike and Brandy. They'll want to see you." She looked down at Luke. "And this guy. Maybe we can sneak him out to the engine bay and set him up in the truck for a minute or two." She knelt down. "But it's a special treat just for you. Okay?"

"Okay." Luke, wide-eyed, looked so much like Kevin that Riley's heart nearly splintered. But he had his mother's eyes, a brilliant blue that glowed with happiness.

Seeing that, Riley's heart mended just a little. She glanced once more around the tent but didn't see Olivia. Holding Luke's hand, she said to Ashley, whose tears had disappeared, "Let's go see the fire station."

❖

"Hey," Olivia said as brightly as she could manage when she found Elizabeth and Kelsey carrying a row of chairs to a storage into a shed behind the firehouse. "What can I do to help?"

"All done inside?"

"Yeah," Olivia said, "and I've got a ton of work to do, so I thought I'd lend you a hand. Unless you're planning to stay later. Then I can get an Uber back to the ranch."

Kelsey chuckled. "An Uber? Yeah, not likely."

"Why not? Ubers are just about everywhere these days."

"There are a couple that service Wickenburg, but usually on runs from the airport into town or out to the airport by appointment. But they're not sitting around in town for a call to come and get me now."

Olivia blew out a breath. "Okay then. Let me know what I can do to move things along."

As Kelsey walked over to a row of folded chairs and two long tables, she called, "This is the last of it. We won't be much longer."

Olivia muttered, "Right," and followed after her.

Walking by her side, Elizabeth leaned close and said, "I thought I saw you headed off for breakfast with Riley."

"Apparently one of Riley's friends showed up. I decided I wasn't that hungry."

Elizabeth frowned. "Riley didn't introduce you?"

"It looked like it was personal."

Elizabeth looked past her to the tent. "Cute blonde, thirty or so, even cuter little boy?"

Olivia didn't turn around to look. She'd already seen the cute blonde with her arms around Riley and her face in Riley's neck. "That would be the one. Do you know her?"

"No, but I don't know all of Riley's…friends."

"You can say girlfriends. I already told you, it's not like that." Olivia paused. "It looked like she was crying, though."

"Okay, well, that's interesting. I guess we'll ask Kelsey. There's nothing that goes on in Wickenburg she doesn't know about."

"Never mind," Olivia said. "It's really not important."

Elizabeth regarded her steadily. "You know, you've never been a very good liar."

"And you have always been entirely too stubborn. I'm serious. Riley's friends are not my business."

"Uh-huh." Elizabeth hefted one end of a long table and Olivia grabbed the other end. Kelsey lifted an impossibly large stack of chairs.

"Show-off," Elizabeth said.

"Just trying to get your attention."

"You don't have to try, babe."

Olivia groaned. "Please, you two. Honeymoon's over."

Kelsey laughed. "Not in this lifetime."

"Hey, babe," Elizabeth said, "did you happen to see the blonde Riley walked by with a minute ago?"

A shadow passed over Kelsey's face before she answered, "Yep."

"Know her?" Elizabeth asked.

"That's Ashley Howard and her son Luke."

"Is there a story there?"

Olivia muttered, "Elizabeth, jeez."

"There is," Kelsey said, "but not mine to tell."

"Okay, well, we're done," Olivia said quickly. "This has been fun. Now let's get going."

Elizabeth shot her a look that said, *You're* really *a bad liar*.

Olivia didn't care if she was being obvious. What she wanted was to settle down at her nice, orderly desk, far from women who smelled too good and occupied far too many of her thoughts.

CHAPTER ELEVEN

Olivia spent the next week in her trailer from six until dinner finalizing the plans to break ground for the new equestrian complex. The plans had expanded as they always did as she and Elizabeth projected future programs and uses for the space. She'd put off requesting the fire inspector's site visit because...well, she wasn't ready. The plans weren't ready, rather.

Today—she'd call the county office and leave a message today. She had to call the county offices anyhow since Elizabeth had asked her to track down the town plot maps. *Efficiency, thy name is Olivia.*

When her phone signaled a call from her mother at six a.m., her stomach twisted. She hadn't missed a call home, and for her mother to call so early, something must be wrong. She pushed accept. "Mama? What's wrong?"

"Your papa is home. I thought you'd like to say hello."

Translation, her mother wanted her to exert her influence— of which she had none, in actuality—over the stubbornest person, including Elizabeth, she'd ever met. "Is he sick?"

"He has the flu."

"It's not the flu," she heard her father grumble in the background.

"And how long has he had the flu? What does the doctor say?"

"He hasn't been—"

"I don't need to bother the doctor over a cold." Louder this time.

Olivia sighed. This wasn't the first time her father had complained of having the flu—or rather, he'd told her mother that was the reason he was tired and short of breath. He worked long hours, longer than most of his colleagues. She couldn't remember the last time he'd taken a vacation. "Let me talk to him."

"I'm not sick," he said an instant later.

"Good," Olivia said, desperately hatching a plan on the fly. "Because I need the two of you to come out here."

"What?"

In the background, she heard her mother's, "What? Are you sick? I knew it!"

Olivia winced. Ah, speakerphone. Nothing was ever private any longer.

"Are you sick?" her father repeated.

"I am. I'm homesick. I didn't think I would be, but this project is a big one and I'm going to be here quite a while. I need to have all my mind on my job, and I haven't been sleeping all that well—" All true, even the not sleeping part, although that had more to do with restless dreams and a constant sense of physical edginess. All things she didn't want to think about. "I know it would be a big imposition, but I thought if—"

"We'll be there in a few days," her father said. "Should your mama make reservations with Elizabeth?"

Olivia grinned. "No, Papa. Just text me your flights. I'll take care of reserving a casita for you."

Her father said goodbye after assuring her they'd be there soon, and she hurried to get dressed. She was already late meeting Elizabeth at breakfast.

"Did you oversleep?" Elizabeth asked when Olivia sat down with her at a small table by the windows in the dining room.

"Emergency call from my parents."

Elizabeth set her coffee cup down. "Is someone sick?"

"My father's been fighting what he calls the flu for a few weeks, and he's too stubborn to go to the doctor. What is with men who think it's weak to go to the doctor?" She poured syrup over the pancakes Maria had set in front of her and instantly thought of the pancake breakfast. And Riley. She hadn't heard from her—not that she had any reason to—or seen her since then. Riley hadn't been out to the ranch, or at least if she had been, she hadn't been to dinner. Olivia could have asked Kelsey about her, but...obvious much? So she'd just tried hard not to think about her, which most of the time did not work. That might explain her restless nights. "He's also a workaholic, and if he's not teaching, he's tutoring four or five kids or teaching Bible school on Sundays."

"Your dad's a good man."

Olivia knew from experience that what Elizabeth didn't add was *not like my asshole father.*

"He is. I know." Olivia set her fork down, suddenly guilty. "I might have manipulated them a teeny bit."

Elizabeth's brows rose. "Really? What did you do?"

"I told them I was homesick."

"Are you?" Elizabeth asked, her expression changing to concern.

"No, but they wouldn't come otherwise, and they need a vacation."

Elizabeth leaned back in her chair, a smile forming. "When are they arriving?"

Olivia grinned. "Soon. I'll give you the info as soon as I have it."

"I'll hold the casita that overlooks the golf course. The view is great, and it's a short walk up to the house for dinner."

"Thank you. I think they need it."

Elizabeth squeezed her hand. "I can't wait for them to arrive. They'll love it."

❖

On her way to her office, Olivia noticed Riley's truck in front of the main stable. Or she thought it was Riley's, except maybe… every truck looked the same, and she'd just been thinking about her, so maybe… No, that gorgeous woman in blue jeans, a tight black T-shirt, and work boots walking out of the barn with Josie was definitely Riley.

At that moment, Riley looked her way and stopped. "Olivia? Hi."

"Hi," Olivia said, walking over to her. "'Morning, Josie."

The small, tight-bodied blonde in a blue cotton shirt, jeans, and chaps waved. "'Morning."

"Taking a group out?" Olivia asked. "Early start today."

"Yep." Josie grinned. "Three-day trail ride. I've got room for one more."

Olivia pretended to look over her shoulder. "Don't see any takers."

Riley laughed along with Josie as Josie strode off.

"You're here early, too," Olivia said to Riley.

"It's shovel the poop day," she said.

"I'm sorry? You're shoveling—"

"Not me. Got a minute?"

She didn't have a minute. She didn't really have thirty seconds, but Riley's warm smile and look of anticipation was enough to make her rearrange her whole day. "Sure."

"Come on in the barn."

Olivia said a prayer for her shoes—at least she had permanently retired everything with open toes—and followed inside. "I've never actually been in a barn."

Riley stared. "Any barn?"

"They're not exactly commonplace in Manhattan—or Istanbul or Tokyo, for that matter. And I somehow managed to miss the pleasure the previous times I've been here." She laughed as Riley rolled her eyes.

"I'd forgotten you're a world traveler," Riley said. "Miss it?"

Olivia thought about it. "No, I don't. Maybe if I'd never seen the places I have, I might want to at some point. But I've done that, been there already."

"So, ah, you're looking to settle down, then."

Olivia tried to read what was behind Riley's question. What was she really asking? Did she want to know if Olivia was available? She remembered the blonde from the morning of the firehouse benefit. How did she know Riley really was even available?

"I have a home in Manhattan," Olivia said to put an end to her going-nowhere mental musings.

"Of course," Riley murmured.

Olivia studied the barn. The huge, soaring space was not what she expected. It had a floor, for one thing. She'd expected dirt. Shavings sprinkled the wide dark planks in places, and a fine, unexpectedly sweet scent filled the air. The ceiling—roof?—rose twenty or thirty feet overhead with exposed beam rafters twelve inches wide. Stalls with open half doors lined one wall.

"Where are the horses?" Olivia asked.

"In the corral or one of the larger pastures."

At that moment a boy of around ten, dark hair flying, his brown face alight with what Olivia could only call joy, hopped out of a stall and called, "Riley! We're done in here."

"Well, let's see how you did."

Other young voices called from farther down the barn, "We're almost done, too."

"Ramon, this is Ms. Martinez. She works on the ranch."

"*Hola*, Ms. Martinez."

"*Hola*, Ramon."

He nearly jumped in place. "Come see."

Olivia followed Ramon and Riley to the stall and peeked in. A red-haired girl with a long braid dragged a big blue plastic bucket filled with horse…dung…to the stall opening. Shavings and straw covered the rest of the floor. It all smelled nice.

She smiled at Olivia. "Hi, I'm Emily Crowley. Are you going riding?"

"Not today." Olivia smiled.

"Good job, guys," Riley said. "Why don't you wait for Julia and Mateo to finish, and the two of you can do wheelbarrow duty."

"Okay, sure." Ramon hurried down the wide aisle yelling for Julia.

"Who are the kids?" Olivia asked. "And how many are there?"

"Wickenburg schoolkids. Six or eight altogether. They rotate depending on how they're doing with their homework or other goals set by the teacher. Could be something practical like learning how to buy groceries or ride a bus. A lot of them need to help out at home."

"You're teaching them to scoop poop?" Olivia asked quietly.

Riley laughed. "That's the fun part. I'm also helping them to organize themselves into groups and work together. And the importance of caring for other living things."

Olivia's throat unexpectedly tightened, and she swallowed hard before she spoke. "That's…you're remarkable."

Riley blushed. Olivia had never seen her blush, and the effect was so tender her throat ached more. She touched her arm. "Do not say you aren't. You want to, but don't. What you're doing for them—the joy you're giving them, never mind the life lessons they absorb—is special."

"Uh, I just wanted to—"

"Hush," Olivia murmured, pressing her fingers to Riley's mouth.

Riley's eyes widened. She leaned into Olivia's hand for a heartbeat before stepping back and said, "If we weren't here right now, I'd ask if kissing you would be out of line."

Olivia's pulse jumped. Now would be the time to back off. To a very safe distance. She knew exactly how to defuse this particular explosive device, one that could easily disrupt her entire life. Wrong person, wrong time, wrong place. "What about the blonde I saw you with at the fire station? I don't get in the middle of people with a thing going."

Riley frowned. "A thing? Ashley and me?"

She actually sounded appalled. "The two of you seemed very close, so I wondered."

"No," Riley said so forcefully Olivia blinked. "Not Ashley— never. She's—her husband was one of my best friends."

Was. Olivia said, "I'm so sorry."

"Is that why you disappeared?" Riley asked.

"Whatever was going on, it seemed very personal. I thought privacy was warranted."

Riley nodded. "Okay. You were right. But just so we're clear— I'm not seeing anyone. Haven't been for a while."

"Neither am I," Olivia said, "just to be clear."

Riley nodded, the look in her eyes dark and hungry. "Now that we're clear, about the kiss."

Olivia laughed. So much for safety. And good sense. "If we weren't likely to be interrupted by a nine-year-old, I might have said yes to a kiss."

"Ten," Riley said hoarsely. "They're ten. God, Olivia, I want—"

Olivia laughed. "You should hold that thought."

"For how long?"

Olivia shook her head. "I don't know. Right now, I have to get to work. And you have kids to mind."

She turned to go. She needed air and a breath of sanity, quickly. She'd actually contemplated dragging Riley into a stall and...What? Kissing her where anyone could walk in?

"I'm not sure I'm remarkable," Riley called after her, "but I have other good qualities."

Olivia smiled and kept walking. She was quite sure those qualities included kissing and other things she needed not to be thinking about but knew she would.

Chapter Twelve

Riley watched Olivia walk away and leaned against the stall door. Jesus, she was so turned on she wasn't sure she could walk. From a little touch on the face. Lips. It had been lips. Way, way better than a touch on her cheek. Her head was spinning. Olivia had said she could kiss her—wasn't that what she said? Okay, not exactly—she'd said might let her—sometime.

Sometime was too damn vague. That could mean next month or next year or, Fates forbid, never. No way. Now she had to kiss her or lose her mind. When? How? She wasn't usually so clueless when it came to seducing women. But she wasn't, was she? She wasn't trying to seduce Olivia. Maybe that was the problem. Olivia wasn't a one-time kind of woman, and Riley was. So what was she supposed to do? Court her? That was not a good idea. Or was it? Courting didn't *have* to mean chapel bells and promises. Courting could just as easily lead to a nice, eyes-wide-open sexual affair.

She could do that, couldn't she? Slow and easy, let Olivia set the pace, keep it light? Sure she could. By the time she'd dropped the kids off back at the school and waited for their parents or sibs to pick them up, she had her hormones under control and her brain mostly online again.

After a quick burger at the Tastee Freez drive-thru, she crossed town to the New Horizons site to get some work in while there was still daylight. She frowned when another truck pulled into the dirt drive a few minutes after her, and Hadley, Sven, Mike, and Travis piled out.

"Hey, Cap," Riley said, walking over to them while buckling on her tool belt. They all held similar wide leather belts with a variety of tools appended. "What's going on?"

"You said you were putting in a few hours today. We're here to help." Hadley leaned into her truck, pulled out a folder, and handed it to Riley. "Time sheets."

"Um—I don't remember mentioning anything about wages," Riley said, staring from one face to the other.

"Oh, I should have mentioned that," Hadley said. "The town board agreed to pay contractor wages for everyone who works on the project. You included."

"You won't hear any arguments from me." Elation swelled within her. With help—experienced help—they'd have the building ready for a certificate of occupancy in weeks instead of months. "Let me show you where to start."

"I spent time as a plumber's apprentice," Travis said, "before I realized how boring it was. I can do the rough-ins, no problem."

"I worked with the power company my first year out of high school," Sven said. "I can handle the electrical."

"I'm a hammer and nail girl myself," Hadley said, and everyone laughed. "Just tell me what you want nailed."

Riley grinned. "All right, follow me."

As sundown approached, Hadley found Riley measuring the counter space in the kitchen. "It's looking good."

"Thanks for all the help," Riley said. "Here and with city hall."

Hadley laughed. "That's a big exaggeration."

"Euphemism."

"It benefits the department, but I'm glad to help, too." Hadley hesitated. "I haven't seen Ashley since the funeral, and I didn't get a chance to say hello before she left. She looked good. A little shaky, though."

Riley winced. "Kev's birthday. She's doing okay, though, and she's made sure Luke is, too."

"Ah, hell. That's tough." Hadley hesitated. "What about you?"

Riley tensed. "I'm fine, Cap."

"Wasn't asking as your captain."

"Same answer."

Hadley nodded. "Good."

"We should wrap up here," Riley said. "Getting dark."

"You ought to swing by the station," Hadley said. "Margie's making tacos."

"I'll be there."

By the time Riley showered at the station house, changed into clean clothes, and had dinner, the night shift had come on duty and someone mentioned a card game. She was still there when the first alarm sounded a little after midnight and the crew on call jumped up, grabbed gear, and loaded onto the engine truck.

Fifteen minutes later the second alarm sounded, and Riley joined the remaining crew to respond. The fire at the Cactus View motel just south of Wickenburg proper was on the cusp of becoming an inferno. Smoke billowed out of the windows on the third and fourth floors when Riley arrived on the ladder truck. She jumped off as the crew engaged the hydraulics to raise the ladders and get the hoses up to douse the fire from above. She scanned the building and the position of the crews already on-site. A flash of movement obscured the glow from a third-floor window for just a second. If she hadn't been staring up there, she would have missed it.

"Hey," Riley said, grabbing a volunteer firefighter dragging a hose past her. "Where's the IC?"

"Over at the command car."

"Thanks."

"Who have you got inside?" she asked Richardson, the incident commander. The heat from the burning building radiated across the blacktop to the command center, and Richardson's face streamed with sweat. Riley already sensed the blacktop getting soft beneath her boots.

"No one. The fire's too hot, and we pulled our guys out."

"Did they get everyone else out?"

"We think so," he said, the flames reflecting in his eyes.

"You *think* so?" How could he not be certain?

"It's a motel, Mitchell. They don't exactly take a head count. No one knows who's in or out half the time."

Riley cursed inwardly and slid her rebreathing gear effortlessly into place.

"Where are you going?"

"Inside. I saw someone at the window." She pointed to the floor two floors above the smoke.

"You can't go in there. The fire's too hot," he repeated. "You could be chasing shadows, for fuck's sake."

"I *saw* someone." She jerked her arm away when he tried to grab her. "No one is going to die while I'm on the line." *Not again*, she thought as she raced toward the motel entrance.

"I'm with you," a young woman called, and Riley glanced over to her.

Dee Crowley, a volunteer firefighter who always responded when her phone rang, ran beside her.

"No. Wait outside and relay messages from me." No way was she going to be responsible for the life of another firefighter.

Crowley slapped down her full-face mask. "Let's go, we're wasting time. I'll be right behind you."

"Channel 3," Riley snapped. With no time to waste arguing, Riley pushed through the dense smoke billowing out the door. She'd kick Crowley's ass later.

"Stairwell on the left." Dee's voice crackled over the radio.

The air was black as Riley climbed the stairs. Some idiot had propped open the doors to the stairwells, and smoke filled their only escape route. She kicked the door closed once Crowley entered. They didn't need more oxygen flowing upstairs to feed the fire. The smoke got thicker and the air hotter as they climbed from floor to floor.

"I saw them on this floor," Riley said, counting the landings as they climbed. "To the left—somewhere near the middle. I'll go left, you take the other end of the hall. There may be others. And for fuck's sake, do not open a door if it's hot to the touch. If there's fire on the other side, we'll have a backdraft and the whole hall will go."

"I got it, I got it," Crowley answered and hurried away.

Thankfully most of the doors already stood ajar. Whoever had been in them had already fled. Riley checked the closed doors, opening each one for a quick search until she finally found an elderly woman unconscious on the floor halfway between the closed window and the door. Riley quickly tugged off her gloves and felt for a pulse. Weak and thready. Ripping off her mask, she placed it on the woman's face, providing her a brief supply of fresh oxygen. Keeping her own breathing shallow to inhale as little smoke and noxious fumes as possible, she keyed her mic.

"Crowley, I found her."

"All clear, this end."

Riley secured the mask to the woman's face as she lifted her into a shoulder carry and lurched out into the hall. Following Crowley's headlamp through the murk, she worked her way down the stairwell as quickly as she could. Eyes streaming from the smoke and coughing from the fumes, she stumbled out into the parking lot and was immediately surrounded by EMTs and other firefighters. On her knees, she breathed into the mask the medic pressed to her face. After a few breaths, she turned and vomited, but her head felt clearer. A few more hits from the oxygen, and she got to her feet. Her chest hurt and her eyes continued to burn, but she'd been through worse, much worse. She tuned out the scene commander chewing her out for going into the building. A chorus of other voices shouted at her, but she waved them all away and headed back to her crew. Richardson could write her up if he wanted. She'd done what she'd had to do.

One voice penetrated though. Hadley's.

"Next time you want to risk your ass, check with me first. You okay?"

"Yeah." Riley coughed. "Fine."

"Bennie," Hadley called to the EMT manning the rescue squad. "Take Mitchell to the ER. Have them clear her."

Riley backed up. "Hell, no, I'm not—"

Hadley's face was suddenly very close to hers. "Not a suggestion. Go."

"Yes, Cap," Riley snapped.

Fortunately, the ER took first responders right away, and after a chest x-ray and a set of blood gases, they let her go. Back at the station, she took a quick shower and filled the water carafe on the station's Keurig. Technically, her twenty-four-hour shift had started when she was at the fire, and she was on duty for the next twenty hours. She should try to get some sleep—another call could come at any time—but sleep would not be her friend that night. It rarely was, especially after a fire. She'd almost certainly recall all the details, as clear as if they had been recorded, except this time, she'd fail in rescuing the woman. In her dreams, she always failed.

Riley pulled clean clothes from her locker. Now that the adrenaline slowed, anxiety threatened to smother her. Every fire she fought was a potential danger to her crew or innocent victims. Even when the outcome was good, her mind conjured disaster. What if they hadn't gotten there in time? What if they hadn't sprayed water in that exact spot? What if she hadn't found the victim? What if she couldn't get inside? What if…?

Closing her yes, Riley focused on her breathing and the cadence of calming techniques. Unexpectedly, an image of Olivia formed in her mind, as if Olivia was reminding her that the past was the past. Now was the now.

"The lady's going to be okay."

Riley jumped. Dee Crowley stood in the doorway of the locker room, her face sooty, her deep red hair a mess from her helmet.

"That's good."

"I can't believe Richardson chewed you out like that," Crowley said.

Riley shrugged. "I deserved it."

She'd disobeyed orders, and it wasn't the first time she'd caught hell for doing something other people considered careless. She supposed it was, but she would do it again. Every time. "I'll be hearing about it from Hadley before the day is out. I'm sorry I pulled you into it."

"You didn't," Crowley said, her dark chocolate eyes unblinking, her voice, with her strong Louisiana accent, firm. "I volunteered. I was there for the same reason you were. To save lives."

Riley nodded. Crowley's words were simple and true. "Then we did the job. So—thanks."

Crowley grinned. "No problem. I think I'll head home before I run into the captain, though."

Riley laughed. Maybe her sleep would be easier after all.

CHAPTER THIRTEEN

Olivia sat down with coffee and her iPad in the restaurant that overlooked the eighteenth green of the golf course to catch up on news while waiting for Elizabeth to join her for lunch. Elizabeth had built the new clubhouse the year before, and though Kelsey hadn't been sold on the idea at first, she'd recently admitted the guests who were less adventure-minded loved it. Olivia could relate. She logged on to the *Wickenburg Daily Star*, a news outlet that covered town news and offered a surprisingly detailed calendar of local and regional entertainment events—the rodeo that she'd gone to on her first tour at the ranch, street fairs with food and art, and community affairs like the firehouse breakfast. Almost every Saturday that it didn't rain—ha ha—which meant almost every Saturday year-round, featured cattle auctions, of all things, and other town events that might interest guests who wanted to take in the local sights. As she skimmed past the news, a single word leapt out at her.

Fire.

At any other time, she might've ignored it. Certainly accidents, violent crimes, and countless forms of destruction to life, limb, and property were the business of the day in a large city like New York, but out here, accidents and other catastrophes very often involved neighbors or friends. And, she thought, sometimes people closer than friends. Her heart pounded, even though she had no reason for the sense of dread that filled her, other than knowing that Riley did a dangerous job that at any time could be the source of injury or worse.

As she skimmed the story, she tried to place the motel that had been destroyed in the fire, but she couldn't quite fix the location. She hadn't really explored beyond the direct route into Wickenburg and around the small town itself. There were several of the drab and somewhat dreary motels crouched beside the arid strip of land that passed as a road on the route into Wickenburg. Below the somewhat dry report of a fire that had completely engulfed and destroyed the Cactus View Motor Court several nights before, the article wasn't very informative. However, the headline just below certainly was.

Hero Firefighter Saves Victim of Fire.

Her body slowly chilled as she read the recount of the hero firefighter who had dashed into the burning building to rescue a guest trapped several floors above the fire. "With only moments to spare, Firefighter Riley Mitchell located the elderly female guest from Tulsa, Oklahoma, and carried her to safety. The victim and firefighter were treated at the local hospital and released."

Hospital. How could Riley have been taken to the hospital and she didn't know about it? Why hadn't Kelsey said something? She rose abruptly.

"Are you leaving?" Elizabeth said as she sat down opposite Olivia. "Has something come up? I can do the interview, but I thought you'd want to talk to her yourself."

"Why didn't someone tell me that Riley was injured in a fire the other night?"

"What?" Elizabeth said. "I don't know anything about it. That can't be right. Kelsey would know."

Olivia turned her iPad to Elizabeth and pointed to the headline. "It says right here."

Elizabeth stared for a moment and then raised her eyes to Olivia. "Tell me."

Heat replaced the chill as Olivia flushed, and reality drove some of the panic away. Of course Elizabeth couldn't read it. Not quickly or easily. "I'm sorry. I wasn't thinking."

"You're upset. Sit down. I'm sure we would have heard something. Riley doesn't keep things like this from Kelsey."

Olivia sat and read the article to Elizabeth.

"That sounds like sensational journalism to me," Elizabeth said when she'd finished. "Call her and ask her."

"Call who?"

Elizabeth stared. "Riley? The person you're so worried about?"

"I can't do that."

Elizabeth cocked her head. "Why not?"

"Because. Because…I just can't. It's not like that."

Elizabeth leaned forward, still studying Olivia intently. "What isn't like that?"

"Whatever it is that's happening between us."

"Oh," Elizabeth said, the word rising slightly at the end. "The *something* that's happening, or maybe isn't happening, between you two prevents you from ordinary interactions like calling up a friend when you're worried that something might've happened to them?"

"It's an invasion of privacy."

"So you need some kind of invitation."

Olivia did not squirm, but she wanted to. Her excuses sounded pathetic to her own ears. "I don't know her well enough to ask her something personal like that."

"You don't know her well enough. After, what is it now, two years of acquaintanceship and, as you so unhelpfully said, whatever the *something* is that is going on between you?" Elizabeth snorted.

Olivia shook her head. "When you put it like that, it sounds ridiculous."

Elizabeth laughed. "For heaven sakes, call her and make sure she's all right. Then you can finally tell me what it is you are trying so hard to avoid saying."

"I guess I can text."

Are you all right?

The reply was instant. *Fine. Something wrong?*

I read about the fire. It said you were injured.

No. Departmental regs. Had to get checked out. Where are you?

Olivia frowned. *At the ranch.*

Where at the ranch?

Restaurant. Luncheon meeting.

Text me when you're done.

It will be a few hours, Olivia replied.

Text me.

OK

Olivia glanced at Elizabeth. "She's fine. She said it was all just protocol or something."

"Good. That wasn't hard, was it."

Olivia narrowed her eyes. "You're enjoying this."

"I'd be enjoying it a lot more if you shared what was going on."

"Nothing is going on, and there won't be."

Elizabeth threw up her hands. "For heaven sakes, why not?"

"Because—"

"You said that."

Exasperated, Olivia blurted, "Because Riley is looking for a good time, and I'm not!"

"You're looking for a bad time?" Elizabeth said, stone-faced.

"Elizabeth, you are not helping."

"So you're not attracted to her?"

"Of course I am." Olivia blinked. Had she ever actually said that to Elizabeth before? Had she ever even said it to herself in those words? "Yes. Yes, I am."

"Is this something new?" Elizabeth asked carefully.

"What? That it's Riley, or that I wanted to kiss her?"

"Well, both, but I meant your interest in women?"

"Not really new," Olivia admitted. "I've had a few...encounters. Brief ones."

"I've wondered. Why didn't you ever tell me?" Elizabeth didn't even try to hide the hurt in her voice.

"I don't know," Olivia said. "I'm sorry. I didn't mean to hurt you—or for it to go on this long, really. The...secret."

"Why has it?"

"I guess I didn't want to hear it from you," Olivia said wearily.

"Hear what?"

"That I should live my life, however I see fit. You know my parents, and their beliefs. I'm a coward, I guess, but I just didn't want to face the drama—and they *would* be hurt—especially when I've never been serious about anyone."

"You're not a coward. It's not easy doing something that will hurt someone you love." Elizabeth laid her hand on Olivia's arm. Her touch, like the caring in her eyes, was warm and comforting. "But what makes you think I'd be anything other than supportive of your decision?"

"Because I tell myself all the time it's not what a strong, independent woman does. Live her life for her parents." Olivia shrugged. "But you know my parents. No way can I have a girlfriend without major family upheaval. And even if I could somehow change their views, I don't live here. Secondly, Riley does. Third, my parents aren't getting any younger, and eventually they'll need me to take care of them, which I can't do if I'm not there. I won't even go down the path that they expect a house full of grandbabies."

Elizabeth tugged at her lip with her teeth. "That's a lot of rationalization over why you can't kiss a girl."

Olivia winced. "I *know*. Even to my ears it all sounds stupid, archaic, weak, cowardly, spineless, and whatever other word I can think of to describe how I feel about myself."

God, she was tired. Exhausted from fighting the internal battle with her parents to live her own life, not what they expected her to do. Tired of fighting her attraction to Riley.

"What are you going to do?" Elizabeth asked again.

"Absolutely. No. Clue."

"Whatever it is, I agree." Elizabeth laughed and finally, Olivia did, too.

"I can't talk about this anymore now. We've got a meeting." She tilted her head toward the entrance where a slender woman with gorgeous auburn hair, eyes so dark they might have been black, and legs that went on forever stood taking in the room. She wore a pale olive-green shirt that complemented her light brown skin, wide-legged ochre pants, and shoes Olivia would kill for. "Adelle Hebert is here."

❖

"I reserved a room for you in one of the casitas," Elizabeth said as she, Olivia, and Adelle walked around the property after dispensing with the usual interview discussions.

"Thank you," Adelle said in her melodious alto. "I thought I'd ride through town tomorrow to get a feel of the place before I head back the next day."

"I'd be happy to show you around," Olivia said. "In fact, if you need a ride to the airport, my parents are coming in the same day you're leaving."

"Oh," Adelle said, "that should be nice for you."

Olivia smiled, thinking, *I certainly hope so.* "They've never been here, so I'm looking forward to their visit."

"I have a rental car I need to return to the airport," Adelle said, "but I appreciate the offer of a guided tour tomorrow."

"Wonderful."

Adelle said, "When do you anticipate the center to open?"

For just an instant, Olivia thought of New Horizons, because almost everything brought Riley to mind. In the next second, she realized they were talking about the equestrian center, where Adelle would be the lead behavioral therapist if she took the job. She was the third candidate they'd interviewed and by far the most experienced. She also espoused a personal philosophy regarding client wellness programs that fit in well with hers and Elizabeth's. "We hope to be ready for clients by the end of summer, assuming no unanticipated major delays."

Elizabeth laughed. "From your mouth to God's ear."

"Well, minor delays are par for the course," Olivia said, "but I've accounted for those in the schedule. I hope. How does that timetable work for you in terms of moving?"

"I'm ready to go any time," Adelle said.

There was a slight bitterness to her tone that Olivia noted but didn't comment on. Everyone had their stories, and certainly someone who was planning to move halfway across the country must have a good reason for relocating other than a good job. But Adelle was perfectly suited for the job, and she hoped she would take it.

"When you've made your decision," Olivia said, "and I hope that will be yes, I'll keep you updated on the progress. We'll be able to talk more about the specifics of hiring other therapists and assistants then."

Adelle paused, shading her eyes with one hand, and glanced out across the desert toward the mountains. "It's quite beautiful, isn't it?"

Olivia was able to appreciate the beauty now, having watched the slow flowering of the desert, the amazing dawns, and the glorious sunsets.

"It's taken me some getting used to," she said, "but I think so, too."

"I want to think it over a little bit and of course see the town and the potential living accommodations," Adelle said, "but I have to tell you, I have very good feelings about this place, your program, and the both of you."

"Wonderful," Elizabeth said. "Let me take you around to the casita, and we'll have one of the staff bring your things over."

Adelle shook Olivia's hand. "It was great meeting you. I'll see you tomorrow morning?"

"Definitely. Six in the dining room?"

Adelle laughed. "Oh my, you are a New Yorker. I think I can manage to get up that early, but you know, in New Orleans, the day doesn't start until eleven."

Olivia laughed. "We all have to deal with culture shock."

Adelle smiled as she and Elizabeth left, and Olivia took a deep breath, mentally reviewed everything she had planned to do that afternoon, and then texted, *I'm free now.*

Good. My truck is parked in its usual spot by the stables. Care for a burger?

Olivia hesitated only a moment. *Absolutely. I'm starving.*

Chapter Fourteen

R iley leaned against her truck, excitement buzzing through her. She'd debated for three hours about making a move after her text from Olivia earlier. Not that a date for burgers was exactly her idea of a sexy occasion, but Olivia had said yes. And anything having to do with Olivia was sexy. And watching her stride down the path toward the stables definitely confirmed the sexy part. Olivia always looked great, but the weather had warmed considerably the last few weeks, and Olivia had opted for a short-sleeved shirt that showed a little bit of cleavage, and that was enough to get Riley revved.

"Hi," Olivia said as she approached.

"Hi," Riley echoed, already all kinds of not-cool. Every time she was alone with Olivia, her brain stopped working.

"Were you playing racquetball?"

"Huh?"

Olivia tilted her head, giving her a questioning look. "What are you doing here? I thought you might be at the sports center with Kelsey."

"Oh. No. Yeah. This." She held out the folder she'd been holding in her left hand.

Frowning, Olivia took it, glanced inside, and actually made a little squealing sound that shot straight to Riley's groin. "You did the inspection! Oh my God, I could kiss you."

"Okay, sure," Riley said hoarsely.

Olivia blushed and pressed the folder to her chest. "You didn't tell me you were coming."

"The request has been in my in-box for a few days, and I had time." She'd hoped she'd run into Olivia when she came out to do the inspections, but this was way better. "So, um, burgers then?"

"Yes. Yes—everything is okay?" Olivia waved the folder.

"Fine. I'll need to come back again—well, you know the deal."

"I do." Olivia's smile was electrifying.

Riley was close to incinerating. "So?"

"Let's go get burgers."

"I can do better than that," Riley said as she held the truck door open for Olivia to climb in. "I'll throw in beer and fries along with it."

"Cheeseburger. Make it a cheeseburger, and you'll score more points."

Riley glanced at her as she headed toward the local burger joint. "Are you keeping track?"

"I might be," Olivia said.

She was flirting. Riley knew flirting when she heard it. The buzzing escalated into uncomfortable pounding a bit lower down. "How am I doing?"

Olivia pointed to the folder that now jutted out of her bucket-sized bag. "Extremely well."

Riley laughed. She'd never looked forward to beer and a burger so much.

They carried their food on red plastic trays to a table under big, multicolored umbrellas on the back patio. Olivia had surprised her by ordering a pitcher of beer. When the waitress, a curvy blonde in a red, barely-there cropped top showing off her toned midriff, brought it out to them, she looked pointedly at Riley.

"How are you doing, Riley? Haven't seen you for a while."

"I'm good, Jean. Thanks."

After an awkward few seconds when Riley didn't say anything else, Jean cast a cutting look toward Olivia and walked away.

"Friend of yours?" Olivia asked with an amused look on her face.

"No," Riley said simply.

"She wants to be."

"Not interested."

Olivia leaned forward. "What type of woman *does* interest you?"

"That's a loaded question."

Olivia smiled, her dark eyes glinting. "I know."

Riley liked a challenge. Okay—she'd play. "Women who are intelligent, who enjoy a little adventure, and who go after what they want when they see it."

"That's pretty broad," Olivia said. "Blond, redheaded? Blue eyes, brown? Tall, leggy?"

"Hmm." Riley pretended to think. "Short or tall, long hair or bald, brown or blue—big boobs or small..." She grinned when Olivia laughed. "It's what's inside that makes me interested." She paused. "Although for quite some time, I've been totally attracted to the not-so-tall, petite, dark-eyed brunette type."

Olivia's very dark eyes widened, and her very lush lips parted just a tiny bit. "Really."

"Really."

Olivia took a long breath. "Well then, some woman is going to get very lucky."

Riley shook her head. She didn't think so. Not for anything serious. Any woman would want more than she had to offer and deserved more than her screwed-up head. "Your burger is going to get cold."

Olivia leaned back as if sensing the topic was closed. She tried the burger and made an appreciative sound Riley couldn't help wishing she'd heard under other circumstances.

"Excellent burger." Olivia wiped her mouth with a paper napkin, and Riley tried not to stare. She had an overpowering desire to feel if Olivia's lips were as soft as they looked.

Olivia went on as if Riley weren't almost drooling. "So—how did you get to be a firefighter?"

"You mean other than the grueling training?" Riley dug into her own order, grateful for the safer subject.

"I expected that part," Olivia said.

"One summer when I was fifteen, my family went on a very rare vacation to Yellowstone. My parents are real estate agents and never took a day off. I don't know why we even went. My brothers were mostly off on their own then, so I had to amuse myself." She paused. "Do you have sibs?"

"Just me."

"I learned a lot from the guys, but sometimes I felt like an only child, too." Riley refilled Olivia's beer. She was driving, so one and done. "Anyhow, I stumbled onto a ranger station. One of the rangers was a woman, and I was...intrigued."

"Was she hot?"

"Very, but hey, I was fifteen and just figuring myself out." Riley smiled at the image of Firefighter Hightower. "They got used to me hanging around and were great about answering my thousands of questions. One day they got called about a missing child staying at the same lodge as me and my parents. Everyone was out watching the search, and I tagged along."

"I hope this ends well," Olivia said.

"It does. I was down by the lake when the firefighters spotted the kid in the water. Jaclyn Hightower, the hot firefighter, never hesitated. She jumped in the lake and in less than a minute was carrying the girl out of the water, performing mouth to mouth at the same time. She laid her on the ground and kept working on her until the girl spit out a mouthful of water and started to cry."

"Thank goodness," Olivia said.

"I decided then and there that was what I wanted to do, be a firefighter and save lives. My parents, however, had a meltdown. They informed me I was going to college and joining them in the business."

"I see how well you listened to them."

"I did. Well, I played the part until I was old enough to join the fire service. I dropped out of school and told my parents the morning I was leaving to start training."

"You're obviously in the right job."

"Why do you say that?"

"Like you said—you want to save lives, and you like to live dangerously." Olivia reached for her beer. "You're a smoke jumper, you run into burning buildings, you fly out of airplanes with a tiny piece of silk to break your fall, and you build a haven for kids to be themselves."

"You make me sound reckless," Riley said, not used to being seen so clearly by anyone—not even Kelsey. And Olivia was right.

"Kelsey said it was a calling. I don't know what else might motivate you."

Riley mentally drew away. That was a story she'd never told.

"Don't tell any of any of my friends, but I kind of miss this," Olivia said after a moment's silence.

"How so?" Ice slid down the side of the pitcher as Riley watched. Olivia was very good at knowing when to back off, and Riley appreciated it.

"Just having a burger and a beer and…talking."

"You don't have burgers and beers in New York?"

Olivia smiled. "No, we do."

"But?"

"Most of my friends are vegan, and beer is a four-letter word."

"And you don't order what you want when you're with them?"

"Sometimes, sure." Olivia waved a hand at her mostly empty plate. "They'd give me crap if I ordered this, though."

"Really?" Riley shrugged. "If my friends did that, they'd no longer be my friends."

"I know it, and you're right." Olivia sighed. "Lately I've been asking myself why I make choices that make other people happy instead of me."

Riley heard the hurt in her voice, and for some reason that made her angry. She slid her hand over Olivia's. "What do you mean?"

Olivia stared at Riley's hand, turned hers over, and gripped Riley's fingers between hers. "I'm not an insecure person."

Riley chuckled. "I've noticed. I've seen you handle butthead contractors and tardy fire inspectors."

"Stop," Olivia said, laughing softly. "I never harassed you about the inspection, although it was coming."

"So you let your friends choose the restaurants. Not a great sin." But there was more, she could tell. "Who else? Who else do you choose over yourself? Elizabeth?"

Olivia jerked back but kept hold of her hand. "Never. She is my best friend, more than a sister—I love her, and she loves me."

"Hey, I know. Sorry."

"It's okay," Olivia said, visibly relaxing. "My parents—who I also love. But they—sometimes I'm not sure they see me."

"How so?"

"My parents immigrated to this country when I was a child in order to give me a better life. They sacrificed a great deal to do that, and they've spent the rest of their lives doing everything they could to help me have that life."

"They sound like great parents," Riley said.

"They are. Your burger is getting cold," Olivia said.

"You're stalling." Riley took a bite of burger. "What don't they get about you?"

Olivia took a swallow of beer. "Everything."

When Olivia didn't go on, Riley said, "Such as…"

"If it were up to my parents, I'd already have six kids."

Riley choked on her beer. Every head turned and looked at her, and she coughed. "Sorry. Just went down the wrong pipe." Finally, she stopped coughing. "Six?"

"Yep. And considering I'm already thirty-six with no desire to be pregnant, that's not happening."

"You could adopt."

"Maybe. With the right partner—who I also do not have. Single motherhood is not for me."

"What would your parents say to the adoption idea?"

"What they always say. 'Find a nice man, get married, and have babies before it's too late.'"

Riley looked at her, eyebrows raised. "Ah, find a nice man?"

Olivia looked away for an instant, as if about to change the subject again, then met Riley's gaze. "They don't know I wouldn't be choosing a man."

"And you've never said anything?"

"I never had any reason to," Olivia said.

Riley frowned, thinking about the almost-kiss Olivia said she might have said yes to. The one she was really hoping they'd get to soon. "You've never…with a woman, I mean."

"Well, yes, but that's hardly something I'd run home to tell my parents about." Olivia withdrew her hand. "Would you?"

"No." Riley had a feeling she was missing something, but didn't know what. She didn't miss that Olivia was backing off, closing up, though. "What about girlfriends? Did you just not tell them about your parents?"

"There weren't any, that's the whole point." Olivia blew out a breath, apparently frustrated that Riley wasn't getting it. "When Elizabeth and I traveled, I'd have a fling or two. That's it. Not anything I'd write home about. And not all that often. My parents expect certain things from me and…"

"Kissing women is not one of them?" Riley said.

"Unfortunately, no."

"Then why are you flirting with me?"

"Three reasons," Olivia finally said.

"Care to share?"

"Well," Olivia said, holding up one finger, "first, because it's fun, second," she added another digit, "I don't always do everything my parents tell me, and—"

Riley interrupted. "Let me guess, it's harmless."

"Wrong," Olivia said firmly. "Because you are not a fling."

"What am I, then?" Riley asked softly.

Olivia answered just as quietly, "I don't know."

CHAPTER FIFTEEN

The drive back to the ranch was silent. Riley had opened the truck windows, and the cold air blew through the cab, carrying the night sounds. In the distance, a pack of coyotes howled. They echoed the loneliness that had engulfed Olivia as she rode through the dark. She'd told Riley things about herself that had taken her years to tell Elizabeth, and she wasn't sorry she'd been honest with her. Riley deserved that. Only now realizing the barrier she'd undoubtedly put between them, she felt the loss of what might have been.

"Do you want me to close the windows?" Riley said after the longest time.

"No, I like to hear them. And the way the night smells."

"You're shivering."

"I forgot how cold it gets at night. It was seventy-five this afternoon."

"There's a denim jacket rolled up in the door pocket beside you. Put it on."

Olivia found it. It was too big, but she wrapped it around her. "Thanks."

Riley pulled through the arched gates of the Red Sky and slowed. "About the fling."

"I should apologize—I didn't mean—"

"What you do or don't tell your parents is your business. But you're right, a fling is not something you need to tell anyone about. It's temporary, right?"

"By definition, yes," Olivia said cautiously. Word traps were the language of negotiation, and she knew better than to fall into one. Riley was going somewhere, and until Riley disclosed the destination, Olivia was not volunteering to go along.

"I live here, in Arizona," Riley said.

"Again, yes," Olivia said.

Riley pulled the truck in before the stables, well outside the circle of illumination thrown by the big halogen light above the closed stable doors. All the horses were bedded down, and the wranglers most likely asleep in the bunkhouse. Lamps glowed in the main house fifty yards away, but to anyone looking out, they would be invisible. Riley turned on the bench seat and faced Olivia. "And you live in Manhattan."

Not at the moment, Olivia did not say. Nor did she add, *I'm not even sure if I'm going back.* She'd have to think about what that meant some other time. "True."

"So a fling is pretty much what we're talking about."

"Were we talking about it?"

"Since it follows flirting, yes." Riley extended an arm along the seat and tangled a strand of Olivia's hair around her finger. She tugged ever so lightly, and Olivia's clit jumped.

Oh, that was bad. And *very* good.

"So, yes," Riley repeated, "I think we were *about* to talk about it."

"Riley."

"Yes?" Riley edged closer, sliding past the wheel and the stick shift. The scent of cactus and evergreen drifted to Olivia, sealing her fate.

"Something comes between flirting and flinging."

"What?" Riley murmured.

Her eyes were very blue—how could that be, when only the moon lit them? Olivia slid her hand to the back of Riley's neck and drew her closer. "Kissing."

Olivia had kissed other women, but nothing prepared her for this. She never acted impulsively. always knew just what she was about, even in the midst of pleasure, but the moment her lips touched Riley's, all thought fled. Only sensation remained. Only Riley. Riley's lips were warm and soft, and she tasted ever so faintly of spices and malt. From out of nowhere rose an overwhelming desire to taste and drink and sate herself in all that was Riley. The mystery of her, her strength, her passion. Even her recklessness stirred Olivia on some atavistic level. Riley was dangerous in a way that made her blood race.

Riley clasped her waist and caressed the arch of her hip with her thumb, pulling her closer until Olivia's breasts pressed to Riley's chest. Olivia's nipples hardened instantly, and the pulsations low in her belly doubled in tempo and pressure. She moaned softly as Riley's tongue swept over her lips and teased into her mouth. Guided by nothing more than the urgency within, she sucked lightly on Riley's tongue and grazed the warm surface with her teeth. Riley groaned, and Olivia shivered, her arousal spinning higher and higher.

She liked when Riley made that sound, liked knowing she had caused it. She inched closer on the bench seat and turned, drawing her leg over Riley's. Half straddling her, she rose above her and pushed her fingers through Riley's hair. She deepened the kiss, her eyes open, heart threatening to burst from her chest. Riley leaned back, both hands on her hips, pulling her snugly into her lap. Riley's leg fit between hers, hard and so, so sexy.

Olivia grasped Riley's shoulders, steadying herself, and pushed down against Riley's leg, the instantaneous pressure between her thighs sending a jolt of excitement through her. Her hips bucked. Riley circled her waist with one arm and cupped her breast.

Olivia moaned. "Oh, you feel so good."

Riley opened a button on Olivia's shirt, and her warm fingers brushed the curve of Olivia's breast.

Olivia gasped. She wanted…she needed…

Too much, too soon.

She pushed back with her arms braced on Riley's shoulders and broke the kiss.

"Don't go," Riley gasped, both hands coming to Olivia's hips again, urging her more tightly into her lap.

"I'm so…" Olivia shuddered. "It's all too good. *You're* too…I have to stop a minute."

"I don't want you to ever stop," Riley whispered, her mouth against Olivia's throat.

Olivia caressed Riley's neck, held Riley's face to her for an instant. "If I don't, I might come right here."

"You're so beautiful," Riley said. "I want to touch you everywhere. I want to hear you come."

Riley kissed the edge of her breast and Olivia arched, pleasure swamping her. Each subtle touch coaxing her closer. One more second, one more caress…

With every ounce of willpower she owned, Olivia shifted away and back onto the seat next to Riley. "I am not going to do that in the car on our first date."

Her words came out between her ragged gasps for air. She needed to clear her head…so wildly, insanely turned on.

"You're right," Riley said, reaching for her hand, gripping it tightly. "But I want you. More than anything."

Olivia turned her head on the seat to meet Riley's incendiary gaze. "I want you, too, more than anything. More than maybe is sensible."

"Fuck sensible. Can't we just take what we want?"

"I don't know. I don't even know if I know how to do that."

Riley gently traced her finger along the angle of Olivia's jaw and leaned closer, kissed her softly, and drew back. "What do you say we practice until you do?"

"You don't mind?" Olivia asked, all of a sudden uncertain and a little afraid. That feeling was so foreign, it frightened her even more. She couldn't really care this much so soon, could she?

"Whatever you want, whatever you need, is exactly what I want." Riley kissed her again. "And I think, maybe, what I need, too."

Olivia reached behind her, found the door handle, and pushed it wide open.

"You know you're a very special woman?" Olivia asked as she slid further away.

"Not so much," Riley murmured, "but I can promise you this. I'll never lie to you. And I meant what I said. I want you more than anything. When it's right for you."

"When it's right for *both* of us." Olivia stepped out. The stars, always so brilliant in the blackest of skies, shone so brightly tears formed in her eyes. That had to be the reason her vision swam.

"Wait," Riley called. "When can I see you again?"

Olivia brushed at the moisture on her cheeks. "My parents are flying in the day after tomorrow. I'd like you to meet them. Come to dinner?"

For an instant, Riley looked stunned, and Olivia laughed. The fear and uncertainty vanished. "It's not what you're thinking. I just… they're the most important people in my life. I'd just like them to meet you. No strings. Remember?"

"Then I'll be there," Riley said.

I'll be there.

The words echoed in Olivia's mind as she hurried up the path to the house. She wouldn't let herself ask for how long. She wouldn't ask any of the questions she couldn't answer.

CHAPTER SIXTEEN

The next morning, Olivia was still thinking about the kiss. About how warm Riley's lips had been. About the taste of her. About the thrill when Riley had had just as much trouble catching her breath as she had. She hadn't fallen asleep right away, had slept restlessly and finally gotten up earlier than usual to wait for Adelle in the dining room.

"Morning," Elizabeth said as she joined her.

"Oh. Morning," Olivia said brightly. She needed to focus. After acquainting Adelle with all the Wickenburg sights, which ought to take less than the entire morning, she had a key meeting with the general contractor, the engineer, and the architect for final review of the construction plans. Excavation was scheduled to begin in the morning. And of course, her parents would be arriving the same day. But she could multitask—that was her main skill set. If only her brain wasn't fogged with runaway hormones.

"You missed dinner last night, and now you're not hungry?" Elizabeth poured coffee into Olivia's empty cup. "Charmaine said you hadn't ordered yet when I stopped in the kitchen."

"I didn't miss dinner." And she was actually plenty hungry. Hungry for Riley in a way she'd never experienced before—for her touch, for the feel of her. The sound she'd made when Olivia had literally climbed on top of her. God, had she actually done that?

"I was here with some of the guests until nine," Elizabeth went on. "I must have missed you."

"I was out with Riley."

Elizabeth's brows rose. "Oh? That's news."

"Not exactly," Olivia muttered. "It was just burgers and such."

"Such?"

Olivia sighed. Really. What was she hiding? "The such might have turned into kissing."

"Now, that *is* news. Which one of you finally made the first move? First kisses can be very telling, you know."

Olivia narrowed her eyes. "You are enjoying this, and there is not that much to tell. One kiss."

"Hmm. Who—"

"I started it," Olivia said.

"Huh. I would have put my money on Riley."

"Well, thank you very much for thinking I'm not able to seduce a woman."

"Did you?"

"No!" Olivia grinned. "I did not. There might have been flirting, and then a little negotiating."

"Okay, this sounds more like you."

"And she was sitting there, all sexy and smelling so good, and talking about flinging—"

"Flinging what?" Elizabeth said.

"Not flinging *things*—a fling. And then it just seemed ridiculous to go there when we hadn't even kissed, so I kissed her."

Elizabeth leaned her chin on her fist. "You know, this does sound kind of sexy."

"It was."

"Are you going to sleep with her?"

"I don't know." Olivia shook her head. "It's complicated."

"How so?" Elizabeth leaned back and sipped her coffee, that speculative look she got in her eyes when she thought someone was holding back information.

"The same reasons I already gave Riley. We live on opposite sides of the country, my parents would never accept it, I'm way too busy to get involved—"

"Do you aways tell your parents when you have sex?"

"What? Of course not."

"So that's not really a worry. Did you ever have sex while we were somewhere on a project?"

"Yes," Olivia said, feeling the heat in her face as she said it. Thinking of the times she'd never told Elizabeth. "I'm sorry."

"We've been over that. You're forgiven." Elizabeth paused as Maria placed waffles and eggs in front of both of them. "I ordered for you. You need your strength. My point is that those reasons are just excuses if you're only talking about having sex with Riley. Are you talking about something more?"

"No, of course not," Olivia said. She wasn't, was she? Nothing else was possible, after all.

"Well, then," Elizabeth said. "Let me know how the negotiations go."

"What negotiations?" Kelsey said as she stopped by the table and kissed Elizabeth. "Morning."

"Hi. How was the dawn trail ride?" Elizabeth stroked Kelsey's arm as she pulled out a chair to join them. She was still wearing her dude ranch cowboy apparel, jeans, boots, and a plaid cotton shirt. On her it looked natural because it was. Kelsey was a woman of the land.

Like Riley was a wildlife firefighter. Born to it. Olivia couldn't see either of them anywhere but in this wild country.

"Gorgeous," Kelsey said. "No problems. What negotiations—is there a new project I haven't heard about yet?"

"Not exactly," Elizabeth said, sending Olivia a questioning glance.

Olivia shrugged. She wasn't embarrassed about her attraction, and Elizabeth wouldn't divulge details, even if she knew any. Which she didn't, because there weren't any. And she could hardly ask her best friend to keep secrets from her wife.

"Olivia and Riley."

"What about them?" Kelsey asked.

"I love you, babe, but sometimes you are clueless." Elizabeth patted Kelsey on the arm.

Kelsey frowned, then broke into a grin.

"Oh, *Olivia and Riley*," she said, as if she had discovered the secret to King Tut's tomb. "When did this happen? Riley hasn't mentioned it."

"Because nothing has happened," Olivia interjected.

"She wouldn't anyhow, you ding-a-ling." Elizabeth rolled her eyes. "Riley doesn't seem to be the kiss and tell type."

"Wait," Kelsey said, looking from Elizabeth to Olivia, and back again, "there's been kissing? How do I not know this? Riley and I definitely have to revisit the best friend code of conduct."

"It won't make any difference," Olivia said as her phone vibrated, "she wouldn't…"

Her voice trailed off as she read the text.

Sorry. Can't make dinner with your parents

Olivia's heart sank. The kiss had been a mistake. Riley realized it, too. They were such a bad fit, even a fling was a bad idea. So that was done. But that was better, wasn't it? To end things before anything started? Even if she already felt as if something big had started.

Olivia took a long breath and replied: *I understand.*

Just until I get back.

What? Olivia frowned. Riley was going somewhere?

Back from where? she texted.

Wildfire in the Kaibab National Forest. Heading in with a drop crew to cut lines.

Olivia reread the words, only understanding the meaning of a few—Riley was going into the forest to fight a fire somewhere. That had to be dangerous, didn't it? Her insides twisted uncomfortably. Riley didn't need her to panic, as it wouldn't change anything. *Just be careful.*

Riley answered, *Always. I'll text when I can. Could be a while.*

Of course. Olivia wished she could see her before she left. Just to…see her. *I'll be here.*

Got to go, Riley replied. *Don't worry.*

"As if," Olivia muttered, setting the phone aside.

"Was that Riley?" Elizabeth asked.

"Yes."

"Problem?"

"I hope not. She's going somewhere to help with a wildfire. Does that happen often?"

Kelsey said, "Every once in a while. The fire departments out here all have crews ready to respond when the forest rangers need help containing a burn."

"How long is she usually gone?" Olivia's nerves jangled. Riley's job was unpredictable and dangerous. Riley had scars to prove it. And if there was trouble of some kind, Riley would be the first one to jump in—just like she had into the burning building.

"It depends." Kelsey shrugged. "Might be just a few days. If it's a big burn, it could be a few weeks."

Kelsey didn't appear too concerned. That had to be a good sign. Kelsey had known Riley a long time. She must be used to this kind of thing. Olivia doubted she'd ever be.

Elizabeth said gently, "You're worried about her, aren't you?"

"Of course I am. Who wouldn't be?"

"Hey," Kelsey said, "try not to. Riley is very good at what she does. She'll check in when she can, but it might be a while."

"I know she's very good. But—I've seen the scars." Olivia tried to sound calm, but Riley'd been hurt, and just thinking about her possibly being hurt again made it hard for her to think of anything else.

"Has she told you?" Kelsey asked quietly.

"No. And I haven't asked. When she wants to—if she wants to—she'll tell me." She pushed her uneaten breakfast away and rose. "Tell Adelle I'll meet her in the lounge when she's ready to leave for our drive to town. She has my number. I have some calls to make before I go."

"Sure," Elizabeth said, the look she gave Olivia telling her she was worried but that she'd let it go for now.

Olivia squeezed her arm as she passed. "Thanks."

She walked outside but didn't go down to her office trailer. Instead, she went to the corral where the horses who would be ridden that day by the guests and trailhands waited. She leaned on the top rail and watched them prance and gallop about. They were beautiful. Majestic in their grace and sleek power. Delicate and yet so strong. Magnificent contradictions.

She had lived a life where the absence of choices, by her own volition, also freed her from conflict and worry. With a kiss, she had opened the door to everything she had avoided—emotions that left her vulnerable to pain, allowing herself a connection that would threaten her ties to her parents, and most of all, the possibility that caring would lead to wounds—like Riley's burns—that might never truly heal.

She still had time to change her mind. That was a choice she couldn't avoid for long.

CHAPTER SEVENTEEN

Riley was emotionally and physically drained but too keyed up to go home, not even to just sit in front of the TV. She'd spent the last four days barely sleeping, checking and rechecking the information coming in from command on the front—wind speeds and direction, distance to the burn, location of the other crews, the evac routes, and safe zones. She'd tried to refuse when Hadley wanted her to lead the crew, even when the rangers only needed them to cut perimeter lines well away from the active front.

"Travis can take the lead," she'd said when Hadley had told her about the request for a fire crew.

"I want you to take it," Hadley said.

"No." Riley went back to polishing the engine truck.

"That's not a request, Mitchell."

Riley stiffened and kept wiping down the already sparkling chrome.

"Unless there's something I don't know," Hadley said quietly, "which I hope there isn't. I need my most experienced firefighter leading the team. Is there something you want to tell me?"

Yes. I'm scared shitless that I might miss something. That I might make a mistake. That I'll get them all killed. All of them. God, all of them.

"I read the reports," Hadley said.

"When?" Riley turned and looked at one of her oldest friends, a cold hand squeezing her heart.

"When I took this position. I also read the performance summaries and the non-confidential counseling sign-offs—on you and every other firefighter in the department. Because that's my job."

"Then you know I got them killed."

"I know you *didn't*. No one did. The fire killed them. It might have been you, too—"

"It wasn't," Riley said bitterly. "It should have been."

"Why?"

Riley stared. "I was in *charge*."

"Yes, you were—and you made the right call that might have saved everyone, but the fire won. No matter what we do, sometimes, the fire wins." Hadley held her gaze. "Muster the team. The chopper is on the way. I'll be in contact with command out there until you bring the crew home."

Riley had gathered her gear and her five-man crew and they'd climbed aboard the state police chopper that dropped them at their position on the southern perimeter. Now they were all back. No injuries. Her body sang with adrenaline, her nerves live wires that sparked and twisted, and beneath it all, the exhilaration of having conquered one of nature's most powerful adversaries.

She needed to blow off some energy, and she knew just the place. If Kelsey wasn't around, she could work out on her own. The beauty of racquetball was she could beat the little blue racquetball to exhaustion. Then a shower, a few hours' sleep, and she'd text Olivia. When she was a little more human.

She jumped out of the truck cab just as Olivia hurried up the path to the rec center.

Olivia stopped and blurted, "You're back."

"Hi. Yes."

"Oh. Well. Good." Olivia started away, and Riley called, "Olivia." Olivia looked back. "Yes?"

"I haven't even been home yet. I…I'm kind of wound up. I was planning to text you when…"

"You look exhausted. Why don't you go home and sleep. Text me later."

"Can't sleep. I was going to work out."

"I have a better idea. Come on."

Riley followed her. "What are we doing?" Not that she really cared. She was too tired to think, and seeing Olivia—just seeing her—had a weird calming effect. She'd have been happy to just walk around with her.

"Yoga. I'm taking over a class for our regular instructor. Fern's daughter is having a baby—a month early."

"Yoga?"

"Yes, you know—strength and flexibility, inner calm, meditative—that kind of yoga?"

"You're a yoga instructor, too?" Riley wasn't quite fitting the puzzle pieces together.

"Why are you looking at me like that? It's not like it's flying to the moon. No, I'm not a certified instructor, but I've been to classes for years, so I can fill in, in a pinch." She tilted her head and grinned. "You've never done it, have you."

"Am I a Neanderthal if I said no?"

"Of course not. Do you have gym shorts in your bag?"

"Sure."

"Good. That will be fine with that T-shirt."

"I don't think—"

Olivia took her arm and pulled her along. "That's the point. I don't want you to think. Let's get you changed. We've only got a few minutes until class starts."

Riley surrendered. If whatever they were about to do involved watching Olivia for an hour, she was all for it. After all, every moment she hadn't been obsessed with keeping everyone safe, she'd been thinking about kissing her again.

❖

When Olivia looked closer, she clearly saw that Riley was more than just tired. Her skin was pale, her eyes missing the usual spark. Even her body language told a story, and it was not one that was explained away by a vigorous hour or two on the racquetball court. She looked like she had been emotionally knocked down and was having trouble getting up. Olivia slipped her arm lightly around Riley's waist and pulled her along.

"I'm not sure about this," Riley muttered.

"Trust me—I have just the thing to not only help you relax, but actually replenish your healthy energy. I am the fixer of all things, didn't you know? Just ask Elizabeth."

"Since I have no idea where you're taking me or what's in store for me when I get there," Riley said, "I must trust you quite a lot."

Olivia slowed and met Riley's gaze, remembering the last time they were alone. "I promise I'll never lie to you."

"I know," Riley said.

"I'm taking you to someplace you have never been and will want to return to again and again." Olivia really did mean the yoga studio, but she couldn't help thinking of what other things they might do together, and her skin tingled.

"In that case, I'm in," Riley said in a husky tone that suggested she was thinking the same thing.

Olivia pulled open the door to the yoga studio and said, "Just grab a mat along with everyone else and do as much or as little as you're comfortable doing. And above all, let your thoughts drift."

"I'll try," Riley muttered as she walked to join the five women and two men already waiting.

Olivia introduced herself, made sure everyone was settled, and asked if anyone had questions. After assuring the novices that there was no right way or wrong way to practice yoga, relying on her memory of her many years of practice, she first took them through a series of breathing exercises to ease them into the poses. She kept a check on all of them, although her attention kept jumping back to Riley, who had set her mat up on the far end of the room. After a few minutes, she was happy to see that Riley looked more relaxed.

As the hour progressed, Olivia took the group through a variety of positions of varying difficulty that would be satisfying for the seasoned veterans and moderately challenging for the newbies. Riley was definitely in the latter category, and Olivia admired her strength, flexibility, and willingness to try.

As the poses grew more complex, she moved quietly around the room, occasionally adjusting the position of a limb or suggesting a modification if a pose seemed too difficult. As she approached Riley, Riley's body jumped into stark relief—the sheer physicality of her momentarily eclipsing every other thought in Olivia's head. The muscles in Riley's long, bare legs were taut and sharply defined, and the few inches of skin exposed above the top of her shorts where her T-shirt rode up revealed chiseled abs.

Olivia stopped a few feet away and instructed the group to lift their hips while lying on their back into a bridge pose, verbally describing the position as she watched Riley. After a quick check on everyone else, she approached Riley, her throat unexpectedly dry as she leaned over her.

"May I?" Olivia asked, as she had to each of the other participants before touching them.

"Yes, please," Riley answered, her voice husky.

Riley's eyes bored into hers as she bent closer, the heat in her gaze making Olivia tremble inside. A bed of sweat ran down Riley's neck. Olivia banished the fleeting image of tracing that trail of moisture down Riley's throat to the hollow at the base of her neck.

With one finger, Olivia gently touched the center of Riley's stomach. The muscles instantly tensed without her asking. "Yes, better. Now, roll your hips under without lowering them."

She touched a spot just below Riley's navel. "Here—this is your center. Breathe in and out from here as you hold your bridge—long in, hold…hold, slow out. Good. Very nice."

Riley was a natural.

"Listen to your body. Listen to your heartbeat. Feel your blood flow through your body, warming you from the inside. Feel your muscles relax and your mind quiet.

"Very good," she murmured thickly as she moved quickly away, the image of Riley arching into her mouth as she made her come nearly making her forget the rest of the class. She collected her wits and hurried back to the front of the room.

"Slowly release and return to savasana," she said, bringing the group into the last relaxation pose to end the class. After five minutes, she continued. "Thank you, everyone. Enjoy the rest of your evening. You can leave the mats if you didn't bring your own."

As the group filed out, she grabbed the disinfectant spray and a cloth from the supply closet to wipe down the mats. Riley was the only one left in the room.

"You're a natural," she said as she cleaned and rolled the mats and Riley came to join her. Why was she so nervous? Riley couldn't have been reading her totally inappropriate thoughts, could she? "So, what did you think?"

"You were right."

"About what?"

"That you'd take me to someplace I've never been and will want to return to again and again."

"Yoga will do that to you."

"Yes, I can see that." Riley took a step closer. "I think the instructor plays a big part in it, though. A very big part."

"I'm glad if it helped," Olivia said.

Riley brushed her fingers along Olivia's forearm. "*You* helped. Especially when I couldn't quite get that last pose."

"God, Riley—I'm sorry if I—"

"Hey, you can offer hands-on instruction any time."

Riley stood very, very close. The intensity in her eyes scorched. Her body radiated heat.

"My parents are here," Olivia breathed, wanting nothing in the world but to kiss her. To kiss her and more. Much, much more.

"Not right behind us, I hope," Riley said, slanting her head as if deciding the best angle for kissing.

"If you do that, I will miss dinner. Possibly breakfast."

"Do what?" Riley grinned and kissed her so quickly, Olivia teetered on the brink of forgetting everything else but how much she wanted her.

"You mean that?" Riley said.

"*That* was not fair."

"Did you not want me to kiss you, because I sort of thought you did."

"Not when I need to meet my parents—" She glanced at the wall clock and groaned. "In twenty minutes."

"I'm going to want more than twenty minutes the next time I kiss you," Riley said, looking very serious.

"So am I."

Riley stepped back. "You should go."

"You should get some sleep."

"You know? I think I'll be able to." Riley traced her finger down Olivia's arm. "I might even have good dreams for once."

"I hope so," Olivia whispered as Riley walked out. Maybe one day, Riley would tell her what haunted her dreams.

❖

Olivia hurried to the locker room, showered, and rushed to make dinner. She even managed to listen to a recap of her parents' adventures at the desert museum that morning and make appropriate noises in the appropriate places. Her father, thankfully, looked healthier than he had in a long time. The climate agreed with him. His breathing was noticeably better after only a week, and his stamina seemed better.

"You'll take us to that little church in town you mentioned tomorrow," her mother asked.

"Yes, of course," Olivia replied. "If you don't mind, though, I'm going to skip dessert. It's been a long day, and if we're going to early mass—"

"That's fine," her father said. "Buck and Kelsey invited me to a card game, so I need to go, too."

Olivia glanced at Kelsey. "Cards?"

"Every Saturday night in the bunkhouse—if you're brave enough." Kelsey grinned.

"I'm not." Olivia laughed. "Mama, will you be okay on your own for the evening?"

"Oh, yes. Charmaine asked me to show her how to make my *pepian de indio.* We're trading family secrets."

Relieved, Olivia said good night and hurried upstairs. Ordinarily she'd read or listen to a podcast in bed before falling asleep. She'd trained herself not to think about work or the many have-tos awaiting her the next day while using the relaxation techniques she practiced in yoga to help her unwind and sleep.

She didn't even pretend that was going to work tonight. The mere suggestion of yoga brought images of Riley in a dozen different positions roaring into her imagination, all of them with Riley in some variation of naked and most of them in Olivia's bed. A few featured deck chairs and kitchen counters. Olivia played a starring role, exploring Riley's body with her hands or her mouth or, in the instantaneous ways of fantasies, coming as Riley did the same to her. She stood in the middle of her room and rubbed her arms, trying to massage away the buzz of excess energy that felt like a hundred bees swarming through her veins.

"Not working," she muttered. She opened the window to the cooling night breeze and took a deep breath of the desert-scented air. That only made her think of the way Riley smelled, and her thighs clenched.

Well then.

In the bathroom, she filled the Jacuzzi tub as she stripped, turned on the jets, and slipped beneath the water. Sighing as the very warm water seeped into her tense muscles, she slid further down into the sculpted surround that mimicked the shape of her body. The pulsing jets on her back and legs echoed the pulsing between her legs that she'd been trying to ignore. Now as she welcomed the vision of Riley naked beside her, she embraced the pleasure of imagining Riley's hands moving over her body, teasing and caressing her. She stretched and shifted as the rhythmic pulsations heightened the urgency building inside.

Closing her eyes, she pictured the hungry way Riley looked at her, envisioning losing herself in Riley's gaze as Riley stroked her breasts.

She cupped her breasts, slowly and firmly squeezing each nipple, tugging until they hardened and ached. Now her clit pulsed in time with the dancing jets of water and Riley's fingers sliding between her thighs.

Oh, she wanted to come now, with Riley's fingers on her clit, pressing and circling. Her thighs tightened and her hips lifted—the warning streaks of electricity streaming from her center and piercing her deep inside. She brushed one hand over her breast, holding back.

Riley's hands, long fingered and tanned, with a pale white scar stitched across her left thumb, slowly stroked the length of her thighs, teasing between them with barely-there touches on her clit.

"Open for me," Riley whispered. "I want to make you come."

"Oh yes, I'm so ready."

"Here?" Riley asked, swirling just inside. "Is this where you want me?"

Olivia lifted her hips, opened her thighs to take her in. "There, yes, deeper. I need you deeper."

Her words turned to whimpers as the pressure soared, searing all thought from her mind. She wanted more. She needed more. "Inside me. I need you inside me."

Riley pressed harder, faster, the orgasm swelling. So close now. So close.

"Harder. I want to come. I can't wait."

Riley's fingers stroked deep inside, taking her higher and higher. Riley's kisses captured her cries as the pressure burst and pleasure flooded her. The orgasm crested, dipped, and built anew, higher, harder, and she shouted hoarsely as she came again.

The water rippled in waves back and forth in the tub as she finally settled back under the surface. She found the dial and switched off the jets, her limbs boneless and her brain fuzzy. Her legs barely held her upright as she quickly dried off and fell into bed.

Well then.

She smiled to herself as she closed her eyes. If that was what Riley could do to her in her imagination, she couldn't wait to find out what Riley would do to her in person. And she was done pretending she didn't want that to happen.

Chapter Eighteen

"It's still early," Olivia's mother said as they left the church after mass. "Let's drive through town. We haven't really had a chance to see everything that's here."

"Sure." Olivia laughed. "There's not a lot to see—not compared to Manhattan, but it's pretty this time of year and still not too hot."

"You like this place, then?" her father asked as Olivia drove down Main Street—didn't all small towns have a Main Street—pointing out a few of the little shops and the eateries. Passing the burger place made her think of Riley. As if she'd needed any prodding, considering she'd awakened thinking about her and the way the night had ended. If she hadn't promised to take her parents to church, she might have had a repeat just remembering it.

Slowing, she pointed out the firehouse. "That's where our friend Riley works—remember me telling you about the pancake breakfast they held here?"

Her mother laughed. "I wouldn't mind some right now."

Olivia didn't see Riley's truck. She hoped that meant Riley was still sleeping in.

"Olivia," her mother said, "turn down this street."

"Here?" Olivia turned onto Santa Rita. "Why?"

"Charmaine told me how that firefighter is building a house—a home—here for the young."

Olivia's breath caught. "She did?"

"Mm, when I told her about my work."

"There," her father said, "on the left. That must be it."

Olivia was sure it was. Riley's truck was parked in the pull-off beside a dirt lot and what looked to be a nearly finished building. The house was framed, the roof gables atop. Several stacks of lumber were laid out by size and length in front of the house, a stack of what looked like flooring material to one side. Several bikes leaned against a temporary fence by Riley's truck.

"That's Riley's truck. Do you mind stopping for a minute? I've never seen it."

"Oh, yes, let's," her mother said.

Olivia parked behind Riley's truck and walked with her parents toward the temporary side porch and the door into the two-story building. Just as they reached the stairs, Ramon came through carrying a bucket filled with wood scraps.

He grinned widely, revealing a missing front tooth. "*Hola*, Miss Martinez."

"*Hola*, Ramon. You're working early this morning."

"Riley's taking us out for breakfast when we're done."

"I see." Another one of Riley's secrets that made her more and more intriguing. "This is my mama and papa."

Ramon smiled shyly.

"What is this place exactly?" her father asked as Ramon carried the scraps to a nearby dumpster, her mother in tow, the two of them chattering animatedly.

"It's called the New Horizon Center," Olivia said. "It's planned to be a place for under-eighteen-year-olds, especially kids from underserved or underprivileged homes. Sort of a rec center with after-school programs and other activities. Riley will be able to explain it better, but she donated the property to the town and is heading up the building construction."

"Hmm," he said, taking in the nearly finished center. "That's quite admirable."

"Yes, it is," Olivia murmured as Riley stepped out onto the landing. She wore a navy long-sleeved tee with the bottom cut off just about belt level, paint-spattered jeans, and work boots. When she put her hands on her hips, an inch of tanned skin showed above her jeans, and Olivia knew exactly how tight the muscles underneath felt. Riley had tied a red bandanna around her forehead, and if she could look any yummier, which Olivia couldn't imagine, she'd be illegal.

Olivia momentarily forgot her parents and gave in to imagining all the things she'd wanted to do with Riley the night before.

❖

"Hi," Riley said, unable to take her eyes from Olivia, who wore a pencil skirt the color of cactus flowers, a print silk shirt with little cut-out places around the collar and along the sleeves that revealed tiny patches of skin, and sandals with blocky heels and open toes. Her hair was down, brilliantly black against all the color in her shirt and shining in the sunlight. Riley's mouth went dry, and her pulse thundered in her head.

"Hi," Olivia said, sounding just a little breathless. "Oh! These are my parents. Mama, Papa—this is Riley."

Crap. Her parents. Riley hastily wiped her hands on her jeans and climbed down the steps to greet them, ruthlessly abolishing images of ravishing their daughter from her mind. "Hello. It's great to meet you."

"And you," Olivia's mother said. "You can call me Consuelo. Charmaine told me of the wonderful thing you are doing here."

"She did?" Riley glanced at Olivia with a *help me* expression.

"Yes," Consuelo said. "I'm in social services. I teach English as a second language, so I know how important places like this can be."

As they talked, two more of the kids appeared from inside and clustered with Ramon around Riley. "Jenny, Ignacio—these are friends of mine, the Martinezes."

Hellos were exchanged, and Riley asked, "Would you like the grand tour?"

Olivia's father looked at his wife, who immediately said, "Yes. Perhaps the children can show me what they've been doing."

All the kids immediately volunteered, and Riley said, "What do we do when we're inside?"

"Watch where we're walking, stay out of any places that are roped off, and…"

"…don't fall through the floor!" they all yelled while bursting into laughter.

"It's really completely safe now," Riley said as she escorted Olivia and her father inside. Consuelo had already gone ahead with the kids.

"Where are their parents?" Olivia's father asked.

"Jenny's mom is at work right now," Riley said. "Ramon is in foster care with a good family—they have three others, too—and Ignacio…well, let's just say he spends a lot of time any place but at home, so I try to give him plenty to do here."

"That is a lot of responsibility," Olivia's father said. "I'm Eduardo, by the way."

That seemed like a small victory. Olivia's father, unlike her mother, struck Riley as being a little harder to impress.

"I just do what I can," Riley said, downplaying her role. These kids deserved so much more. "Here, let me show you around."

For the next few minutes Riley took them on a room-by-room tour, explaining as they went what programs and activities she hoped the center would provide. "Of course, a lot of that will be decided by the people actually running the place."

"Not you?" Eduardo said.

"Oh he—heck no. I'm a firefighter. I figure this place will need counselors and teachers and such."

"Hmm. Yes," he said.

The kids' voices echoed throughout the building as they excitedly pointed out to Olivia's mother everything they had done to help.

Ramon announced loud enough for the neighbors to hear, "Riley won't let us help if we don't bring our homework in to show we did it."

Riley laughed and looked at Olivia. "They clearly like your mother."

"They adore you," Olivia said softly.

"They just need a little guidance and a few kind words of encouragement."

"Well, you're giving them that and a lot more."

Riley warmed to the praise. "Thanks."

"Thank you for the tour," Consuelo said as they all walked outside a few minutes later.

"My pleasure," Riley said.

"Eduardo and I will be leaving for home in a few days. I hope we see you again."

"As a matter of fact," Olivia jumped in, "you should come to dinner before they leave. When do you go back on shift again?"

"Not for a couple of days."

"Great—tomorrow night, then?"

Dinner with her parents. Ookay. Anything for a chance to see Olivia again, even if it meant keeping her fantasies to herself when she looked at her.

"I'll be there."

❖

"Your friend Riley is very nice," Olivia's mother said as they sat on the porch of the casita waiting for Olivia's father to finish golfing with Elizabeth.

"She is," Olivia said, wishing she could tell her mother all the things she found wonderful and exciting about Riley. She'd never been in a position to discuss anyone whom she'd cared about in that way with her family before. Discovering she had to censor her feelings with her mother left her sad and a little angry.

"Your father has enjoyed being here," her mother went on.

"He seems more relaxed than I've seen him in a couple of years," Olivia said.

"I have been hoping he would retire."

"Did you ask him to?"

Her mother made a pfft sound. "Your father is a stubborn man."

"He is a proud man," Olivia said. "But he is a caring man, too. If he knew you worried, he would listen."

Her mother studied her curiously for a moment. "You haven't been gone quite two months, but you have grown wiser."

Olivia laughed. "Oh, Mama, I only wish that was true."

"Next you will need to learn patience. And perhaps I need to learn less." She cocked her head. "I hear the little cart coming. They must be done with their game."

"You wait for them. I'm going to walk down to the stables and wait for Riley."

"The stables?"

"Mm. She always parks there when she comes."

"Go then." Her mother made shooing motions. "I will see you at dinner."

Olivia didn't need to wait long. Riley was just parking as Olivia arrived. She walked over to the driver's door, leaned in as Riley opened it, and kissed her for a little while longer than she'd intended. But she just smelled so damn good, and tasted better.

"Hi."

"Holy crap. Parents!" Riley jumped as if she'd found a poisonous reptile in her lap.

Olivia laughed. "God, you're adorable when you're flummoxed."

"I am not…that." Riley glowered.

"If you say so. My parents are nowhere around."

Riley climbed out. She'd dressed for dinner in black chinos and a light blue open-collar shirt, black belt and boots.

"You look great," Olivia said. "And I'd really like the chance to kiss you again."

"If I survive dinner," Riley said, "how about we go on a real date. I promise there will be kissing."

"How long will I need to wait for this date?" Olivia asked as they walked toward the house. She loved the idea of a date, but kissing definitely took first place on her wish list, and any-old-where would do just fine.

"Less than a week. The town is having a birthday party at the town hall on Saturday night."

"Whose birthday?"

Riley gave her a look that meant she had missed something vital. She blamed it on the kiss, which still tingled all the way to her toes.

"Wickenburg."

"Oh. Of course." Olivia smiled. "How old is the town?"

"Depending on which town historian you ask, one hundred sixty, one-hundred and sixty-one, or one-fifty-nine."

"Will there be dancing at this party?" Olivia's stomach flip-flopped at the possibility of dancing with Riley again.

"Yes, there will be," Riley said, not taking her eyes off Olivia. "And as I mentioned, that could be followed by kissing."

"Then I'll be there." Olivia hoped she could wait a week without some part of her incinerating, because right at that moment, all she wanted was another wild taste of Riley Mitchell.

CHAPTER NINETEEN

Riley washed the truck, vacuumed it out, and shined her boots. The rest of her date night preparations meant grabbing a new pair of black jeans—washed twice to break them in, an emerald green shirt with white trim on the cuffs and collar, and a wide black belt that matched her boots and black Stetson. She drove up to the main house instead of parking in her usual spot by the stables. She couldn't have Olivia walking down in the heat and the dust. As she hopped up onto the wide porch, Kelsey hailed her from her spot on a bent-cane rocker where she sat sipping a beer.

"You look like a dude," Kelsey said with a hint of laughter.

"Fuck you," Riley said. "You planning to take your wife out wearing your shit-kickers?"

Kelsey craned her neck to examine her boots. "She likes my rugged look."

"Does she like the smell of horse shit, too?"

"Point taken. You here for Olivia, then?"

"Yes, why?" Riley said, unaccountably uneasy. She hadn't changed her mind, had she?

"She and Elizabeth are family, so Olivia is family, too."

Riley's back went up as she slid her hands into her pockets. "You have a problem with something?"

"Of course not. I'm kinda wondering, though, why you haven't mentioned anything about her." Sighing, Kelsey stood and walked to the railing. "You generally do when you're hitting on someone new."

"I'm not hitting on her. I'm taking her to the damn dance." Riley braced her arms on the railing and watched the sky bleed red over the mountains. "It's not like that with her."

"So what is it like?" Kelsey asked conversationally.

"Like I like her…a lot."

"Me, too. I like you a lot, too. So I hope it goes the way you both want it to."

Kelsey was her best friend—had been since they were kids, but that didn't mean she opened up to her about her deepest feelings on the regular. They didn't probe, they waited for the other to say what they needed to say, or not. And they always, always, had each other's backs. "You think I'm going to screw something up?"

"I know you wouldn't on purpose." Kelsey looked her in the eye. "I think Olivia could be the best thing that's ever happened to you."

The idea of anyone getting that close—close enough to see how fucked up she really was inside—scared Riley down to the toes of her gleaming boots. "That's just you being married talking."

"Could be, but doesn't mean it isn't true. Give yourself a break. It's time."

"I'll be careful, okay?" Riley said. "I'm not planning to go anywhere Olivia doesn't say she wants to go."

"Take it from someone who's been there—sometimes you end up where you never thought you'd want to go, and then you find out that's just where you want to be." Kelsey clapped her on the shoulder. "Now I better go change my boots."

Riley watched her best friend walk off in the direction of her casita and shook her head. That had to be one of the weirdest conversations they'd ever had. But she'd meant what she'd said. Olivia was in charge. That way nobody would get hurt.

"Hi," Olivia said as she came through the door, a quizzical smile on her face. "Have you been waiting long?"

"Just got here," Riley said.

"I love that hat," Olivia said.

"You look amazing," Riley said, wishing she had a better way with words. Olivia wore a sleeveless black dress that left a little bit of her shoulders bare, dipped just low enough in the front to be a heart-stopping tease, and hugged her body ever so gently as it fell to mid-thigh. Another pair of strappy shoes with heels high enough to bring her mouth within kissing distance if Riley dipped her head just a bit completed the look. Riley decided to test the theory and kissed her.

"Was that the kiss you promised," Olivia asked, "because I rather thought there'd be dancing first."

"Nope. That was just hello. The kisses I'm saving for later will be a whole other conversation."

"Oh good," Olivia said, looping her arm through Riley's. "I love pillow talk."

Yep, Riley thought as they walked to her truck, Olivia was in charge. And from the way her insides twisted into knots of wanting and amazement every time she looked at Olivia, Riley figured she might be the one ending up getting hurt.

❖

The mayor was finishing up his speech when Olivia and Riley walked into the civic center. Multicolored streamers draped the walls and cascaded from the ceiling, with a large *Happy Birthday Wickenburg* sign hanging behind the stage. A five-piece band was getting ready to play what Olivia suspected would be "Happy Birthday."

"Good timing. I've heard this talk about twenty times," Riley said, making Olivia laugh.

Elizabeth waved from a table as Kelsey rose and headed their way and the band broke into the expected song.

"If you want to join Elizabeth," Riley said, "I'll go fight my way to the bar—what are you having?"

"White wine is good."

Olivia joined Elizabeth while Riley and Kelsey squeezed into an empty place at one of the three bars set out around the room.

"Hi," Elizabeth said as Olivia slid onto the high-top stool. "You look great."

"Thank you. I wasn't sure if it was a little black dress or jeans and boots type of celebration." She wished she'd chosen the jeans. Sitting on a bar stool in a dress was always a modesty challenge.

"The way Riley is staring at your legs, she's glad you opted for the dress," Elizabeth said, nodding as Riley made her way back to them carrying the drinks.

"She's definitely hot tonight in that shirt—I wonder if she knows how it brings out the color in her eyes."

Elizabeth laughed. "I'm betting that is pure accident."

"Lucky me, then," Olivia said.

"You know what?" Elizabeth said. "You've been working nonstop since you got here. Go dance with Riley and have some fun tonight."

Have some fun? How did Elizabeth read her mind? Kissing would definitely be called fun. As would what she really wanted to happen next. What would it hurt to have a little fun? Riley understood nothing but fun was on the agenda—Olivia had already pointed out the reasons why. Riley hadn't objected. She'd been the one to say the word *fling*. With the year Olivia had had, she deserved some fun. And watching Riley looking at her changed her thinking from deserving it to wanting it.

"Hi, Olivia." Kelsey set a drink in front of Elizabeth and said to her, "I volunteered us to help out at Horizons tomorrow."

"Oh? Doing what, exactly?" Elizabeth sounded just a bit suspicious.

"Painting," Riley said, handing Olivia her drink. "We're pushing to get the place done before the end of the month so when the kids get out of school for the summer, we'll be ready."

"Sure," Elizabeth said.

Riley glanced at Olivia. "You in?"

"How can I refuse? But if I'm working tomorrow, I want to have fun tonight." Olivia held out her hand. "Would you like to dance?"

Riley barely waited a beat before taking her hand. "Absolutely."

The band had switched to a popular Top 40 song as Riley led Olivia to the crowded dance floor and Olivia stepped into her arms. When she put her hand on Riley's shoulder, Riley tensed, not as if she didn't like it—but as if she did. Their height difference put Olivia's cheek just at Riley's chin, and she inhaled the scent she had come to recognize as Riley's.

"The last time we danced was at Elisabeth's wedding," Riley murmured.

"I remember," Olivia said. "You looked all kinds of sexy in a tux."

Riley chuckled. "I felt all kinds of awkward. But I'm glad you liked it."

"Oh, I did." Olivia moved a little closer into Riley as they danced. Riley's hand pressed more firmly against the small of her back, and a frisson of excitement shot through Olivia's middle. "Handsome, striking, stunning, and *fine* are the words that come to mind. Just like tonight."

"You put me to shame," Riley whispered, "with a line like that."

"No line." Olivia tilted her head to search Riley's face. "And hot. Definitely hot."

The look in Riley's eyes now told Olivia that she wanted to do more than dance with her.

"I should have told you earlier that you looked so beautiful when you walked outside tonight my heart about stopped," Riley said.

"Thank you." Olivia's throat was tight and her skin heated. She tightened her hold where her hand rested in Riley's. "And you smell delicious."

"Do you know," Riley said softly, "I really like it when you say that?"

Olivia lightly brushed the underside of Riley's jaw with her lips. "And you taste good."

"Olivia," Riley said with a warning tone in her voice, "unless you're ready to leave right now, do not do that again."

"Oh? Problem?" Olivia had never felt so powerful. She'd never wanted to arouse a woman so much or loved knowing that she could. Not just any woman—this woman. "How long before we can properly leave?"

"No one is taking attendance," Riley said.

Olivia raised up on her toes, letting her breasts brush against Riley's chest, and put her mouth close to Riley's ear. "Then now would be a good time to say good night to our friends."

CHAPTER TWENTY

M y place okay?" Riley said as they headed out of town.
"Perfect. If I brought you up to my room at the ranch, we'd
be tomorrow's news at breakfast." Olivia turned in the passenger seat,
bending her left knee to look directly at Riley. The movement caused
her dress to hike up, revealing a good part of her thigh. Riley couldn't
help but notice and had to swerve to keep her truck in the correct lane.

"Yeah, no," Riley said, studiously keeping eyes front. Didn't do
much to keep her from imagining what Olivia's legs would feel like
wrapped around her. The cab was cool but she was sweating.

"Not that I care what people think," Olivia said quickly. "I just
happen to prefer to keep my private business private."

"I'm with you there." Riley turned into the trailer park and drove
down the row to her lot.

"You live in a trailer?"

"It's a fifth wheel," Riley corrected as she unbuckled her seat belt.

"And that makes a difference how?" Olivia asked.

"I'll have you know, that is the Rolls-Royce of travel coaches."

Olivia pursed her lips. "I can't say I know much about these things,
but this one looks like it's never even been on the road it's so spotless."

"It's home—I like to keep it neat."

"Isn't it a little small to actually live in?"

"Nope. It's just the right size for me. It's all I need. Well, almost
all."

"What else do you need?" Olivia's voice was barely above a
whisper that drifted over Riley's lips as she leaned closer. Tension filled
the air inside the small truck. Olivia's eyes searched hers, and Riley
hoped she liked what she saw.

When Olivia's gaze moved to her lips, Riley gritted her teeth to hold on to a little control. Jumping Olivia in the front seat of her truck was not in her game plan. "I need to be somewhere I can kiss you again and not stop until you tell me to."

"Then I guess we'd better go inside," Olivia murmured, her throaty tone turning Riley on more than getting naked with any other woman ever had.

"Come on, then. I'll give you a tour."

❖

"Wow, this *is* impressive." Olivia looked around the small space, noting the leather recliners, what looked like high-end appliances, and the kitchen area. The lighting was subtle yet efficient. A laptop lay closed beneath a large monitor on a small desk tucked into an alcove. She pointed to a container on the counter, surprised and not knowing why. "You have a cat!"

"What? Oh, not really. That's for Artie. She lives…around."

"She? And where's around?"

"Artemis. And she's feral. Desert cat."

"But you feed her."

Riley shrugged. "Sure. Why wouldn't I? We have a casual relationship. She comes and goes as she pleases."

Olivia doubted Riley thought anything of the remark, but how typical. Riley and casual—no strings, no expectations. That's what she wanted, too, of course. She pushed the slight unhappiness away. "And you can live anywhere, too. Come and go anytime. Like a nomad."

"That's a little extreme. I've been here for years."

"Are you intending to stay?"

Riley looked at Olivia as if she were searching for the answer to her question. Instead of replying, she said, "The bedroom and bath are through there."

Riley pointed to a small doorway and Olivia wondered how many women had been in the bed that she could barely see. That wasn't any of her business, but she couldn't seem to stop wanting to know more about Riley—worse, wanting more than was wise. She smiled. "Well, I think you ought to show me the rest, then."

Riley took her hand and led her back to what turned out to be a fairly spacious sleeping area that didn't look the least bit claustrophobic, which was what Olivia had imagined. "You're right. This place is pretty amazing."

"Thanks," Riley said.

Olivia turned. Riley was only a few inches away. "Are you going to kiss me again?"

❖

Olivia's voice was quiet, her eyes intensely searching. Riley's chest tightened. She never hesitated with women, not when the chemistry between them was working. And working was a poor word for what was happening between her and Olivia. Exploding might be more like it. And still she hesitated. Because, damn it, this mattered in a way she didn't want to think about. Not right now, at least.

"Do you want me to?"

"Yes, very much." Olivia threaded her arms around Riley's neck. "I really want to know if your lips on mine will make me forget everything except having your mouth all over my body."

Olivia's breath ghosted across Riley's lips. Something shifted in the air that she was powerless to stop. A force drawing her into Olivia's orbit she didn't *want* to stop. Heart hammering in her chest, Riley gripped Olivia's waist and pulled her close. "I've been wanting to taste you again since the first time we kissed. Everywhere."

"Do you still want to?" Olivia asked, drawing one bare calf up the back of Riley's leg. The heat penetrated to Riley's skin through her pants, and she groaned.

"Yes, but you're going back to New York," Riley murmured, her lips on the soft skin beneath Olivia's ear.

Olivia gasped. "Not tonight I'm not."

"So it's a fling," Riley persisted, needing to be sure.

"As we agreed." Olivia arched her neck. "This is not my first rodeo. I want your hands on me *tonight*. I want your mouth on me tonight. I want *my* hands, my mouth on you—all over that gorgeous body. *Tonight.* Clear enough?"

"Crystal." Riley cupped Olivia's breasts and kissed her.

Olivia pressed closer, her nipples pebbled beneath the soft fabric of her dress, hard against Riley's chest. When Olivia's lips parted, Riley deepened their kiss, rubbing her thumbs over Olivia's nipples. Olivia moaned, and fire leapt in Riley's center. She tugged one shoulder of the black dress down and fondled Olivia's breast. Heat and need flashed through her. "You're perfect."

Olivia's hips rocked, and she tugged Riley's bottom lip with her teeth. "God, I want you. Please touch me."

Riley spun around and sat down on the bed, pulling Olivia down beside her. She guided Olivia to her back and leaned over her, resting her hand on Olivia's calf. Her palm tingled as her skin touched bare flesh. Her head buzzed, and she gripped the tatters of sanity. "Where? Where do you want my hands?"

Olivia cupped the back of her neck, met her gaze with fierce certainty. "I want your hands on my breasts, on my thighs, between my legs. I want you inside me, making me come. Can you do that? Can you?"

Riley bent her head, kissed Olivia's breast. "I can do whatever you need."

"All of it, then. I want all of it. Now. I need you now."

Riley stroked the inside of Olivia's leg from the inside of her knee to the satin-soft curve of her inner thigh. Every inch was a wonder, and a twist of need fisted in her gut. She wanted to feel her heat, slide her fingers through the silky wetness, stroke the places that made her cry out. And she waited, fingers feather light, up and down, up and back, higher and higher. Her clit swelled, pounded, ached. And still, just the slightest brush of her thumb over the silk covering Olivia's sex.

Olivia's face, cast in moonlight, glowed. Riley kissed her again, pressing her fingertips to the sheer fabric over Olivia's clit. "You're beautiful. You feel amazing."

Olivia arched into her hand. She was hot and wet in anticipation of her touch. "I need your fingers on my skin. Touch me."

Olivia lifted her hips, and Riley slipped her fingers beneath her panties and drew them off. Slowly, ever so slowly, she caressed the flesh made bare. Olivia trembled, her legs open and tight.

"That feels so good," Olivia said, her lips against Riley's neck. "Be careful. I don't want to come until you're inside me."

Riley groaned and closed her eyes. Blood pounded in her head. Her clit felt spring-loaded, ready to explode. "I want to make this good for you."

Olivia gripped her hair, tugged. "It already is. I'm seconds from coming. Hurry."

"Hold on to me." Riley wrapped one arm around Olivia's shoulders and tugged her against her chest, holding her close as she filled her.

Olivia in her arms, Olivia surrounding her deep inside, Olivia rising and falling to the rhythm of her strokes. Olivia was everything.

"Oh, you're making me come." Olivia buried her face in Riley's neck, shuddering as the orgasm rocked her. "Yes, oh, yes."

Riley held her breath, absorbing every cry and shiver.

"Oh my God, that was good," Olivia gasped. "Give me a minute. I'm not done."

Riley laughed. "Amen to that."

❖

Olivia caught her breath. Had she drifted? Oh, God, she couldn't have fallen asleep. "Riley?"

"Right here."

Yes, right next to her. Riley was there. Relief flooded her. Olivia turned on her side and faced her. "You're still dressed."

"You, too. I didn't know how to get you undressed without waking you up."

Olivia groaned. "How long?"

"Just a few minutes."

"Oh, thank God. I'm sorry."

"For what?" Riley kissed her. "I've been lying here congratulating myself for being such a stud."

Olivia laughed. "And well deserved. You're...well. You're incredible."

"If you're awake now, we can do that again," Riley murmured, kissing her throat.

"Oh, can we?" Olivia worked on the buttons of Riley's shirt. "I'd like to do it again without clothes. You can start with the boots."

Riley turned on her back, kicked off her boots, unsnapped her pants, and pushed them down.

Olivia lifted her dress over her head and dropped it beside the bed. "You weren't wearing underwear."

"Does that bother you?" Riley asked. "Because I usually don't."

"It's sexy as hell and is going to make me crazy every time I look at you from now on."

"Good. Because every time I look at you, I'm going to be thinking about being inside you again."

Olivia's sex clenched. Damn it. She wanted Riley to make her come right this instant, but she wanted one thing more. She got the last button on Riley's shirt undone. "Lie back down." She could almost hear Riley frown and grinned. "I have plans for you."

Riley pulled a pillow behind her head and lay back. "Whatever you want."

Whatever she wanted. Olivia was afraid to even think about how much she might want. Naked and feeling more gloriously free than she ever had, she straddled Riley's hips. How could she ever have thought that a brief tangle with a stranger in a strange land was enough?

Riley sucked in a breath, and those amazing abs tightened. Olivia rocked slowly, teasing herself as she watched Riley watch her. The muscles in Riley's neck stood out like sculpted columns of granite. Her eyes flashed in the moonlight.

Olivia leaned forward, spreading her palms over Riley's breasts, smoothing the hard muscles beneath as she caressed the amazing softness. The back-and-forth friction on her clit was maddeningly good. "I might come on you just from this."

"Please," Riley groaned. "Do it."

"Do you need to come yet?" Olivia asked, reaching behind her to stroke Riley's thigh with one hand.

"Like you wouldn't believe."

"I might." Olivia shifted higher on Riley's body, rubbing her engorged clit faster over Riley's stomach. "Because I'm going to any second."

Riley gripped her hips, pulled her harder against her. "That's it. Come on, baby. Do it."

Olivia cupped Riley's sex and slipped her fingers around her clit. The pressure ballooned inside her. She squeezed and stroked, and Riley groaned. Olivia cried, "Come with me?"

And then Riley shouted and she exploded, and the only sound was her own sobbing breath and Riley murmuring her name.

CHAPTER TWENTY-ONE

I hate to get you out of bed this late," Olivia said, "but I'm going to need a ride home."

"Not a problem," Riley said. "I'm used to getting up in the middle of the night."

Olivia dressed quickly, thinking how different this moment was than all the other nights when she'd left a stranger's room. Riley wasn't a stranger, and what had passed between them was nothing like what she'd experienced before. Partly exhilarated and partly terrified by the intensity, she climbed silently into the truck.

As they pulled away, Riley said, "Are you okay?"

"Of course. I'm sorry. I'm a little tired and…" She laughed. "Well, you probably know why."

"If you mean the last few hours were blow-your-mind amazing, then, yeah, I know."

"I think that covers it."

"I don't want this to be one and done," Riley said.

Olivia shifted on the seat to look at her. Riley's profile in the moonlight was stark and tight. She gripped Riley's forearm and squeezed lightly. "Neither do I. Is that what you thought I would want?"

"I guess I wasn't sure. I didn't mean to insult you."

"I'm not insulted. There is one thing we should discuss."

Riley laughed. "Only one?"

"Well, for starters, yes."

"Okay, I'm listening."

Riley's words repeated in her mind. *I'm listening.* Riley *did* listen and never tried to change her mind about how she felt—about her parents, about her future, or even about what would happen between them. Riley had given her all the power, and knowing that humbled her, made her grateful, and turned her on in a way she hadn't expected. "If we do this, I have to say something to Elizabeth."

"*Do this*. You mean keep doing what we're doing together?"

Olivia laughed. "To be more precise, if we're going to keep having sex, I'm not going to sneak around or pretend it's not happening when we're all together. That isn't fair to either of us or the friends we share."

"And you want Elizabeth to know."

"I want her to hear it from me. She's my best friend."

"Are you afraid she won't approve?"

"No. Or at least I don't think so. In fact, I think she's always been in favor of something happening between us."

"Really. I think Kelsey is worried that if we get together, it's going to fuck something up between the four of us."

"What? Did she say that?"

"No, but she kind of pointed out to me that you were Elizabeth's best friend and family. As if I'd somehow missed that." She sounded a little insulted.

Olivia sighed. "That, I think, is the cost of having friends. They're supposed to worry about us."

"Are you worried about it?"

"That us seeing each other's going to be a problem for them, or become one if we *stop* seeing each other? No. I trust them to trust us."

Riley let out a long sigh. "Good. Because with the slightest encouragement, I could have sex with you right here, right now."

Olivia's insides fluttered. Amazingly, she was ready for sex again, too. The lights of the Red Sky Ranch came into view, a hazy glow against the black sky. "I've never had sex in any kind of vehicle, and it sounds somewhat appealing. I'm afraid if we tried it, though, we might make a commotion, and I'd rather not have an audience for my first time."

Riley laughed. "I'll keep it on my to do list, then." She stopped the truck in front of the main house, let it idle, and slid across the seat to Olivia. She framed her face and kissed her. "I'll see you in a few hours at Horizons, right?"

"You will," Olivia said. "I've got an enormously busy week coming up. We're getting ready for our certificate of occupancy inspections. Are you working shift soon?"

"Day after tomorrow."

"Can I see you later in the week?"

"I'll text you when I'm free, if I can't figure out a way to get you into the truck before then," Riley said.

Laughing, Olivia climbed out of the truck and hurried inside. She had time for a few hours' sleep, a shower, and undoubtedly the conversation that was coming with Elizabeth in the morning.

❖

"Have a nice night?" Elizabeth said as she settled into the breakfast nook across from Olivia with her coffee and toast.

"Yes, the celebration was everything I expected it to be, especially the happy birthday song." She sipped her second cup of coffee and felt far more awake than she had any right to be. She had slept, if for only a short period of time, and she hadn't dreamed.

"Oh, you left before the fun really began." Elizabeth sipped her coffee while watching Olivia over the top of the mug. "There was a conga line."

"Oh my God," Olivia said. "I'm so glad I missed that."

"Big day today, painting and all," Elizabeth said casually.

"You're not going to ask?"

"You mean, how was it?" Elizabeth grinned. "That would be crass. Was she good?"

Olivia knew she was blushing. "Yes, I spent the night—well, part of the night, with Riley, and yes, she was wonderful."

Elizabeth's brows rose. "Wonderful. Now, that's an intriguing word. I was expecting hot, sexy, magic hands, something along those lines."

"She was all those things." Olivia shook her head. "She's just… more than that."

"Is it serious?"

"How could it be? That was the first time, after all, and you know, everything is temporary."

"Well, sometimes the first time is the *last* first time when it's with the right person, and no, I don't know that everything is temporary. I want you to stay when this project is done. I have another one in mind that I think might interest you."

"How can I stay? My parents—"

"Your parents," Elizabeth said, "love you and have always wanted the best for you. If you tell them this is where you want to be, where you need to be, they will understand."

"I know you're right," Olivia said. "They *would* understand, but that doesn't stop them from needing me and deserving me to be with them when they do. Am I wrong to think that after everything they've done for me, it's my turn now?"

"Are you wrong for loving them? Of course not. And I know absolutely that they feel your love for them. Just think about talking to them. Just think about it."

"They don't know about me and…women." Olivia steadied her voice. "I don't think they'll take that very well."

"That might take some time," Elizabeth said gently. "That's a conversation you owe yourself as well as them."

"I've always thought I would know if the time was ever right," Olivia said quietly. "Now I think I might just end up running away."

Elizabeth shook her head, her expression fond. "You have never run away from anything in your life. You've always just needed a reason to do something. Maybe now you'll have one."

Olivia hoped she would have the courage to know when the time was right.

Kelsey pulled out a chair. "You don't look like you're wearing painting clothes."

"I wasn't aware there was a uniform requirement," Olivia said.

"You must have an old T-shirt with holes in it, the arms cut off, the bottom raggedy, and possibly sweat-stained."

Olivia made a face. "That sounds disgusting, and no, I'm afraid I forgot to pack that particular item."

"Are you sure you're up for this?" Kelsey teased.

"I'm a New Yorker. We have many skills. I can take on any challenge. Other than desert creatures."

"Never mind her," Elizabeth said affectionately. "Just change into shorts and something you don't care about throwing away, because I can promise you'll get paint on it."

Olivia stood, a surge of excitement warming her at the thought of seeing Riley again. "That I can manage."

❖

To Olivia's surprise, a row of cars lined the pull-off in front of Horizon House and a chain of bicycles leaned against the board fence that separated the construction site from the neighboring lot. Mildly disappointed that she wasn't going to be able to see Riley alone, she reminded herself she was actually there to work. Oh goody.

The disappointment faded instantly as Riley came out through the now functional front door onto the porch and down the temporary stairs. Olivia climbed out of the truck and hurried to meet her.

"Hi. It looks like you're having a party."

Riley slowly took her in, a grin forming. "Some volunteers from the station, and some of my kids and their friends."

Riley's kids. The term never failed to make her smile. "Who else is here?"

"Hadley's around somewhere with Sven and Travis. Ignacio, Mia, Jenny, and—"

"Riley," a young boy called as he dashed out the front door, "Hadley wants to know—"

Riley looked over her shoulder. "Hey, Luke. I'm talking to Ms. Martinez just now. So what's the rule?"

Luke looked from Riley to Olivia, and his smile disappeared. "Sorry. I forgot. I'm not supposed to interrupt."

Olivia took a few steps forward. "Hi, I'm Olivia."

Luke glanced at Riley and must've gotten the go-ahead sign because his grin returned. "I'm Luke. Very nice to meet you."

Kelsey and Elizabeth joined them as Riley said, "Come on, let's go inside and see how everybody's doing."

Riley dropped her hand casually on Luke's shoulder and he smiled at her, hero worship plain on his face. All the kids looked up to Riley, but it seemed Riley had a special bond with this boy.

Olivia found herself stationed in the room with Jenny and Luke, who chattered away about kid things that she was amazed to realize she knew nothing about. A television show she'd never heard of and apparently the most popular recording artist in the universe, also completely unknown to her. She was impressed, though, that despite their excitement and conversational level, they were able to paint efficiently and far more neatly than she appeared to be doing. Thus far she had a paint smudge on her bare knee, one on her elbow and, she feared, more in her hair.

When Riley appeared in the doorway, she stopped painting just to indulge in looking at her again. As usual when she was doing physical labor, she wore a low-slung pair of faded jeans, a leather tool belt, and a green T-shirt washed so many times it resembled the color of a sun-bleached lime. The sleeves were shorter this time than she usually wore, revealing the scars on her forearms. Her hair was a little shaggy. Olivia liked it that way. It gave her a wild look, and she was discovering she very much liked wild in a woman. At least, this particular woman.

"Status reports," Riley called, her attention on Olivia. The gleam in her eyes suggested she knew Olivia had been checking her out.

Olivia smothered a smile as Jenny and Luke tumbled over each other telling Riley everything they had completed so far. Riley took a slow walk around the room, apparently checking out everyone's work. She stopped where Olivia had been painting the trim around the windows.

"Very nice," she murmured, and Olivia knew damn well she was not talking about her painting skills.

"Thank you," Olivia said just as quietly. "I was just thinking—"

"I know what you were thinking," Riley said. "And the answer is—"

"Luke," a woman called from behind them.

Riley stiffened and moved away. The blonde she'd seen at the fire station, definitely *not* wearing painting clothes, stood in the doorway in pale yellow capri pants and a simple white shirt that showed off the honey brown hues of her skin and the very nice body beneath. "Oh hey, sorry."

"No problem," Riley said. After a pause, she added, "Ashley, this is Olivia Martinez. She works out at the ranch. Well, kind of runs a part of it."

Ashley smiled a little uncertainly and held out her hand. "Nice to meet you."

She slipped a hand onto Luke's shoulder and turned to Riley. "How's he been doing today?"

Riley said, "Great."

"Thanks for letting him spend the morning here," Ashley said.

"Hey, always happy for another good worker."

Olivia couldn't help but listen, considering she was standing two feet away. The conversation seemed casual, but their body language spoke volumes. Riley had gone from her usual upbeat, easygoing self to quiet and almost sad as soon as Ashley appeared. Ashley seemed uncomfortable, as if talking to Riley took effort.

"Luke," Ashley said, "we need to get going. Still some chores to do at home."

"Can't I stay here? There's lots more to do," Luke said.

"There'll still be more to do the next time you come," Riley said. "Make sure you clean up."

"Okay." Luke put his paintbrush in the tray next to the paint can.

Ashley shook her head. "I don't know how you do that."

"I'm not required to negotiate," Riley said.

"Good point," Ashley said, finally smiling. "Ready, Luke?"

"Thanks, Riley," Luke said. " 'Bye, Ms. Martinez."

" 'Bye, Luke."

"Jenny," Riley said, as Ashley and Luke left, "go find Ignacio and Mia and let them know we're finishing up. You all need to bike home together, okay?"

"I'll tell them," Jenny said, hurrying out.

"You're really great with the kids," Olivia said. "Luke especially adores you."

"He's a kid. They all just need attention."

"Kelsey told me Ashley's husband was killed," Olivia said carefully. "I imagine it's a big help to her for Luke to spend time with another adult."

Riley looked past her as if seeing another place—or time—in the distance. With a shrug, she focused on Olivia. "Least I can do. Come on. Let's get everyone else and go find some food."

"Sure," Olivia said. "Let me finish cleaning up here. I'll be right down."

Riley left without another word, making clear the topic of Luke and Ashley was a conversation for another time.

CHAPTER TWENTY-TWO

Hadley and the other firefighters all had plans, so Olivia, Kelsey, Elizabeth, and Riley drove to Cowboy Cookin' for lunch. Olivia recognized the burned-out motel across the street from the photo in the newspaper as the place where Riley had rescued the trapped woman.

Riley paused as Olivia fell behind Kelsey and Olivia. "Everything okay?"

"Seeing it like this," Olivia said quietly, "is so much worse than a photograph. I can't believe you were inside there."

"I wasn't—not when it was like that. I—"

"Don't treat me like I'm one of the kids. You ran in there when it was burning, didn't you?"

"Yes, but—"

"Then don't try to pretend that wasn't dangerous," Olivia said. "You tried that route with skydiving already, and it didn't work then either."

"This is my *job*," Riley snapped.

"I know. And I respect you immensely—you and all the other first responders. And I still get to be afraid that you might be hurt. Just like everyone else who lo—" Olivia stopped, shocked to her core. Oh no. Absolutely not. No. "Who cares about you and everyone who does what you do."

"I'm trained for this work," Riley said in a gentler tone.

"I know." Olivia hurried to catch up to Kelsey and Elizabeth. She did not want to talk to Riley any longer about something she didn't even want to think about. For so many reasons.

While they waited for their beer and assorted burgers and sandwiches in a booth at the back of the restaurant, Elizabeth said, "I've got an interesting new project I think you'd be up for, Olivia."

"Oh?" Olivia waited for details. Why did she think the road ahead should be marked with caution signs?

"Mm," Elizabeth said, grabbing some nuts from the bowl the waitress had set on the table. "I had a chance to go over those plot maps I asked you to dig out for me."

"Plot maps," Kelsey said. "Of the Red Sky?"

"No—of the area northwest of the golf course that runs between the Red Sky property line and the old state road. The one that doesn't see much traffic since the bypass went in."

Olivia asked, "How much land are we talking about?"

"Somewhere in the neighborhood of a hundred and fifty acres."

"We don't need any more land," Kelsey said, "and that parcel isn't much good for anything with the road so close."

Riley sipped her beer. "Nice access to town on that road, though."

Elizabeth grinned at her. "I'm looking for investors for the Sunset Vista Development corporation, and since you have experience with the town officials, you'd be a perfect candidate. Interested?"

"I might be," Riley said.

Olivia filed that away under one more interesting thing about Riley she hadn't expected.

"Wait," Kelsey said. "Who owns it now? And what are you... we...building?"

"That land was once part of a larger parcel that was sold off in pieces over the last seventy-five years or so," Elizabeth went on in her presentation voice. The one that always ended with her closing exactly the deal she wanted. "Preliminary inquiries suggest the far-away and completely disinterested inheritors would be happy to sell it at a very reasonable price."

"Houses," Olivia said, visualizing the site plan of the community as if it was spread out on the drafting table already. "Mostly three bedroom, two and a half bath, some larger for those expecting bigger families to visit. What do you think—three-acre lots?"

"Two to four, depending on the buyers' interests. We don't want them crowded, and we'll need forty percent of the land as undeveloped common ground to maintain the natural landscape. Once we have the area surveyed to determine the best location for structures, wells, that kind of thing, we can determine how to subdivide."

"And of course," Olivia said, "the homeowners association would be under the management of the Red Sky Ranch and Resort, and the property owners would all have full access to the Red Sky's programs, including meals. For an annual fee scaled to their interests."

"Of course."

Riley turned to Kelsey. "Do they share a brain?"

"Pretty sure," Kelsey said.

"It's exactly your kind of project," Olivia said.

"Our kind," Elizabeth said quietly. "Think about it?"

Olivia considered what a project of that scope would mean—two, three years' commitment at least. Time for her to decide about so many things. But a long time away from home. Beside her, she sensed Riley waiting. "I can't say just now. I'll need to see the prospectus."

"As soon as you're ready," Elizabeth said.

"Now that we've settled that," Kelsey said, shaking her head, "let's talk about the camping trip."

"You're going camping?" Riley said.

"Yep. Want to come along? We can always use skilled labor."

"If I can make it work with my schedule, you bet. They're a lot of fun."

"Is this a new event package?" Olivia asked. The Red Sky had a variety of packages guests could select including accommodations, meal plans, and resort activities ranging from easy day trips to extreme adventure outings.

"Yes. You should come," Kelsey added.

"I don't think so." Olivia held up her hand as if it was a stop sign. "I'm a New Yorker, not a cowgirl."

"Didn't you just say that about helping out at Horizon House? That you were a New Yorker and could do anything?"

Riley cocked her head. "Did you now? Anything?"

"That was different. That was doing a little bit of manual labor, then going home to a hot bath and a glass of chilled wine." Olivia waved a hand at the array of food the waitress had delivered. "Or local cuisine, as the case may be."

"Never heard it called that before." Riley laughed. "But I'm pretty sure there will be hot water, and as I recall, Chuck always stocks wine in the chuckwagon."

"I still can't believe you have a guy named Chuck who runs the chuckwagon." Olivia tried to see the appeal of the whole idea and wasn't finding any.

"Come on," Elizabeth said, "it's a lot of fun, and the moon will be full. It'll be so bright you can read a book, not that anyone does. If I can do it, you can, too. Live life on the edge."

"I have electricity in my room if I want to read at night," Olivia said mildly.

"It's more like glamping anyway," Riley said.

"Glamping? You mean with luxury tents, real beds, and dare I say, bathrooms?" Olivia looked at Elizabeth. "Since when?"

"We still have the rough-rider experience and the three-day trail hikes, but we added this luxury excursion for the guests who want the gourmet food, the cocktails, the wine," Elizabeth said.

Kelsey added, "You can either take a Jeep or horseback to get there."

"Or you can ride with me on a motorcycle," Riley said.

"In the desert?" Olivia said, intrigued by the idea of going somewhere new with Riley. Even on a motorcycle. At least she wouldn't have to worry about traffic.

"Sure." Riley caught her eye and grinned. "You can share my tent. I'll make sure it's creature free."

"Come on, Olivia," Elizabeth and Kelsey said together.

Olivia pretended to think it over, but Riley had her at *share my tent.* "I suppose if you're providing security, I can't refuse."

Riley smiled. "I personally—" She broke off as she reached for the beeper hooked on her waistband. "Sorry. Looks like I've got a call." She rose and pulled out her wallet.

"Go," Kelsey said. "I've got it."

Riley glanced at Olivia. "Sorry. I'll text you."

"Of course." Olivia smiled despite the sudden unwarranted twist of fear. The call could be anything. Riley had said most calls were medical emergencies, not fires. "Be safe."

After a moment of awkward silence, Elizabeth said, "You're still worried."

"Every time she gets called." Olivia rubbed the space between her eyes. "Sorry. I wasn't expecting her to just…disappear like that. And don't say I'll get used to it, because I don't think I can."

"You're not supposed to get used to it," Kelsey said matter-of-factly. "You're just supposed to trust her to do her job and come back when it's done."

"That's going to take some time," Olivia said. Possibly more than she would ever have.

CHAPTER TWENTY-THREE

When Riley arrived at the base camp, she was assigned to an eight-man crew, given a radio, and directed to a briefing room with twenty other firefighters. Everyone wore yellow brush coats and pants over their shirts and pants, along with boots and chainsaw chaps. Their helmets rested on the tables nearby. When Riley shouldered the bag that held her emergency fire shelter kit, a sudden surge of nausea swept over her. Despite the accompanying dizziness, she forced herself to focus on the fire crew chief as he described the location of the fire, the weather forecast, and the deployment routes for each crew. Concentrating on the job she was about to do helped the familiar anxiety to pass quickly.

The briefing over, Riley gathered up her gear and pocketed her phone. For a fleeting second, she thought of texting Olivia just to feel connected to her, but she had no time. Her crew was moving out.

For the next three days, Riley thought of little but fighting the fire—where she needed to be, what she needed to do, and what danger she needed to be on the lookout for. Smoke filtered out the sunlight, giving the sky an eerie glow that made it impossible to tell night from day. Choking on acrid air, eyes burning, and nearly deafened by the roar of the fire, the crackle of limbs burning, and trees exploding from the heat, Riley was marooned in her own circle of hell. Like the day she lost her crew. The panic gripped her by the throat and squeezed the last bit of air from her lungs. For a heartbeat she was back with Kev and the others, just before...*no*...she wasn't there. The voice of her first trainer sounded in her memory.

Situational awareness. Never forget where you are and what the fire is doing around you. Are you in a good spot? What is your escape route?

She knew who she was, where she was. She knew what she was

doing, and she knew what she wanted when this was over. She knew who she wanted.

Finally off the line, Riley grabbed some food and headed for the crew tent. The tent was empty and she ought to try to sleep, but her nerves still sizzled like live wires. As she lay on her cot trying to quiet her mind, her thoughts drifted to Olivia as they always did when she had even a second to breathe free. Recalling Olivia's face, her smile, her laughter soothed her even as the memory of making love with her excited her. Making love—when had she ever used that term when thinking about sex with a woman? And they had great sex, amazing sex, sex she'd like to have again as soon as possible once she got out of this inferno. And after the sex, she wanted to fall asleep with Olivia beside her. And wake up to find Olivia still there. Fuck, what was she thinking? This was not the picture of a fling. And she sure as hell didn't need to worry about that now.

Riley sat up and texted Olivia. As she waited in anticipation for Olivia to respond, hoping this time she'd get a connection, she chugged a bottle of grape Pedialyte. Cases of it filled the corner of the tent for quick rehydration and electrolytes.

Olivia: *hi how are you?*

Riley: *I'm fine. First chance to text*

Olivia: *Thank you I was worried*

Riley: *No need all good*

Olivia: *How is the fire?*

Riley: *Almost contained. Lost some homes though*

Olivia: *I'm sorry. Are you okay?*

Riley: *Mostly yeah*

Before Riley had a chance to delete what she hadn't meant to say, Olivia texted again.

Olivia: *What aren't you telling me?*

Riley: *I stepped in a hole and my knee is killing me. My eyes are burning from too much smoke and my back hurts. This is a job for the young*

Olivia: *But you're okay? Are you safe? Sorry just had to ask that —again*

Riley: *I'm okay. good to know someone cares*

Olivia: *I do*

Riley reread Olivia's words. *I do.* When was the last time she'd talked to anyone about this—even to say she was fine? Not since she'd lost Kevin and the others. Just connecting with Olivia like this had blown away the ever-present cloud of anxiety that had hung over her since she'd arrived. The excitement pulsing through her body was warm and welcome. The feeling of rightness, she realized with a shock, wasn't new. Being with Olivia anchored her.

Olivia: *Still there?*
Riley: *sorry yes thinking about coming home*
Olivia: *soon?*
Riley: *a day or so I'll text you as soon as I know*
Olivia: *please be careful*

Riley stared at the screen. She had never told anyone she'd be home. *I'll be back* or *back in town*, but never home. What was it about Olivia that made her think that way? What should she say? *I keep thinking about kissing you*? *I want a whole lot of things with you I never wanted with anyone else*? Hell no. That would be one quick way to chase Olivia away.

Riley: *I will. I'll text you when I can. Don't worry*
Olivia: *Sorry, can't help it. I don't want anything to happen to you*
Riley: *It won't be back soon*

The screen remained blank and Riley mentally cursed. What was she supposed to say? She already had scars Olivia could see. What about those she couldn't? How could she pretend to be someone Olivia would want for more than a fling when she couldn't even tell her the truth?

Two days later, Riley finally got the all clear. Within the hour she texted Olivia.

Riley: *I'm OTW.*
Olivia: *Right now? Where are you?*
Riley: *Packing up my gear. I'm on tomorrow's flight out.*
Olivia: *OMG the best news I could get. you're all right?*
Riley: *just tired and really need a shower. dinner when I get in? I'll pick you up*
Olivia: *you can shower here*
Riley: *at the ranch?*
Olivia: *With me.*

Riley's pulse kicked into overdrive. She'd spent more than a week driving herself beyond exhaustion, fighting the fire and her own demons, and every moment she wasn't doing either, she'd been thinking about

Olivia. About losing herself in the indescribable wonder of touching her and being touched by her.

She texted: *People will talk*

Olivia texted back a smiley face and *Possibly but who cares*

Riley didn't, and when she got the chance to jump on an earlier flight, she grabbed it. As soon as she landed, she texted *Just landed*

A minute passed. Now? *You said tomorrow*

Wanted to surprise you. Riley followed the trail of deplaning people through the airport to baggage claim.

You did I'm in the car on the way back from Phoenix

Riley's stomach burned with disappointment. *Well hell I'll head home and come by later seven okay?*

yes fine

Riley left her bag outside the trailer to let it air out. At Dr. Townes's suggestion, she'd started doing that and laundering her uniforms at the station house to avoid triggering flashbacks inside her home. In a hurry to meet Olivia and almost as eager to wash the grime and lingering sense of devastation away with steaming hot water, she jumped into the shower. She was rinsing out her hair when she sensed movement in the small space and the stall door opened.

"I thought the plan was for you to shower with me," Olivia said.

Riley turned in the adequate but far from spacious shower stall as Olivia, naked and more beautiful than her memories, stood with the door half open, brazenly observing her. Olivia's gaze traveled the length of her body, then slowly rose to focus on her breasts. Riley's nipples hardened and her breath quickened. Olivia smiled, a decidedly appreciative smile.

"I was in a hurry." Riley's words sounded raspy, and she swallowed around the arousal threatening to make her dizzy.

"Is that right." Olivia's gaze dropped to a point Riley could almost feel between her legs, and her clit swelled. "This is a very acceptable alternative to my room."

"There's room in here." Riley backed up as far as she could and held out her hand. The invitation was something else she hadn't done with anyone else. She was offering to let Olivia see all of her, scars and all. She hadn't showered or even gotten shirtless with anyone since the fire, not because they were disfiguring but because they invited questions. Questions that required explanations of things she couldn't share with anyone.

Olivia's hand fit perfectly in Riley's as she stepped in and closed the door behind her. Pressing against her, Olivia fisted her hands in Riley's hair and pulled her head down for a kiss that left Riley reeling. Breathless and just a little dizzy with sheer need, Riley lifted her up and Olivia wrapped her legs around her.

"At this moment," Olivia whispered between kisses, "I'm glad to be smaller."

Riley nuzzled her neck and kissed her again. "You're perfect. Fuck, I've been thinking about this for days."

"About what?"

"About touching you everywhere. About making you come." Olivia's smooth breasts against hers made her head spin. "You skin is like silk. I can't stop touching you."

"I love your hands on me." Olivia's breath against her neck made her blood race.

"I'm not going to be able to wait," Riley warned.

"Then put me down," Olivia said after one more quick kiss.

"Why?" Riley nibbled on her neck in that sensitive spot just below her ear.

"So you can touch me everywhere."

Riley eased Olivia down and slid her thigh between Olivia's, who instinctively rocked against it.

"Fuck, you're so hot," Riley said. She drew Olivia's nipple into her mouth and Olivia arched into her with a small cry. Riley's clit gave a warning twitch, which she ruthlessly ignored. She wanted Olivia. Wanted her like air, like the next beat of her heart. She cupped Olivia between her legs and stroked through the satin heat.

Olivia gasped. "God, that is so good."

Olivia cried out when Riley lightly bit her nipple and wrapped her arms around Riley's neck. "I need you to make me come. I'm close."

Riley stroked her, and Olivia rocked against her hand. When she entered her, Olivia stiffened in her arms and came hard.

"That was…" Olivia sagged in Riley's arms. "Fantastic."

Grinning, Riley leaned back against the shower wall and rubbed her cheek against the top of Olivia's head. "Yeah, it was."

"My legs are shaking."

Turning, Riley said, "Hold on," and sat on the wide bench on one side of the shower with Olivia straddling her thighs.

Olivia leaned back far enough to meet Riley's gaze. Her eyes were hazy with satisfaction, and Riley grinned. Olivia's brows rose. "Proud of yourself?"

"Yep."

"Good." Olivia spread her fingers over Riley's middle, and Riley jerked. "Hold still."

Riley's stomach tied itself in a neat knot, and her clit turned to stone. "I don't think—"

"Don't think. Just feel."

How could she not, when every place Olivia touched turned electric. If she hadn't been immobilized in a space the size of a phone booth with Olivia in her lap, Olivia's hands all over her, Olivia's mouth doing—

"Olivia, I'm about to explode here." Riley sounded like she was begging, and she was. "Please, have mercy."

Laughing, Olivia shook her head. "I've waited a long time for you to get back, and you're not rushing me."

"I'm about to…"

Olivia silenced her by lifting up off Riley's thigh and sliding her fingers down and around her clit. Riley's head snapped back against the shower wall, and she cursed. Olivia lightly bit her neck. Stroke after stroke, teasing bite after bite, Olivia drove her higher. With one last flick on her clit and thrust of Olivia's fingers, Riley came.

Riley's mind blanked. Sounds faded, and she lost track of where she was.

"Riley?"

Riley blinked a few times, her eyes clearing. Olivia looked worried.

"Is everything okay? Did you not want—"

Riley kissed her hard. "You're what I want. All I wanted. All I thought about out there. You and getting out of that fire. You're my reward." She kissed her again. "No, you're a gift."

Olivia buried her face in Riley's neck. "I was so worried. I don't know what I would have done if—"

"I'm right here," Riley whispered.

"Then take me to bed and hold me."

Riley couldn't think of a single thing she wanted more.

CHAPTER TWENTY-FOUR

B linding smoke. Heat and roaring flames.

"Alex! Kev! Shelley! It's everywhere. Clear a spot and deploy your shelter. Now!"

Riley rolled onto her stomach. "Get your tent under your feet and over your heads. Wrap up in a cocoon.

"Is everybody good?"

She pressed her face to the ground, still screaming. "Stay tight and let the fire roll over you. Keep your head down and your face in the dirt. Breathe shallow and stay calm. We *will* get through this."

Her skin streamed with sweat. "Jesus, it's hot."

So hot, so hot, no air.

Don't die, don't die, don't die.

Time collapsed into an abyss of scorching air and mindless terror. Silence finally pulled her back from the void, and she cautiously pushed her tent aside.

"Is everyone okay?"

The inferno had moved on, leaving nothing, not even sound, behind.

"Alex? Shelley?...*Kev!*"

"Please, someone answer me." *Someone answer me. Someone answer me.*

"Riley, Riley," Olivia said soothingly. "Sweetie, wake up. You're dreaming."

Riley bolted upright and yanked at the sheets twisted around her waist. Sweat and tears streaked her face. "*Fuck.*"

Olivia reached out but didn't touch her. "Are you awake?"

"Yes," Riley said hoarsely. "Yes, sorry."

"No, no. Not your fault." Olivia stroked her arm. "Lie down. You're cold."

Riley shivered. It was not a dream. It couldn't be. The sound, the smell and heat were real. Just like she remembered. Panic surged, and she shoved her way upright on the side of the bed.

A warm hand touched her back. "What is it?"

Olivia's voice was crystal clear, penetrating the cloud of dread pressing in on her from all sides. Riley took a deep breath and ran through the familiar techniques. *What do you see?* The numbers on the clock, moonlight coming through the window, her running shoes on the floor. *What do you hear?* Olivia.

Riley instantly calmed. Olivia was in her bed. Naked in her bed. She cleared her throat. "I'm okay."

"Are you sure?" Olivia turned on the light beside the bed.

Riley took one more breath before turning to her. This was why she didn't spend the night with anyone. "Yes. Sorry that I woke you."

"Don't apologize. It looked like it was scary for you." Olivia sat up, the sheet falling to her waist, exposing her breasts. She ran her hand through her hair. "Do you want some water or anything?"

"I'll get it."

"Do you want me to leave?" Olivia asked when Riley returned with two bottles of water.

Yes, no, yes, no, yes, no. "It's the middle of the night."

Olivia's gaze didn't leave hers. "You didn't answer my question."

Yes, no, yes, no, yes, no. Riley expected panic, but it didn't come. Since the fire, she'd never awakened next to a woman. She always left after sex as soon as she could without seeming like an asshole, but she never let her guard down, never took a chance that she'd fall asleep. She feared a scene just like this, or worse.

But this wasn't just anyone—this was Olivia. And weirdly, she was embarrassed, but she wasn't incapacitated by the dreams or the anxiety that always followed.

"No, of course I don't want you to leave."

Once the words were out of her mouth, Riley knew they were the right ones. She gathered Olivia in her arms, and after a few minutes, Olivia fell asleep.

Sleep wasn't happening for her now, and when she was sure Olivia was sound asleep, she eased out of bed, pulled on sweatpants and a tee, and made her way through the trailer to the back patio. She settled into one of the patio chairs, stretched out her legs, and replayed the night in her mind. The hurried flights back, unable to think of anything but getting home to Olivia. Olivia surprising her and blowing her mind with white hot sex in the shower. Her body started to tingle at the memory. Did everybody have sex in the shower? It was probably the most dangerous place in the house, but she'd never even considered not touching Olivia. Her hands ached to touch her. She craved the feel of Olivia's skin against hers. She hungered to feel her come apart in her arms. Every damn thought, every desire, had been for Olivia.

And then the dream. The thunderous roar of the fire, the overwhelming heat, the choking smell of death. The terror and self-loathing she'd awakened to so many times, except for tonight. Tonight Olivia had been there. And Riley had conquered the secret that haunted her, if just for a second.

"Hey," Olivia said as she slid the door closed behind her. "What are you doing out here?"

Riley turned her head. Olivia had found an old button-up shirt of hers and looked rumpled and beautiful. "Just watching the sun come up."

"Want company?"

"Yep." Riley pulled another aluminum chair closer. "Sit down."

As Olivia got comfortable, Riley opened the plastic container of cat food she'd brought out with her and tossed some a few feet away on the patio pavers.

"Will she come, do you think?" Olivia asked quietly.

"I never know," Riley said. "She's got her own timetable."

A minute passed in silence as the sky above the distant mountains burst into color.

"I never get tired of that," Olivia said.

"Me nether."

"Look." Olivia gasped and gripped her arm. "There she is."

Riley tensed, more from the surprise than the slight discomfort. No one ever touched her there. "Hey, Artie. Good morning."

"Oh, she's beautiful."

The ginger cat padded directly to the food, meticulously snatched up each piece, and sat for a moment cleaning her paws while watching them. When she'd finished, she rose and danced off into the brush.

"You're definitely special," Riley said. "I had to wait two months before she sat with me out here."

"Thank you." Olivia ran her hand over the scars on Riley's arm.

"You don't have to tell me, but I was wondering how you got these scars?"

Riley's first instinct was to minimize the event like she did every other time she'd been asked that same question and blame it on some trivial accident. But she couldn't lie to Olivia.

"Six years ago, we had a pretty big fire up in the mountains. It started small and spread fast. I went up with a crew when it had involved ten thousand acres."

"From a lightning strike?"

"No, it was manmade." The fury rose as it did every time she thought of the damage and devastation. Of the men and women who'd died.

"And you were hurt fighting the fire?" Anger showed in Olivia's tone. "That's...terrible. That must be infuriating for you and the other firefighters."

"It's the job," Riley murmured, not wanting to be cast a hero when she was anything but.

"You said that before, but it's more than a job for you, isn't it?"

"Why do you say that?"

"Did you ever consider anything else?"

"No."

"Not since you were a teenager and saw that little girl who would have drowned except for the firefighter." Olivia smiled. "The instinct to protect and serve is part of you. It's admirable."

Riley shrugged, uncomfortable with the praise. She sure didn't deserve that.

"It's okay," Olivia said lightly. "I won't tell anyone."

Riley didn't really mind if she did, as long as Olivia didn't ask her what caused the nightmares.

CHAPTER TWENTY-FIVE

G ot a minute?" Elizabeth asked as she entered Olivia's trailer office.
"Just barely." Olivia gestured to the drafting table covered
with blueprints and site plans. "I just got off the phone with the county
inspector. I told him we're going to have the new horses on-site in three
weeks, and I need the certificate of occupancy before that." She paused.
"Are we going to have the new horses?"

"I've talked to the breeder every day. They're ready to transport
whenever we're ready. Josie says the wranglers and stable crews are
ready."

"Are the new hires working out all right?"

"Kelsey and Josie are happy with all the new stable hands, and
I've got another little bit of good news." Elizabeth smiled. "Adelle
wants the job and is ready to move whenever we give her the word."

"That's great. I'm saying word right now." Olivia let out a long
sigh. "She's just the person we need."

Elizabeth pushed aside a stack of folders and settled a hip on
the edge of the counter that ran below the trailer windows. "I'll call
her today. I think we should wait to interview any further staff for the
behavioral program until she's on board."

Olivia pointed to one of the stacks by Olivia's left leg. "Those are
the ones we winnowed out from the first run-through. She can review
them."

"One other little bit of news."

"I could use some, hit me with it."

Elizabeth frowned. "Wait a minute, what's wrong?"

Olivia sighed. "Nothing to do with the ranch."

"That's not what I asked."

"My personal life is going to hell," Olivia said.

"Aha. Does this have anything to do with the nights you haven't been sleeping here?"

"That's very subtle of you. Yes, partly due to Riley and partly due to my parents."

"Riley first," Elizabeth said. "What has she done?"

"Nothing, that's just it. She's practically perfect."

"Let me see if I can translate that," Elizabeth said. "She's wonderful in bed, she's great looking. She's kind and considerate, loyal and honest. So what am I missing?"

"The obvious—in a few months we'll be living at opposite ends of the country, so a long-term relationship is not really something I'm looking for. If I was looking for a long-term relationship at all. She's wedded to her job, and I can't fault her for that, but it also happens to be a job that's pretty damn scary." Olivia hesitated. There were some things she wasn't sure she should share.

"And she's been hurt," Elizabeth said quietly. "Anyone can see that, and I don't just mean physically."

Olivia nodded. "She's strong, but she suffers."

"Doesn't everyone in their way?" Elizabeth said quietly. "And I can't believe that her being involved with you doesn't help her. Being cared about goes a long way toward helping us heal. Ultimately yes, we have to do it ourselves, but there are some places that simply need love."

"I don't think we're talking about love."

"Aren't we?"

"God, I don't know," Olivia said. "I've never been in love before." She leaned back and closed her eyes. "Does it involve emotional roller coasters, feeling exhilarated one minute and terrified the next? Does it hurt sometimes, when you're apart and all you want is to just see her?"

Elizabeth smiled. "Yes, all those things. And the sense of rightness and hope that goes with it. So any of that?"

"Not that I can see," Olivia said quietly.

"Then what you need is time." Elizabeth rose, hugged her, and stepped back. "And a little bit of camping. Fresh air and the outdoors. Are you ready to leave tomorrow?"

"I'm to be at Riley's at six a.m.," Olivia said, "for what I've been told will be the adventure of my lifetime." She shook her head. "Really,

I don't need any more adventure. I need some order and reason in my life."

Elizabeth opened the door and looked over her shoulder with a broad grin. "Then you've come to exactly the wrong place."

"You're right about that," she said to the sound of Elizabeth laughing as she disappeared.

Alone again, Olivia turned back to her unfinished work and so wished Elizabeth was right about everything.

❖

"Thanks for seeing me," Riley said. She hadn't once in her long association with Dr. Townes asked for a session outside of the regular time. She still couldn't believe she'd done it.

"Of course," he said in his usual unruffled fashion. He looked like most fifty-year-old guys who kept in shape. A golfer's tan, sandy-brown hair full on the top and neatly but not too closely trimmed at the back, and deep blue eyes that watched without judgment. Nothing ever seemed to surprise him, but that was probably just his professional façade. And that really wasn't fair. One thing she was certain of was that he did listen, and she'd felt his sympathy even in the things he never said.

"So," he said after a few moments of silence. "You want to start with how you're doing? Or would you rather talk about why you decided to come in today?"

"Pretty much all the same thing," Riley said. "I got called up on the fire up in the Kaibab a month or so ago. Hadley wanted me to lead the crew. We weren't front line, but close enough."

Even now, remembering her awful fear that she'd miss something and her crew would suffer on her watch, made her queasy.

"How did that go?"

"Took a while for my nerves to recover, but okay. I made it through. I was worried and a little paranoid and maybe hyperalert, but nothing I don't usually feel when I'm running a crew. This last time, though…" She shook her head and ran a hand through her hair. "I just got back from a jump on a big fire a week and a half ago. That one was rocky for a while."

"Rough?"

"Yeah, you could say that. It was a lot like Colorado. The fire, I mean. Big bad bastard of a blaze. Jumping around, eating up the acreage. I had a few minutes of disorientation at one point. Not exactly a flashback, and not enough to endanger anybody else."

"What about yourself? Were you in danger?"

Riley did a mental rewind. She hadn't really been thinking about herself, because she rarely did. She cared about what happened to everyone else, but her own well-being wasn't on her mind. She'd just wanted to do her job and get everybody else home safe. "No, I don't think so."

He paused a minute, and she got the message. Like maybe getting *herself* home mattered, too.

"Were you able to contain the anxiety?" he asked.

"Yes, pretty quickly. Like I said, I always knew where I was, what was happening." Riley blew out a breath and figured she might as well just get to the core of things. "Something else is going on. I got involved with someone. A woman." She chuckled. "You probably figured on that part."

He smiled. "How is it going?"

Riley smothered a grin. Yeah, no, she for sure wasn't going to talk about the great sex. "It's different than I expected. The relationship's not like anything I've ever had before."

"How so?"

"It's…personal." She shook her head. "That sounds ridiculous, doesn't it."

"No, not at all. So is this personal relationship troubling you?"

"No, just the opposite. It…Olivia…*Olivia* has a strange effect on me." She laughed again when his brows rose. "Yeah, I know. Sure, I have butterflies and am excited, but besides that. Being with her, even when I'm not *with* her, helps me work my way out of the anxiety stuff faster. Calms me somehow."

She'd spent a lot of time since that night in the trailer trying to figure out how being around Olivia had changed so many things she'd felt about herself. About her past. After searching and failing to find any better way of explaining it, she simply said now, "I feel good around her. The anxiety disappears. The anger is not as strong. I'm in the moment."

He nodded. He'd know what a big deal that was. They'd been working on Riley being in the moment, especially when events were potentially triggering, and not what Dr. Townes called "what-iffing," for years.

"Does that make any sense to you?" Riley said.

"Strong positive relationships, particularly intimate ones, are one of the things that help us deal with the harder things in life. This sounds like good news. And the relationship with Olivia sounds like something new for you, too."

"It is. *She* is what's different," Riley said, having no trouble finding words to describe Olivia, the things they had done together, and the way she felt around her.

"Have you shared with her what happened in Colorado?"

"No, not the details." Riley frowned. "I had a nightmare when I was with her. She asked about the scars."

"How do you feel about telling her? Confiding in someone?"

Riley tried to laugh, but it sounded more like choking. "Remind me why I pay you to make me feel uncomfortable?"

"What do they say in training?"

"Yeah, thanks," Riley muttered. "No pain, no gain."

"I don't necessarily recommend it in every circumstance like this, but I believe you'll know when the balance tips."

She didn't have any difficulty knowing where he was going. They'd spent many of those early sessions talking about her need to feel strong, and how showing vulnerability didn't mean she wasn't worthy of respect. Or love. Those sessions had been more grueling than any training she'd ever completed.

Riley sighed. "I feel like I should tell her all of it."

"That you *should* tell her?"

"That I need to tell her." Riley winced. Why did she have to suffer through these fucking sessions to arrive at what she should have figured out herself?

Dr. Townes regarded her as if he knew exactly what she was thinking and didn't hold it against her.

"News flash, huh?"

"Why do you think Olivia came into your life now?" he asked, surprising her. "You've known her for quite a while. Why not when she was here the first time? Or when she came back for the wedding? What's so special about now?"

Riley didn't have to think about the answer. "Because I'm ready for a relationship."

She wished she knew if Olivia was. Or what the hell she was going to do about all the reasons Olivia believed a fling was all they could ever have.

CHAPTER TWENTY-SIX

O livia stared at the duffel—correct that, saddlebag—that Riley had provided her, helpfully telling her everything she needed would fit inside. Obviously Riley didn't know very much about the way most women packed. Kelsey and Elizabeth were dropping her off at Riley's on their way to the campsite, and she had exactly fifteen minutes to decide which part of the mountain of clothes and other absolute essentials arrayed on her bed she was going to be able to pack. When her phone signaled, she almost ignored it, but with a sigh, checked the caller ID. She had too much going on at the ranch to ignore a phone call. When she saw it was her mother, her heart kicked as it always did now whenever she got an unexpected call from her.

"Mama? Is everything all right?"

"Eh. It's starting to get hot here, and you know what that's like in the city."

Olivia did her best to decipher what that meant. She didn't think her mother was talking about summer city smell or the sense of being wrapped in a wet blanket almost every time she stepped outside. "Is the weather bothering Papa?"

Translated, is he not doing well again?

Her mother sighed. "He doesn't sleep so good anymore, and I think the breathing is getting harder again, too."

Olivia sat on the edge of the bed, pushing the clothes aside with one hand. "Is he home? Let me talk to him."

"No, he had an early morning meeting. But I'll make sure he talks to you soon."

"Good. I'll be away for a few days, but I'll text when I get home."

"Oh? Where are you off to? Not one of those foreign countries again."

Olivia laughed to herself. A year ago she would have said the desert was the same as a foreign land, but as the weeks had passed on this trip, she'd begun to feel at home. "Believe it or not, I'm just about to leave for a camping trip."

Her mother laughed and she actually sounded happy for a moment, which made Olivia's heart hurt less. "Did Elizabeth talk you into that?"

"Her and Kelsey and Riley."

"Oh, everyone is going."

Olivia detected just the slightest bit of probing in her mother's tone. Interesting. "It's actually an event for the guests, but we're all going a little bit earlier to get things set up and maybe have a couple of days of relaxation."

"That sounds nice. You work too hard."

Olivia laughed. "That runs in the family."

"How is that new project you said Elizabeth was working on?" her mother asked.

"Elizabeth is always working on new projects. Do you mean the one for the planned community development I told you about?"

"Yes, that sounds brilliant to me, but then Elizabeth has always been brilliant."

"Elizabeth sees the possibilities in things," Olivia said.

"And she chose you to make sure all those possibilities come true."

Olivia smiled. That was her mother's way of saying she was proud of her. "We do work well together. And it's coming along very well. We have approval from the town planning board to expand." She laughed. "After all, luxury homes will bring in more taxes. And once the surveys are done, we'll be able to begin selling lots and thinking about construction."

"So you will be busy there for quite some time."

Olivia caught her breath. That must be the second reason for her mother's call. "I haven't made any decisions about that. I don't like being so far away from the two of you, you know."

"We know that. And we miss you, too." Her mother paused. "Well, you must be getting ready for that trip of yours. It is safe, right?"

"I'll be well protected by the veteran campers."

"As long as you're happy, then I won't worry."

"I'll call you when I get back," Olivia said.

"Go have fun and don't worry."

As soon as she ended the call, Olivia made a hasty decision as to exactly what essential meant in terms of camping and piled items into her saddle bags. *Don't worry.* That was essentially impossible. Her father was ill and not getting any better. Her mother was distraught. She had decisions to make and didn't know how to make them, and that was not how she lived her life. No way could she not worry.

But she promised herself that for the next few days, she'd think about nothing except being alone with Riley and hopefully having enough privacy to show her exactly how much she'd been missing her.

❖

"If someone had wagered that I would ever see you on a motorcycle, I would have bet a million dollars against it," Elizabeth said to Olivia as Kelsey pulled into the motorhome park and drove down toward Riley's trailer.

"I would have doubled the bet," Olivia muttered.

Kelsey laughed. "You'll like it. It's a great way to get a feel for the desert."

"Oh, just what I've always wanted," Olivia said. Then she caught sight of Riley standing in front of the trailer by a very large gleaming black and silver motorcycle and decided at least part of the day to come was exactly what she wanted. Riley looked unusually attractive, which was going a long ways, as she always looked attractive to Olivia. Today, though, she wore blue jeans with black leather chaps, a denim shirt with the sleeves rolled up, a black leather vest, and heavy black motorcycle boots.

"I'll see you later today," Olivia called as she dragged her saddlebag out of the truck.

"Hi," Riley said, her eyes on Olivia as Kelsey and Elizabeth drove away.

Olivia loved the way Riley always watched her—as if she was seeing her for the first time. "You look incredibly sexy."

Riley glanced down at herself and then back to Olivia, grinning. "If I'd known this was what it took, I would have tried leather a lot sooner."

"It's not like you had to wait very long," Olivia said.

Riley gripped Olivia's shoulders and kissed her. "Considering all the time I've missed since first meeting you, I think it's taken me way too long."

"I'd say the timing's perfect." Olivia held out her saddlebag. "I don't have enough in here to last a day, so I'm going to be borrowing clothes from you."

"There's no way my clothes are going to fit you, but if you get desperate, I could probably dig out a T-shirt or two that'll work." Riley reached behind her and picked up a dark gray leather jacket off the seat and held it out. "Here. Try this on."

Olivia frowned. "I'll never fit into a jacket of yours."

"I know. That's why I got you this."

Olivia's stomach turned into a flutter of butterflies. She took the jacket, which was butter soft and far sleeker than the heavy black one Riley wore. "You bought this for me?"

"Try it on," Riley said.

"It's perfect," Olivia said, and it was. Everything about it was perfect—the color, the cut, and most of all, knowing that Riley had bought it for her. She hugged herself. "I adore it. I'm never taking it off."

Riley laughed. "Oh, yes you are. Later."

The butterflies took flight, and Olivia jumped into Riley's arms. "I can't wait to thank you properly."

"Whoa!" Riley steadied herself as Olivia wrapped her legs around her waist and kissed her.

"How long will it take us to get there?" Olivia murmured, her arms around Riley's neck.

"Not quite an hour if we detour for a little sightseeing. We're headed to the farthest stretch of the ranch, so it's a good time for you to see the wilds."

"The wilds. Oh, yes, please," Olivia said and rolled her eyes.

Riley grinned. "And we have to help set up camp when we get there. You'll have to wait to thank me."

"Mm, some things are worth the wait," Olivia said as she slipped back to the ground and studied the motorcycle. It's not like she'd never seen one before, and she knew where she'd be sitting. "Anything I need to know?"

"Put your arms around my waist, lean a little when I do, and enjoy the ride. Okay?"

"I've got this." Olivia decided if she was going to be hurtling through the desert with her arms around Riley and her breasts pressed to Riley's back, she would damn well be enjoying herself.

❖

"Holy crap, *this* is what you call camping?" Olivia asked, astounded by her first look at the Lodge at Red Sky. The expansion had happened while she was back in Manhattan, and she'd expected a few wooden platforms for the tents, a fire pit or two, and basic bathroom and shower facilities. "Kelsey grossly understated the description of this place."

"That's the whole point. The experience can be whatever you—or the guests—want it to be," Elizabeth said. "Come on, I'll walk you around."

Elizabeth linked her arm through Olivia's as they strolled about, Elizabeth pointing out the different types of structures to choose from. Each tent, situated an ample distance from its neighbor to afford plenty of privacy, sat on a raised deck with room for several comfy-looking chairs in front. A few sites also offered individual fire rings while a much larger brick ring capable of holding a bonfire occupied the middle of the spacious grounds. Several picnic tables flanked the larger tents. Mesquite chips covered the ground to keep the dust and dirt down. Breathtaking views of the surrounding Black Hills mountains created a picture-perfect backdrop.

"It's a gorgeous location," Olivia said. "And so many options for accommodations. I need the details."

"Of course you do. We have our large family tent over there," Elizabeth said, indicating a huge sand-colored canvas tent flanked on three sides with a large wooden deck. Despite its size, the color so closely resembled that of the surrounding desert, it barely left a mark on the terrain. "They're called bell tents. That one has four double beds and one king and can sleep ten."

"If you have a lot of cousins and want to spend the entire vacation listening to them all snore," Olivia said. She hoped beyond hope she and Riley were not expected to share a tent with anyone. As to eight other people? The thought made her shudder.

Laughing, Elizabeth went on, "And for those wishing a smaller but still intimate gathering—our traditional family tents boast a queen and two singles, the majestic a king bed, and for the truly adventurous, the covered wagons sleep four in two stacked bunks."

Elizabeth didn't need to point those out to Olivia. She might be a city girl, but she knew a covered wagon when she saw one.

"All of our tents, except the covered wagons, of course, have a private bathroom inside. Nothing special but beats an outhouse. The king and queen beds have high end mattresses and linen."

"This is spectacular," was all Olivia could say.

"I know, pretty cool, isn't it?" Elizabeth said. "Ever since we announced the opening, we've been booked solid. It's amazing how many people want to unplug and get away from everything. Guests are making reservations even in the summer when it's still pretty warm at night. We have heaters for our winter visitors for when it gets a bit chilly."

"I can just imagine the sky at night out here," Olivia said. "Not a single artificial light for fifty miles."

"There's a hot tub behind that fence over there," Elizabeth said, pointing, "so you can enjoy the view. Most nights there's not a single cloud, and of course, no air pollution."

"I think this might be the most amazing thing you're done so far," Olivia commented.

"Thanks, but it was Kelsey's idea. She and Riley constructed it almost by themselves. It turned out even better than I'd hoped."

"If this is camping, I'll do it all day, every day." Olivia turned in a circle as she spoke, impressed all over again. Despite the upscale amenities and programs offered at the Red Sky Ranch, none of the development had impinged on the natural beauty and wild spirit of the land. "I love this place."

Elizabeth gave her a slow smile. "Gets to you, doesn't it?"

"Where am I staying?" Olivia asked.

"The other tents are all made up for the guests. We put you and Riley in one of the traditional tents. Plenty of space so you won't be on top of each other." She paused. "Unless you want to be, then you'll have some privacy. Nice jacket, by the way."

"Thank you." Olivia decided to make her ask and said nothing more.

"Riley?"

Olivia grinned. "Yes, it's awesome, isn't it?"

"Iced. The guest tents are already made up, so you're free for the afternoon."

"I'll catch you in a little while. I want to see the tent."

"Have fun," Elizabeth said.

Olivia lifted the flap of the tent Elizabeth had pointed to and found Riley waiting.

"I brought your saddlebag in," Riley said. She'd removed her chaps and leather vest and looked just as hot in plain denim as she had earlier.

Olivia took in the interior of the tent. Mesh windows let in plenty of light and enough air flow that the heat wasn't stifling. A partitioned area in the far back corner must be the bathroom. The beds looked like...beds. And Riley was standing next to one.

"Hey," Olivia said. "This looks pretty comfy. Thanks for bringing in my things."

"Sure. Ah, you can have the big bed. I'll take this one." Riley pointed to the queen size bed on the left side of the room. A thick canvas curtain could be pulled between the sleeping areas for a semblance of privacy.

"Why would I not be in the one that you're in?" Olivia had just expected they would share a bed, but obviously Riley thought differently. Was it because of her nightmare the other night? Not something she could just assume, and not something she wanted to ask if Riley didn't want to bring it up. "Unless you don't want to, and that's fine, too."

"Of course I want to," Riley replied. "I just didn't want to presume."

Olivia crossed to Riley. "Is everything okay?"

"Sure, why wouldn't it be?"

Despite what she'd said, Riley seemed tense and uncomfortable.

"I don't know. Are you afraid you'll snore?" Olivia laughed.

Riley looked around the tent as if she wanted to escape. Olivia reached for her hand. Her skin was cool and clammy.

"Riley, are you okay? I didn't mean to—"

"Of course I'm fine. It's not like I haven't shared a tent with anyone before."

Olivia had seen Riley do this before—refuse to talk about something that was obviously bothering her—and by the set of Riley's jaw, she was not ready to talk about anything now either. Olivia longed to help, if she could, but pushing Riley to share was not what Riley needed, no matter how much Riley's distress bothered her.

Olivia nudged her shoulder. "But you've never shared a tent with me. A city girl from Manhattan. That could be an all new experience."

"No, I haven't, and I'm looking forward to it."

When Riley laughed and the color returned to her cheeks, Olivia sighed with relief.

The thought of the two of them alone in a tent in the middle of the desert, despite the proximity of other people, lent a magical air to the whole experience. She was suddenly very ready to explore the pleasures of private glamping.

Riley tossed her bag onto the large bed. "Let's hit the trail, city girl from Manhattan. We're burning daylight, and we still have work to do."

"Wait a minute. Elizabeth said the guest tents were all set up. And you know, free time." Olivia glanced meaningfully at the bed.

"That's because she was going easy on you. There's still plenty to do. Of course, if you're too tired—"

"As if. Wait—if I'm doing manual labor, I'm not doing it in these clothes."

"I'll wait outside."

"Why?" Olivia smiled and pulled off her top.

❖

"What are you doing?" Riley cringed at sounding just a bit squeaky, but she couldn't help it. Olivia was killing her.

"It's not as if you haven't seen me naked," Olivia said with a shrug, "I'm covered."

Riley could not *not* look at the lacy red bra that covered the essentials but made the essentials look like a feast to a starving woman. And she was suddenly very, very hungry.

"That"—Riley swept a hand in Olivia's direction—"is cruel."

Olivia dug an olive-green T-shirt with a Jefferson Airplane logo on it out of her saddlebag and looked over her shoulder at Riley.

"Really?" She pulled on the T-shirt. "Better?"

Riley gritted her teeth. "No. I know what's under there, and I'm not going to be able to look at you without seeing it."

"Well, I hope you haven't forgotten that you know what's underneath."

"Believe me, I haven't forgotten a single minute."

"Neither have I." Olivia brushed past her on her way toward the front of the tent, her fingers lightly stroking Riley's butt. "I'm looking forward to tonight."

Riley followed her outside. At that moment, she would have followed her anywhere. Olivia in charge, teasing her, flirting with her, seducing her right in the damn tent, was the sexiest thing she'd ever experienced. Now she just had to figure how she was going to have sex with her at the first possible minute without sleeping with her. She hadn't thought about the sleeping arrangements when she'd offered to share a tent with Olivia. She'd been too caught up in the idea of being away with her, anywhere. She could have another nightmare—probably would. She didn't want Olivia witnessing another one of those. She'd just have to stay awake. She'd brought her headphones and iPad. No one would be the wiser.

Kelsey spied them and called out, "About time. I thought you two were going to beg off the hard work." She tilted her head. "Excellent T-shirt, Olivia."

"Thank you," Olivia said, casting a sideways glance at Riley.

Riley laughed, and Kelsey shot her a look.

"What?" Kelsey said.

"Never mind," Riley said, "just tell us where to start."

The work wasn't really hard—the staff had already done the early prep. Since the guests weren't due to arrive until the next day, they didn't have to rush to get everything ready. Olivia and Riley checked the accommodations against the reservations, making sure any special needs or requests were taken care of. The chuckwagon had arrived, and Elizabeth supervised the setup there while Chuck got the solar water heaters turned on. Kelsey reviewed the next day's events with the staff and assigned group leaders for each excursion. By the time dinner time came around and amazing smells emanated from the chuckwagon, Kelsey had a fire blazing in a large pit in the center of the grounds.

Out of habit, Riley surveyed the setup. The pit itself was framed by large rocks Riley had located around the ranch, and the surrounding ground had been cleared of shrubs or anything that could catch fire from a wayward cinder. A fire extinguisher was discreetly located on the other side of the freshly cut pile of mesquite. Satisfied, she took over the ministrations of the fire, keeping it fed and burning to maximum effect.

Dinner done, the four of them sat around the fire until the conversation slowed, and Riley let the flames die down.

Kelsey rose and held out her hand to Elizabeth. "Ready to call it night?"

"Yes," Elizabeth said.

" 'Night," Riley said, watching the fire as the embers glowed.

"Are you having a good time?" Olivia asked quietly, linking her arm through Riley's.

"Excellent." She glanced at Olivia. "You?"

"So far I've found camping to exceed my expectations. Can't wait to see what the night brings."

Riley's vital parts woke up with a kick. "Are you ready to go in?"

"Can we sit and watch the stars for just a few more minutes?

Elizabeth said the sky would be incredible, but even at the ranch it never looked like this. So...pure."

Riley held out her hand. "Anything you want. We can sit right outside our tent on the deck as long as you want."

Olivia took her hand. "That sounds perfect."

"It does," Riley said, leading the way through the dark and quiet campsite. Perfect was Olivia's hand in hers. Perfect was lying naked with her, touching her and being touched by her. Perfect, Riley was coming to think, could be a single night when shared with the right woman.

CHAPTER TWENTY-SEVEN

Is this okay?" Riley said, indicating a lounger slung with heavy canvas on the deck in front of their tent. "Room for two."

Olivia laughed. "Who could ask for more?"

Riley stretched out and Olivia, smaller and shorter, fit seamlessly beneath Riley's arm. Olivia cradled her head on Riley's shoulder and took in the sky revolving overhead.

"The stars are so bright—and the sky a true black. Amazing," Olivia said.

"Do you know there are whole groups of people called Dark Sky gazers who search out the best spots in the world to see a sky like this? A lot of those places are in Arizona."

"Are you a stargazer?" Olivia asked.

"I like looking at them." Riley stroked Olivia's arm. "Right now, I'm a little distracted. I know what you're wearing under that T-shirt, remember."

Olivia shifted to face Riley in the surprisingly comfy chair. "I did say I was going to thank you for that incredible jacket. I think now would be a good time. Any requests?"

"You could start with kissing me," Riley said, her voice deep and husky. As she spoke, she tugged up the bottom of Olivia's T shirt and ran her fingers along the few inches of bare skin.

Olivia shivered, not the least bit cold, and kissed her. She wanted soft, and to her surprise, so did Riley. Olivia teased her tongue along the seam of Riley's lips, lightly biting the warm inner edge. Just as tenderly, Riley fluttered feather-light kisses along her cheek, to the corner of her eye, to the curve of her temple. Her mouth was so gentle, Olivia shuddered with the intensity.

"How can anything so tender drive me out of my mind," Olivia whispered.

"The waiting makes the having so much better."

"I'm not so sure I'm good at waiting." Olivia could not get enough of Riley's kisses. She wanted—no, *needed* to feel skin on skin, to feel Riley's mouth everywhere. Leaning away, she pulled her T-shirt over her head. "Kiss me everywhere, and maybe I can be patient."

In the starlight, flames flared in Riley's eyes. She tugged the lacy cup of Olivia's red bra down and took a nipple into her mouth. Olivia just barely stifled a cry, remembering in some corner of her brain that they were fifty feet from Kelsey and Elizabeth's tent. Riley's teeth closed slowly on her nipple, and Olivia arched in her arms.

"That's so good, too good," Olivia murmured. "Keep it up, and I'll come right out here."

"We should take this inside, then," Riley said, "because I don't want to stop."

"All right." Olivia drew in a deep breath. "I haven't finished saying thank you yet."

"Oh, I think you've been thanking me just fine." Riley stood, her hands on Olivia's waist. When she urged her up, Olivia wrapped her legs around her waist.

"Is this the traditional fireman's carry?" Olivia asked as Riley pushed aside the tent flap and carried her inside.

"It is now."

Olivia felt the rumble of Riley's words in her chest. The web windows let in just enough of the sky glow for her to see as Riley headed for the larger of the beds. "I could get used to this."

"Wait till I throw you over my shoulder."

Laughing, Olivia held on as Riley leaned over and settled her on the bed. "Next time."

Watching Riley, Olivia reached behind her, unhooked her bra, and slid it off. "Your shirt."

"Right," Riley said, sounding a little disoriented. "You're beautiful, and the killer lingerie has nothing to do with it."

With Riley looking at her the way she was, as if Olivia was a delicacy she wanted to devour, Olivia *felt* beautiful. She pushed off her capris and bottoms all at once and tossed them aside. "Boots. Pants."

Still looking at her, Riley somehow got naked and stretched out beside her. Olivia arched above her and took her mouth. Not gently this time, not slowly. Not teasing kisses. Fast and hungry and demanding. "God, I love your mouth."

"I love what you do to me with yours," Riley said.

Olivia cupped Riley's breast and rubbed her thumb over Riley's hard nipple. Riley's sharp intake of breath made her clit pulse. Still fondling Riley's breasts, she dipped her head and kissed Riley's stomach. The muscles she'd felt during yoga quivered beneath her lips. The power of Riley's arousal made her head swim.

"You are so unbelievably sexy," she muttered, kissing the soft skin lower on Riley's belly.

Riley ran her fingers through Olivia's hair. "If you keep that up, I can't be responsible for my actions."

Olivia laughed. "Good, because you don't have to be. I'm in charge."

Riley cupped the back of Olivia's head while she explored with her mouth and tongue. When Olivia pressed her fingers to the inside of Riley's thigh, Riley opened for her. Resting her cheek on Riley's thigh, Olivia looked up to see Riley's gaze on her. The trust in her eyes humbled her as much as the need in them aroused her. Trust and need. To be given that. To offer that. What else was love?

Her heart seized, caught between joy and sorrow. "I'm going to show you just how much you make me want, and how much I want you. I'm going to take my time while I enjoy you, until you shatter like you've made me shatter. Into a million pieces."

Riley gasped when Olivia's tongue flicked over her clit. "Pretty sure of yourself, aren't you."

"Absolutely."

"Then do it."

Riley choked off a whimper when Olivia took her into her mouth, and the sound sent ripples of pleasure through Olivia's clit. She followed the rhythm of Riley's heart beating between her lips, and when she felt her getting close, slipped inside her. Riley thrust against her and came with a muffled shout.

Holding her, Olivia watched in awe as Riley's breathing slowed. She had never felt as satisfied or as content as she did at that moment. Riley—an amazingly strong, smart, beautiful woman—lay in her arms, for just a moment, hers.

"Hey," she whispered. "How are you doing?"

Riley chuckled and kissed her. "Can't remember being better."

"That's perfect, then," Olivia said.

"Pretty much."

"Oh? Not totally sure? Did I forget something? Because I'm not tired." Olivia wanted, *needed*, for her to come again. Having sex with Riley was more than she imagined it to be. And she had imagined it plenty of times these past few days.

Riley sighed. "We probably *should* get some sleep."

"But what if I don't want to sleep?"

"Oh yeah?" Riley raised her eyebrows. "What do you want to do?"

"Exactly what we just spent the last two hours doing." Olivia pushed aside the fleeting sense of desperation. This wouldn't be their last night. Not with the way Riley looked at her. Not with how much she needed to touch Riley again. How much she needed to feel that incredible sense of oneness. She had months before she needed to decide what she was going to do.

"I've got a better idea," Riley replied, pushing Olivia onto her back and climbing on top of her. "I'll show you what *I* want right now."

Olivia wrapped her arms around Riley's shoulders. "I can't wait."

Riley wasn't lying. Her lips and tongue were everywhere. Warm fingers slid over Olivia's skin, heating her flesh, sending electricity spiking into her clit. Soft kisses turned into taunting nips across her breasts. Her hips bucked as Riley stroked between her thighs—close but oh, God, not quite close enough.

"Riley, please," she gasped. "No more teasing."

"Sure? Now?"

"Yes, yes, now." Olivia had trouble catching her breath. Her heart hammered in her chest. She grabbed a fist full of sheet to keep from flying away. Pleasure engulfed her as Riley's mouth worked magic on her body. Every nerve felt exposed. Riley's tongue circled her clit as she slipped her fingers into her. Olivia lifted her legs to take her deeper. She looked down, mesmerized at the view. It was impossible to look away. Riley's mouth was between her legs, her fingers moving inside her.

Olivia felt the orgasm roar to the surface like a nonstop train on a slick track. She clung to the precipice of pleasure for as long as she could before one final flick of Riley's tongue pushed her over the edge. Remembering where they were, she put her hand over her mouth to muffle her climax. Wave after wave of pleasure crashed through her with no beginning and no end. Exhausted, too sated for words, she clung to Riley and finally floated away.

Chapter Twenty-eight

Riley woke before dawn, surprised that she'd fallen asleep with Olivia. Even more surprisingly, she hadn't dreamed. Carefully, she slipped out of bed, pulled the light blanket over Olivia to ward off the chilly morning air, and carried her jeans and shirt out to the deck to dress. She stretched out in the same lounge chair where the amazing sex with Olivia had started, and as she watched the majestic saguaro cacti emerge from the dark and heard birds begin chattering in a nearby bush, she couldn't help but relive the night, moment by incredible moment. She'd never had a night like the previous one. Never gotten so lost in the wonder of a woman the way she had with Olivia—every sound, every touch, every word between them had been magical. Unforgettable. And damn, wasn't that a terrifying problem, because now that she knew what sex—what *lovemaking*, because how could she call it anything else?—could be like, she'd want that, want her, always.

"Why are you not in bed with me where you belong?" Olivia, wrapped in a blanket and looking impossibly sexy in a sleepy, disheveled way, appeared beside her.

Because I was thinking that I'm in lo—

Riley jerked her brain back to reality. She'd just been daydreaming, that's all. "I didn't want to wake you up."

"Want company?"

"Are you wearing anything under that blanket?"

Olivia smiled, an altogether self-satisfied smile. "Not much."

"Then there's definitely room." Riley shifted over, and Olivia crawled onto the lounger while pulling the blanket over them both. "I believe I caught a glimpse of a T-shirt and shorts."

"They're doubling as pajamas. I'm not wearing anything else, though."

Butterflies darted around in Riley's stomach at the soft, still-sleepy tenor of Olivia's voice. Her actual words heated the blood in her veins. "The camp is going to wake up soon."

"That's okay," Olivia said. "I can wait." She kissed Riley lightly. "Not too long, though."

"Count on it," Riley said, wanting to take her back inside the tent instantly. If only Kelsey wasn't likely to pop out of her tent and start looking for her any minute. She rested her cheek on the top of Olivia's head and idly followed a cottontail running off across the sand at the edge of the clearing. Minutes of silence passed, and she thought Olivia had fallen asleep.

"Did you sleep at all?" Olivia asked.

Riley hesitated. She could just follow the script. She didn't have to open the door she vowed never to walk through. She could keep her pain and her guilt to herself. And she would never be free to give Olivia what she deserved. "I don't sleep much. I have nightmares. That's why I never—why I didn't stay the night with a woman before you."

"Will you tell me about your dreams?" Olivia's voice was soft, her breath warm against Riley's chest.

Riley's pulse skyrocketed. Olivia's hand, nestled between Riley's breasts on top of her shirt, felt like an anchor and a heavy weight bearing down on her.

Fuck. Deflection would get her nowhere, but she couldn't help but try. "How long are you staying?"

"I don't know."

God damn it. Olivia always told the truth even when a lie would be kinder. How could she tell Olivia about the horrors that haunted her? What would she think of her? Would she look at her differently? Think her weak? Think her a coward? Would she want her less? Would Olivia see her as she saw herself—broken somewhere deep inside, ashamed, and afraid?

Dr. Townes's words came back to her. *Why do you think you're involved with Olivia now? Why not a year ago?*

Because she was ready. Riley sucked in a breath. Olivia hadn't moved, still gently lying in the curve of her body. Waiting.

Something else Dr. Townes had once said. That the people who matter will not pity you or blame you, and the people who will, don't matter.

Go big or go home, Riley thought. She needed to trust Olivia, even if it turned out there was no future. Olivia deserved it, and so did she.

"I was almost killed by a falling tree once. Another time the smoke was so bad I coughed for a week. It was the hardest job I've ever had, and I loved it. Sixteen-hour shifts wearing thirty-pound packs and digging in the dirt. When we were deployed, there was always a chance we weren't coming back, but we didn't think about that. We had to believe we were. I read once where someone described wildfire fighting as chasing an adventure. And God, was he right. My best friend Kevin and I were part of a six-man crew that deployed all over the country, fighting some of the biggest fires on record."

Riley faltered. Chasing an adventure. Yeah, and daring death. That was part of the thrill, too, but one she'd never thought much about. "I suppose I worried sometimes about dying out there, but I never imagined being the sole survivor."

Olivia wrapped an arm around her, pulling her closer. "What happened?"

Riley closed her eyes.

"There were six of us fighting a fire in Colorado. I was the crew chief, and we'd been on the line for weeks. Just when we thought we'd gotten it under control, she would flare again and eat up another few hundred acres. Seventy thousand acres burned before it was under control."

Riley shuddered. The memories were never far from her mind, but she was barely able to breathe.

"Stop if you need to," Olivia said quietly. "But I'm not going anywhere."

The compassion in Olivia's voice and the comfort she imparted with her embrace helped Riley fight through the agony. Gave her the will to get it all out.

"It was a Thursday. We were due to rotate out the next day. We were on the north ridge when there was a blow-up. The fire exploded around us. No one saw it coming. In an instant we were trapped." She opened her eyes, saw not the charred ruins of the forest and the bodies of her friends, but Olivia's steady, *unpitying* gaze on hers. "I never should have let us get in that position. I should have—"

"No one saw it coming, you said," Olivia murmured. "What did you do?"

"We deployed our shelters," Riley said. "We all carry these fire-resistant blankets, like a cocoon that we're trained to use if…" Riley stopped, her throat tight. "They were a part of us. We were trained to deploy them in less than a minute. We were *trained* how to survive when you became fuel for the fire. We deployed and dug in and waited. I dug a hole and buried my face in the dirt and prayed."

The sound of the fire that day filled her head. The roaring that blocked out the screams, until all she heard was her own helpless pleas.

"Riley, hey. Riley?"

Olivia's voice. Olivia was there.

"It's as clear as if I'm back there, that day, every time I think of it. The sound was deafening, the heat unbearable. The fire was on us so *fast*, and when it passed, in its place was a quiet I had never heard before. I was the only one that crawled out from under their shelter."

Riley hesitated, fully expecting to begin sliding down the familiar dark hole, but she didn't. She felt it coming, and she focused on the now. The here. The heat of Olivia's body next to hers. The birdsong. The scent of fresh air and horses. She had never been able to do that before. Stronger now, she finished.

"Kevin, Ashley's husband and Luke's dad, died that day with the rest of my crew. My friends. Luke was just a baby. It should have been Kev that survived, not me. I knew they were gone. All of them. I don't know how I survived, but they all died." Riley took a deep breath before continuing. "Everyone except me."

Several minutes passed before Riley finally said the words she never thought she'd say out loud.

"If I could have one day to do over again, it would be that day. And I would die with my crew."

❖

"I'm so sorry," Olivia whispered, holding Riley close as much to ease the ache inside herself as to comfort Riley. The tears that flooded her heart and threatened to flow burned her eyes, but she held them in. Her pain was nothing to what Riley must have endured, and she didn't want what she was feeling to cause Riley any further distress. And she knew Riley would hurt, thinking Olivia hurt. All that mattered in this moment was Riley. Riley's agony was palpable in every word, and all Olivia could do was be there for her. Knowing Riley relived that indescribable horror and suffered the unimaginable loss over and over again, asleep and awake, ripped at her heart. "I don't know what you feel, and I'm not sure if I did that I could bear it. But you *do* bear it. You honor them by bearing it."

"I'm no hero," Riley said. "Sometimes I have trouble concentrating.

I'm constantly on edge. I see a shrink. I have to. I owe it to the people that are beside me on the line every day. I work too much because I can't stand the thought of anyone else dying because of a fire."

Riley didn't move for a long moment, and Olivia feared she'd said the wrong thing. "I know I can't understand what—"

"You're listening." Riley turned to face Olivia. "That's the first time I've actually told the whole story to anyone, even my shrink."

"Any you told me because?"

"Other than you asked me?"

Olivia nodded.

Riley kissed her gently on the lips. "Because you matter."

"I always want to hear whatever you want to tell me," Olivia said, cupping Riley's jaw. "Whatever it helps you to say, whenever you need to say it, I want to hear. There's probably nothing I can say that your fellow firefighters or your therapist hasn't said about that day, but I *know* with all that I am that you did everything you could to save them."

"I'm not sure I'll ever believe that." Riley paused. "How long are you staying?"

"I don't know," Olivia said, because honesty deserved honesty.

Riley nodded. "I guess we both have decisions to make."

Olivia kissed her. "But not today. Let's go back to bed."

CHAPTER TWENTY-NINE

Riley woke to the smell of coffee. For an instant, she wasn't sure where she was.

"Hey, sleepyhead." Olivia stood beside the bed, a cup of what had to be heaven in her hands. She wore the T-shirt and shorts Riley distinctly remembered removing right before the repeat of last night's amazing sex.

She shot up in bed. "What time is it? Is that for me?"

"Seven and yes, you want?" Olivia held out the steaming mug.

"Yes, and you're damn right I want. Are you still naked under there?"

Olivia laughed and handed her the mug. "No and, sadly, no, we can't right now. Kelsey threatened to come in here and drag you out. I thought I'd better warn you."

"Hell." Riley made it a point to touch Olivia's fingers when she took the mug. Since the fire, she hadn't allowed herself to be in a position where a woman could even bring her morning coffee. She hadn't realized how much she missed the connection and the slow, comfortable morning sex that often followed. Her body remembered, though, and a twinge of arousal shot between her thighs. "I can't believe I fell asleep."

"Thank you," Olivia said, looking smug.

Then she pulled off her T-shirt, unhooked her bra, and pushed down her shorts.

Riley swallowed a large gulp of hot liquid and winced. Olivia, naked, stunned her at the same time her simmering arousal detonated. "I thought you said we didn't have time—"

"We don't." Olivia winked as she turned and walked unhurriedly away. "I'm going to take a luxury shower in our luxury bathroom."

Riley watched, a huge case of lust searing all coherent thought from her head. Then memories of her confession that morning obliterated every sensation except regret. She'd shared more than she'd ever intended, more than she ever had before, and with the one person who could hurt her the most if the truth of her past, of her guilt and apathy, forced Olivia to run for cover.

Sweat misted her face and chest, her heart raced, and her vision wavered. What had she done? How could she fix this? How could she make Olivia unhear what she'd told her?

She couldn't.

Because Olivia had heard her. Olivia had *listened*. Olivia had not turned away. She'd acknowledged Riley's loss, recognized her pain, and accepted that her guilt and shame still affected her. The one thing Olivia hadn't done was turn away. Olivia had held her, comforted her, and given herself without restriction. She reveled in Riley's body a few hours ago, and she'd just teased her by getting naked when she damn well knew that would make her crazy.

Riley usually lived in a constant state of hypervigilance, always on edge in anticipation of the next trigger that would send her spiraling, but surprisingly, the overwhelming cloak of anxiety and guilt was gone. For the first time in a long time, she felt like she could actually breathe without the weight and burden of keeping her nightmares a secret that was suffocating her. She had stepped out of the dark night of her past into the sunlight.

Riley bolted out of the bed. The water shut off just as she reached the small shower enclosure. She grabbed the plush gray bath towel Olivia had left draped over a camp stool and stepped through the opening in the canvas flap into the shower stall.

Olivia squeaked and reflexively folded her arms over her breasts.

"Here," Riley said, holding out the towel. "Let me."

She'd feared what she might see in Olivia's eyes when Olivia had had a chance to think about what Riley had told her. What she found when she met Olivia's gaze was anything but rejection. The heat in Olivia's eyes telegraphed desire that matched her own.

"We're a little crowded in here," Olivia murmured, her voice as heated as her gaze.

"Just enough room." Riley slowly ran the towel over Olivia's shoulders, her arms, her chest, her breasts. When she knelt, naked, to dry Olivia's legs, Olivia gasped and set her hand on Riley's head to steady herself.

Riley's vision wavered, from need, not anxiety. Olivia's scent floated to her on the steamy air. Her clit swelled and pulsed. Hoarsely, she ordered, "Hold on to me."

Olivia's fingers twisted in her hair, and Riley opened her with her fingers and took her into her mouth.

"Oh God." Olivia groaned, her thighs trembling.

Riley gripped her hips, steadying her as she licked her. When she held her between her lips and sucked, Olivia cried out. Wild with the taste of her, with the power of the orgasm rising between her lips, Riley shot one hand between her own thighs. One swift stroke brought her over as Olivia came in her mouth.

❖

"Are we alive?" Olivia croaked, not entirely certain since she still couldn't hear and could barely see. She was somehow still standing, leaning into Riley, who held her up with her arms around her waist.

"Mm-hmm." Riley kissed her. "And if we're not, I don't care."

Olivia sighed, her cheek against Riley's shoulder. "Was it the coffee? Because I'll figure out how to bring you coffee every day, even if it's takeout."

Riley laughed. "The guys at the station will die of jealousy."

"I know it wasn't the outfit."

"I loved the way you woke me up," Riley said, "and the coffee helped. But mostly I was thinking about earlier, and at first I was worried, until I remembered how glad I was I'd told you. And how great you were."

"Are you all right now?" Olivia leaned back to look at her. Riley looked…peaceful. She'd never seem her look quite that way, not even after they'd made love.

"I'm here. I'm okay, really." Riley added after a second, "Well, I think I'm on my way, or at least managing it better."

Olivia kissed her. "Good morning then."

"An excellent morning," Riley said, her voice low and suggestive. "Maybe we have time—"

"Yo, the tent," Kelsey called, obviously right at the main entrance. "Do you plan on doing any work today?"

Olivia kissed Riley quickly and shouted, "We'll be right there."

When Riley cursed inventively, Olivia laughed, happier than she'd ever been and determined not to think about why. Just to feel.

❖

Olivia spent the morning helping Elizabeth welcome guests and get everyone outfitted for the afternoon events. Riley, Kelsey, and several ranch hands tended the horses. After they'd all been fed, watered, and checked to be sure they'd made the trip in the trailers without incident, Kelsey and the trail guides saddled up five of the gentlest ones for a trail ride.

Kelsey led the riders to a trail on the left of the campground with one of the ranch hands bringing up the rear. Elizabeth took another group for an offroad adventure, leaving Riley and Olivia alone. Chuck hadn't yet returned from a grocery run for fresh vegetables he needed for the dinner meal.

"You know we're alone," Olivia said.

Riley lounged in one of the chairs by the fire pit, legs stretched out in front of her, eyes closed as she enjoyed the warmth of the afternoon sun.

"Don't get any ideas," she warned without opening her eyes. She had felt Olivia approach and stop beside her. She was acutely aware of any time Olivia was near. "Sound carries out here."

Olivia took Riley's hand and tugged her up.

"Then I guess I'll have to put something in my mouth to keep quiet."

"Race you," Riley said an instant before running toward their tent.

"Hey, no fair," Olivia called from behind.

They were both laughing when they tumbled onto the bed, and Riley caught a glimpse of herself before her life went to shit. Before the fire and the baggage that clung to it. A brief moment of the fun she used to have with a woman in bed.

Riley weakly tried to resist, still laughing, as Olivia tickled her while simultaneously getting them both naked.

Breathless, Riley rolled onto her back and grinned at Olivia, whose face was flushed and her eyes dancing. "I love it when you get ideas."

Olivia straddled Riley's stomach. "There is just something about sex in the afternoon that's almost decadent."

"Decadent?" Olivia was hot and wet, and a fist of need knocked the breath from Riley's chest.

"Yeah," Olivia began, leaning down and kissing her on the mouth. She pulled away and kissed the underside of Riley's jaw. "Decadent."

She kissed her neck. "Erotic." She moved to her collar bone. "Spicy." She kissed the outside of her left breast. "Titillating." Her lips did the same to the other breast, this time sucking her nipple before she spoke. "Double titillating."

Riley laughed and fought to hold still.

Olivia's hands and lips blazed a path down her stomach, each kiss punctuated with a word. "Shameless, brazen, lascivious, tasty."

Riley parted her thighs in anticipation of Olivia's mouth.

"And my favorite two." Olivia paused, looking up at Riley as she slowly lowered her head. "Wicked and nasty."

Riley moaned when Olivia's tongue touched her clit.

"Shh, sound carries out here," Olivia teased.

"I can't swear I'll be quiet." Riley raised her shoulders and looked down at Olivia, poised between her thighs and smiling up at her. She'd never seen a more beautiful woman. Never wanted a woman to take her as much as she did in that moment. She cradled Olivia's head with both hands and guided her to where she needed her. "In fact, I'm pretty sure I won't be."

CHAPTER THIRTY

Just coming off a four-day shift, Riley was two miles into a five-mile run at a little after six on a bright sunny June day when the sound of screaming brakes and rending metal pulled her from the meditative cadence of footfalls on asphalt and her own rhythmic breathing. A car had passed her moments ago, but she'd barely registered it going by. As long as no one was about to run her off the road through inattentiveness, carelessness, or malice, she didn't let them intrude on one of her few peaceful hours. Besides, on the relatively deserted stretch of road that ran out of town through unpopulated desert, there was very little through traffic.

The sounds were unmistakable. Somewhere up ahead a car had crashed. She picked up her speed and raced around the curve, heat waves already shimmering on the surface of the pavement, making her feel as if she was running into a dream. Her heart pounded but her mind was clear and automatically switching into action mode. She yanked her phone from the pocket of her shorts and was already pressing 911 as she rounded the bend. Smoking rubber debris cluttered the ground. A car rested upside down at the bottom of a steep embankment in the scrub by the side of the road.

"What is your emergency?" the calm, steady voice of the dispatcher asked.

"This is Firefighter Riley Mitchell. I am west on Stonehenge, three miles from town. One-car accident, unknown injuries."

"Keep your phone open, Firefighter. I'll dispatch fire rescue and emergency personnel to your location."

Riley didn't wait for an answer but shoved the phone, the call still open, back in her pants. She heard the screaming now. Saw a woman next to the vehicle, and as she drew closer, the screams became words.

"My baby, my baby. I can't get my baby. Somebody please help me. Help me."

Riley took in the scene like a series of snapshots, analyzing the images in rapid succession. A young brunette in pink shorts and a flowery halter top, blood streaming down her face and neck. Probable forehead laceration, possible closed head injury. Ambulatory, moving all four extremities, and obviously alert, although how oriented remained to be seen, as she wrenched at the rear door and screamed semicoherently. Smoke billowed from underneath the hood of the upside-down hatchback. The front tire had blown. Riley smelled the fire before she saw the flames reaching out from beneath the crumpled hood.

"Get away from the car," Riley yelled as she half slid, half tumbled down the slope from the road toward the wreck.

The woman continued screaming while tugging at the door.

"Move away from the car," Riley shouted as she drew level with her. "I'll get your baby."

The woman turned glassy, uncomprehending eyes toward her as the flames spread from beneath the hood into the passenger compartment. Riley gripped the woman's shoulders and forcibly pushed her away from the car. "I'll get your baby. Do you hear me? I'll get your baby. Stay back here."

She couldn't wait for the woman to acknowledge her but ran to the vehicle. She peered into the smoke-filled interior. Front passenger compartment empty. A baby—toddler by the size—dangled in an infant carrier suspended from the rear seat that now formed the ceiling of vehicle. Riley yanked on the handle of the same door the woman—presumably the mother—had tried to open. The metal was hot, and the door held firm.

"Fuck," she muttered. If she'd had the hydraulic jaws, she could pop it in a few seconds, but she didn't have any equipment, and she didn't have a few seconds. If the fire hit the gas tank or the gas line, the entire car would go up in less than that. She sprinted around to the other side of the car, saw that the window in that door had shattered and, turning her face away, jammed her elbow against the fragments still attached. Once most of the fragments were clear, she levered her upper body into the back seat. The fit was tight, but she was able to reach the car seat where a toddler, red-faced and tear-streaked, screamed as loud as their mother.

"I got you," Riley repeated over and over as she methodically unclipped the various buckles and straps one-handedly while holding the baby in place with the other hand. She carefully took stock in the few seconds she needed to free the child. Breathing was just fine, if the screams were any indication, although they both were starting to cough from the black smoke that filled most of the interior. Arms and legs all waving in the air. No blood anywhere. The baby, it seemed, was okay, although she knew better than to make snap judgments. As the last strap came free, she cradled the writhing, now hiccupping toddler against her chest with one arm, and pushed herself back through the window. Her gym shorts caught on something, and a searing pain streaked down her leg. Ignoring the pain, she got herself and the baby back on the ground and raced to get clear. A quick visual check as she sprinted showed the baby coated in sweat and looking a little stunned, but their breathing still seemed okay. She continued to cough as she backpedaled away from the car and then ran back toward the road. The mother hadn't moved from the spot where she'd left her and blessedly had also stopped screaming.

"I got them, I got them," Riley shouted. "Climb up to the road. Now." Because she kept moving with the baby, the mother finally moved as well, scampering up the sandy slope. In the distance, sirens wailed.

❖

"You need stitches there," Crowley said, indicating the long gash in Riley's thigh. Blood streaked down her leg and into her shoe.

"Oh, fuck me," Riley muttered. "That's the last thing I need."

"Sorry, but you are going to have to get in the bus," Crowley said, indicating the EMT vehicle.

"Come on, don't get all technical on me."

Crowley shook her head. "Sorry, Riley, but you need to go to the ER."

"Fuck," Riley muttered again. The mother and baby had already been transported, and the road crew was starting to clear the wreckage. "Fine. Let's just get it over with."

"Here," Crowley said, handing her an 02 mask. "You sound like a frog, and you're wheezing a little bit."

"You're starting to be a real pain in my ass." Riley clamped the mask to her face, breathed deeply, and coughed. Fuck.

"What else is new," Crowley said as she walked Riley to the open back of the EMT van, escorted her up the two steps and into the rear. "You know the drill. Lie down on the stretcher."

"You're kidding me, right?"

Crowley shook her head. "You know you have to be secured before transport. Do you have to make this any harder?"

Riley sighed and stretched out so Crowley could secure the safety belt across her hips. In truth, her chest burned almost as badly as her leg. She knew the gash needed to be cleaned out. But a dose of antibiotics, a little bit of saline irrigation, and some freaking Steri-Strips, and she'd be fine. The whole ambulance bit was just embarrassing.

"Who do you want me to call?" Crowley said as the driver hit the siren, and they pulled away.

"Call? What do you mean? Nobody."

"Going to need a ride home from the hospital. I'll have to head back to the station once we get you unloaded, or I'd do it."

"Oh, come on," Riley said. "Now you're really busting my stones."

"Okay, let's see, I'll start with a call to Had—"

"Fine, call Kelsey. No, never mind, I'll call her."

"Okay, you could probably do that while we're on the way."

Riley closed her eyes. This was not going to be a good day.

❖

As soon as she was offloaded into a cubicle and Crowley left, a nurse came in to do the initial assessment.

"Listen," Riley asked him, "what's the status of the mother and the baby from the accident?"

"They're in trauma one. You the firefighter who got them out?"

"Yeah. Can you get me a status report?"

"I can, as soon as I get you checked in."

"Look, I'm fine."

He looked up from where he was taking her blood pressure. "Then why are you bleeding all over the bed?"

"Right." Riley hated hospitals. She'd spent far too much time in the burn center recovering from injuries she sustained in the Colorado fire. Was it only six years ago? Every time she walked into the ER with an injured or sick patient, the memories came back so strongly it was like it had just happened that morning. Lying on the stretcher made her antsy and angry, even though her working brain knew she needed treatment. Some jagged piece of metal had snagged her as she'd crawled back through the window with the kid. Mostly, she just wanted up and out of there. Sweat popped on her forehead, and her pulse raced. Fuck, not now. She did not need to lose it now.

"Can I go in?"

The voice came from outside the curtain, and for an instant Riley thought she'd imagined it.

"She can probably use the company," a voice Riley recognized as Crowley's said. "Olivia, right? I remember you from the pancake breakfast."

"Yes," Olivia said.

"Hey, Riley," Crowley called, parting the curtain and looking in. "You've got a visitor."

Riley wanted to shout no. And she desperately wanted to see her.

The curtain parted further, and Olivia stepped in. Her hair was down, she was makeup free, and she wore a tank top and skimpy shorts. She looked like she'd just rolled out of bed and had never been more beautiful.

"Hi," Riley croaked.

Olivia bit her lip. She looked around the treatment room as if uncertain what to do next and then took Riley's hand. "Hi."

"What are you doing here?"

Olivia looked surprised, and Riley knew she sounded angry. *Jackass.* Not Olivia's fault she was freaking out. Quickly, she added, "How did you hear?"

"Kelsey. I was having breakfast with them when you called."

"Of course." Riley sighed. "You didn't need to come."

"Didn't I?" Olivia asked softly, watching her intently.

Riley realized she was gripping Olivia's hand so tightly she had to be hurting her. She loosened her hold but didn't let go. "I'm fine. It's just a…a cut."

"Really?" Olivia looked down at Riley's leg propped up on a pillow at the end of the stretcher. Her leg was wrapped in a sterile dressing from the top of her thigh to her knee. "It looks like a big one."

"It's not that bad." Riley hated people making a fuss over her. Injuries, usually minor, were a consequence of her job and nothing special. Maybe if she said it enough, everyone would believe it.

"I understand you're used to this," Olivia said, "but from what I heard—and you know how fast news travels around here—you climbed through a window into a burning car, cutting your leg on something while freeing an infant, and have smoke inhalation. Don't tell me it's nothing."

This conversation was making Riley more uncomfortable than waiting for the doctor. "Because…"

"Because nothing. You're hurt. That's not a crime or a weakness or…or a sin. People care about you. *I* care about you. Don't pretend you don't matter."

"I'm not…"

"Yes, you are." Olivia let out an aggravated sound. "I know your job comes with risks. It frightens me, and that's my problem. But you also take unnecessary risks—like skydiving and…and riding your dirt bike out in the desert alone. You insult every person who cares for you when you act like *you* don't care what happens to you."

"I don't know if I can change that." Riley stared at her. "I didn't ask you to care about me. I've been honest about why."

Olivia's head snapped up and her eyes flashed. Anger? Hurt? Riley couldn't tell.

"I see," Olivia said quietly. Way, way too quietly.

"Look—" Riley began.

"Hello," a hearty male voice called as a balding man in rumpled green scrubs pushed through the curtain. His name tag read D. Herrington, ER MD. "Heard you were here, Riley. Thought I'd take a break from back pain and UTIs to sew you up." He glanced at Olivia. "Sorry to interrupt."

"That's all right. I was just leaving."

Riley gritted her teeth as Olivia turned and left.

"Girlfriend?" Don said as he pulled a sterile suture tray from the cabinet.

"No," Riley said. At least, maybe not any longer.

CHAPTER THIRTY-ONE

Olivia watched along with Elizabeth as Josie, Buck, and several of the other wranglers unloaded the new horses from the two trailers that had arrived at dawn. In an abundance of caution, the staff at the equine rehab center had wanted the horses to travel at night when the temperatures were cooler, despite the vehicles being air-conditioned.

"They're beautiful," Olivia said.

"Mm. I think all horses are, but the thoroughbreds have a grace that the trail horses don't bother with."

Olivia laughed. "An attitude, you mean?"

"Exactly."

"They all seem very healthy."

"Our vet will certify them, but the rehab center has a great reputation."

"It makes me sad," Olivia sad, "to know they needed to recover from what should have been simply joy for them."

"Racing? Yes," Elizabeth said. "They love to run, but racing, especially when so young, takes its toll." She smiled at Olivia. "But they'll have a cushy life here now that they've got a new job. All of them are now certified therapy animals. They won't be trail ridden, and most of them won't be ridden at all, but they'll all be free to run for the rest of their lives."

"That helps me feel better," Olivia said.

Elizabeth hugged Olivia with an arm around her shoulder. "You broke speed records getting this place ready for them."

"The stables, maybe," Olivia said grumpily, "but we're delayed *again* on the materials delivery for the indoor ring."

"You won't need that until these horses get acclimated to the staff and the routine here, and Adelle arrives, hires *her* staff, and starts working with them." Elizabeth gave her an appraising look. "How's Riley?"

Olivia tensed. Elizabeth hadn't even pretended to know she wasn't upset. "I haven't seen her since the hospital."

"She didn't call?"

"No."

The drivers closed up the trailers, and one walked over to Elizabeth with a clipboard and a sheaf of papers. "You want to sign for the stock?"

Elizabeth handed the clipboard to Olivia. "Would you?"

"Of course." Olivia flipped through them. "I want to talk with Josie a moment."

The driver shrugged. "Take your time. We get paid by the hour."

Olivia found Josie talking with the stable hands about feed schedules for the new arrivals. When the tanned, wiry blonde in a plaid shirt with cut-off sleeves, dusty jeans, and dustier boots finished her instructions, Olivia asked, "Hey, got a minute?"

"Sure," Josie said with a warm smile. "What's up?"

"Quick question," Olivia said. "Before I sign off on the delivery, I wanted to check that none of them have any immediate issues."

Josie shook her head. "I've had a quick look at all of them, and they all look great. You probably ought to add on there 'accepted pending vet check' or something like that."

"And that's why I asked you," Olivia said, adding the codicil beneath the signature line before signing and dating it. "Thank you."

"No problem. And hey, Olivia?"

"Yes?"

"This place is amazing. Great job."

Olivia flushed. The project had become much more than a project over the last weeks as she, Elizabeth, and Adelle, via online meetings, had outlined the plans for the equine therapy program. Her part in building it had given her more satisfaction than any of the multimillion-dollar spas she and Elizabeth had spearheaded for Sutton ever had. Thinking about not being here when the program went live left her feeling sad and a little lonely. "Thank you."

"All set?" Elizabeth asked as Olivia rejoined her and the driver.

"Yes." She handed him the papers back. "Here you are."

"Have a nice day," he said as he climbed into his truck cab and drove away with the second trailer following.

"Now," Elizabeth said, "back to your personal life."

Olivia frowned. "Please. There's nothing to tell. I've been busy."

She waved at the new stables and the almost finished adjacent indoor riding facilities. "With my *job*."

"Why haven't *you* called Riley, then?" Elizabeth said, picking up their previous conversation without missing a beat.

"Because..." Olivia made the mistake of meeting Elizabeth's sympathetic gaze, and her throat tightened. "Damn it—why do you pester me all the time?"

"Best friend job." Elizabeth bumped shoulders lightly. "And you look sad."

"I'm not...yes, I am, I guess." Olivia walked with Elizabeth along the stone path back to the main house. "We'll wrap this up soon, and I'll...miss the place. Miss you, and Kelsey, and everyone."

"I'm going to skip over all the logical arguments, since we've already had that discussion, and cut to the chase. What about Riley? The woman you've been sleeping with lo these many weeks?"

"Yes, Riley. Sleeping with being the correct term." Olivia had the insane urge to kick a small rock in her path out of frustration and anger. How had she let this happen? "We both agreed our *thing* was a fling. And now the fling has gotten complicated."

"Complicated how?"

Olivia stopped and looked her closest friend in the world in the eye. "I screwed up."

Elizabeth waited.

"I don't think I'm having a fling any longer, and when whatever this *is* ends, I'm going to get hurt."

"Does Riley know?"

Olivia shook her head. "It's complicated."

"Love is."

"I never said *love*," Olivia said instantly. She distinctly, absolutely did not say that, because then what was she going to do about the mess she had created for herself?

"Uh-huh. I noticed. I love you, Olivia, and I know you are no coward. I'm going to breakfast. You coming?"

Olivia stared after her. Coward? Coward!

"Can I borrow the SUV?" she called after Elizabeth.

"Keys are in the visor. Take your time. You don't get paid by the hour."

❖

Riley heard the vehicle pull into the drive. She hadn't expected anyone and put the glue gun on the spanking new counter in the kitchen that was still covered in thick cardboard to protect it from people just like her who put tools down on any handy surface. Not that she would have if the cardboard *hadn't* been there. She looked out the window and, when Olivia climbed out of Elizabeth's SUV, walked outside to meet her. Olivia looked, as always, great in a sleeveless royal blue dress with thin white stripes and sandals. She'd left her hair loose on her shoulders, and Riley immediately thought of running her hands through it when they were in bed. The fist of want hit her hard, the way it always did when she first saw Olivia. She swallowed around the dryness in her throat. "Hi. What are you doing here?"

Olivia took off her sunglasses, as if she wanted Riley to see all of her face.

Uh-oh. That little gesture meant something serious was coming. Not that Riley was surprised. She'd spent two restless nights wondering what the hell she was supposed to say. Or what she wanted to say. Time had run out.

"I drove by the trailer first," Olivia said, stopping a few feet away. "You weren't there, but Artie was."

"I left food out for her this morning," Riley said, feeling that was somehow important for Olivia to know. That she took care of the ones she loved.

"And then I tried the station—sorry, I know that might have been overstepping." Olivia shrugged. "Hadley said you were on sick leave until next week."

Riley ground her teeth. *Thanks, Had.*

"I didn't really think you'd be here, considering you were in the ER two days ago, but it's on my way home. Why *are* you here? You just had surgery on your leg, and you're supposed to be on sick leave."

From Olivia's tone, she sounded confused and a bit angry. Wonderful.

"It was just a big scratch," Riley said. "And it was stitches, not surgery."

Olivia's brows rose. "I'm sorry. We're parsing semantics now?"

Riley's jaws were starting to ache from clenching them. "It was not a *big* deal."

"Is it part of the first responders' code that you need to be tough and strong all the time? You're just people. Your bodies are not made of steel."

"It's a little laceration." Riley held up her hand and stopped Olivia from contradicting her. "Okay, it's a *medium* laceration. It's not serious anymore, and I'm taking care of it."

"Is working on a construction project when you're on sick leave taking care of it? Taking care of *you*?"

"What is this really about?" Riley didn't think for a second Olivia drove all over town to tell her to put her leg up, for fuck's sake. "Is this about me getting hurt or something else? Because if it's about the former, it's happened before and will probably happen again. I'm trained to do the things I do, and I know I'm not invincible, but I will continue to run into burning buildings or jump out of the sky into a burning forest if that's what's in front of me."

Olivia was so quiet for so long, Riley feared she might leave.

Riley grimaced. "I should have called you sooner—thank you for coming to the ER."

"I know what you do is who you are," Olivia said. "I told you before that it frightens me, but I'll wager it frightens a lot of people who care about the people who do what you do."

"Okay, I get that," Riley said cautiously.

"But what frightens me more is that you might not care if a situation is so dangerous you might not survive, and you'll do it anyhow. I can't live with that."

Riley took a long breath. "You might have been right, once. I—"

Olivia's phone rang and she automatically turned it over in her hand and looked down. "Sorry—it's my mother. Hello, Mama? I'm not...what? What? When?...Yes, yes, of course. I'll be there as soon as I can."

Olivia ran toward the SUV, calling as she hurried away, "It's my father. He's had a heart attack."

"Call me!" Riley wasn't sure Olivia even heard her. As she watched the SUV disappear, numbness spread through her. What if Olivia never came back?

CHAPTER THIRTY-TWO

Between the time it took Elizabeth to drive her to the airport, the actual flight, and getting to the hospital, a few hours turned into a dozen before Olivia reached the admissions desk at NYU. She'd tried texting her mother but got no response. She must be in the hospital somewhere with her phone turned off.

"Can I help you?" asked the thin, sandy-haired man with the pleasant voice and vaguely weary gaze behind the desk.

"My father—Eduardo Martinez. Can you tell me where he is?"

"Just a moment."

Olivia bit her lip. The trip had mostly been a panic-filled nightmare that she'd be too late. *Please, please, don't let me be too late.*

"He's in the intermediate cardiac intensive care unit on five." He handed her a red badge to pin on her shirt. "This will allow you to visit after regular hours."

"Thank you."

Intermediate intensive care. That was good, wasn't it? The intermediate part sounded hopeful. Right now, she needed a lot of that. Her mother sat in the family room outside the IICU, sitting ramrod straight with both hands clutching a Coach purse in her lap. Olivia remembered buying her that as a birthday gift and her mother chiding her that it was much too expensive. As if anything could be too much for a gift for either of her parents. "Mama?"

Her mother sprang up and rushed to her. Olivia swung her carry-on shoulder bag to the floor, the only thing she'd bothered to pack before Elizabeth rushed her to the airport, and enfolded her mother in her arms. "How is he?"

Her mother trembled and drew a shaky breath. "They only let me see him for a few minutes about two hours ago. He was still sedated."

"What did they tell you?" Olivia ached to hurry inside, to see her father for herself, but her mother needed these few minutes with her. Her mother was the strongest woman she knew, but Olivia saw the fear in her eyes.

"Not very much. There was a blockage"—her voice caught—"*four* blockages, and they did an operation to bypass them."

Four. Olivia closed her eyes. He could have died—could *still* die. The idea was unimaginable. "I'm going to go see him."

"Yes." Her mother stepped back, kissed her cheek. "I'm so glad you're here."

"Of course I am. I'll always be here."

Olivia hesitated at the door to the cardiac IICU. She desperately wanted to see her father and tried to prepare herself for what might be waiting. Her childhood image of him had never changed even as they'd both aged—that of a big, robust man with a big laugh and a bigger heart. Both her parents were her heroes, and she would do anything for them. Being strong for her mother was exactly what she needed to do now for both of them. She gathered her strength, took a deep breath, and pushed the doors open.

Bright lights in the tiled ceiling illuminated the long, rectangular room like it was the middle of the day, not approaching midnight. A curly-haired, muscular man who could be anywhere from forty to sixty in baby-blue scrubs and a stethoscope dangling around his neck sat at a counter in front of an array of beeping monitors and scrolling EKG readouts. He gave her a kind smile as she walked over. The name badge clipped to his pocket identified him as Ron Lee, RN, ANCC.

"May I help you?" he asked.

"I'm Olivia Martinez. Eduardo Martinez is my father."

"Visits are five minutes on the hour between seven a.m. and eleven p.m., but you can see him now since you won't be able to see him again until morning. He's still recovering from the procedure." He rose. "Follow me. He's still sedated, so don't be concerned if he doesn't seem to know you're there."

The nurse took her to one of the private rooms opposite the monitoring station. Each cubicle held one patient. The partial glass wall allowed the staff to continuously observe the occupants without actually entering the room unless necessary. Her father lay with his eyes closed on a large bed with metal siderails beneath a crisp white sheet that covered him to his shoulders. His arms lay outside the covers with multiple intravenous lines running into each one. A pulse oximeter sat on the first finger of his left hand, and a small patch of dried blood spotted the dressing around the IV in his right hand. A tube the diameter of her thumb snaked from beneath the sheet, running to a plastic chamber hanging from the bedrail that held fluid the color of Kool-Aid. His cheeks appeared sunken beneath an O2 mask. He looked very pale and vulnerable surrounded by half a dozen different beeping machines and monitors. Her father seemed a shell of the man he'd been the last time she'd seen him. Had that visit to the ranch only been two months ago?

She slowly approached the bed.

"Papa," she said quietly. "It's Olivia."

Her father gave no sign that he'd heard her.

"May I touch him?" she whispered.

"Yes," the nurse said. "Right now he's on various medications to stabilize his blood pressure and support his cardiac function. Over the next few days, those will be adjusted as he recovers."

Olivia's hand shook when she reached for her father's hand. She was careful not to dislodge the oximeter as she wrapped her hand around his. Her stomach lurched at the nonexistent tightening of his fingers around hers. As a child, and even as an adult, every time Olivia took his hand, he would squeeze hers as if to say *I love you.*

"I'm here, Papa. I love you." Olivia kept her voice from breaking. This was her time to be strong. "You're going to be okay. Don't worry about anything. I'll take care of Mama until you come home."

When the nurse gently told her the five minutes were up, she kissed the back of her father's hand and left the room. When the door to his room closed behind her, she asked, "Is he in any danger tonight? Should we stay here?"

"He's stable and the procedure, according to the surgeon and the cardiologist, went well. That means his heart is healthier tonight than it was twenty-four hours ago." He studied her as if looking for something. Whatever he saw must have satisfied him, as he added, "The best thing you can do is take your mother home, and both of you get some rest. His recovery is going to be a marathon, not a sprint. You'll all need to save your strength when you can. I'll be here until seven when the doctors make rounds. If there's any change between now and then, I'll call you right away. You can see him at eight after the staff make rounds. One of them will give you an update then."

Olivia looked back at her father on the other side of the glass wall.

She wanted him home again, and when he did come home, he would need her and her mother to be his support system. "We'll be back at seven, then."

❖

"Do you want me to fix you some tea?" Olivia asked her mother after the silent cab ride home and the elevator ride to her parents' apartment.

"No, I don't want anything," her mother said quietly.

"Have you eaten today?"

"I'm not hungry either."

"Do you need me to say out loud that it's important for you to take care of yourself? For *you* most of all, and for Papa and for me?"

Her mother sighed. "Toast."

"Wonderful. I don't suppose you have any of that orange marmalade that you're partial to."

Her mother smiled, a wistful smile. "I believe I do."

"Then I'll have some with you."

Olivia didn't have any more appetite than her mother, but she hadn't eaten anything, not even the free pretzels on the flight. They sat side by side on the sofa, eating the toast. When they'd finished, she pressed her mother's hand. "You should try to get some sleep."

"I'm not sleeping in that bed until your father is, too," her mother said in an absolutely unswayable tone.

Olivia's heart ached for her. Her parents had been together since their teens, and they bragged that the only nights they had spent apart were when her mother remained in the hospital after Olivia was born.

A few months ago, Olivia couldn't have come close to understanding what her mother must be feeling, but now she believed that she could. Two days ago, she'd had a gut-wrenching moment of fear when Kelsey had said Riley was being taken to the hospital. Losing Riley would devastate her. How could she have ignored what she felt for Riley? And why, *why* did she need to feel it all now when it was too late?

"On the sofa, then," Olivia said, focusing on what she needed to do and pushing her own pain aside. "I'll get your pillow and a cover from the linen closet. At least, close your eyes for me."

"Yes, all right," her mother said.

"I'm going to take a shower, and then I'm going to put you to bed," Olivia said with a small laugh.

To her amazement, her mother laughed a little, too. So strong. Olivia hoped she could be as strong.

The shower washed away the grime and some of the weariness of the long day of travel and anxiety, but she doubted she could sleep. When she carried the pillow and a light throw out to the living room, her mother stretched out on the sofa. Olivia kissed her on the forehead. "Do your best to rest."

When her mother nodded silently and closed her eyes, Olivia let herself out onto the narrow balcony overlooking Fifth Avenue. The sky looked completely foreign to her. Hazy with barely a glow from the moon or the stars. Too much city light. Too much pollution. Nothing like the beauty of the deep dark she'd grown to love out on the ranch. Noise—so *much* noise—funneled up from below. Not the occasional nicker of a horse or the far-off howling of a coyote pack, but car horns, engines revving, a cacophony of sound melded from hundreds of voices. In this place where she had grown up, she now felt the stranger. Loneliness pierced her, and she did what she had done so many times in her life. Reached for her to phone to call Elizabeth.

Realizing the lateness, she texted instead. Just that connection would help, and Elizabeth would get the message in the morning.

I'm here. Papa is in the intensive care unit. He's stable.

Elizabeth replied a few moments later. *Oh that's wonderful. How are you?*

Scared. Tired.

Want me to come? I can be there by midmorning tomorrow

Olivia's eyes filled with tears. Yes, she desperately wanted her to come. She wanted not to be alone. She wanted not to be the one who needed to be strong.

No, she texted instead. *I know how much you have to do there. I'm all right. I'll tell you if anything changes.*

Promise?

Swear. She texted their decades-old response.

I love you, Elizabeth replied.

I love you too.

Their exchange eased much of her heartache, but her soul still felt empty. She should text Riley, too. Riley had asked her to call, and she hadn't even answered. She lifted the phone to text but instead touched Riley's number before she could overthink her actions.

What felt like only a second later, Riley said, "Olivia?"

"Hi. I know it's late. Were you sleeping?"

Riley laughed. "No. How are you? How is your dad?"

"He's in the intensive cardiac care unit. He had a big surgery, so I couldn't really talk to him yet. The staff said that the procedure to correct the blockages in his heart went well, and he was stable."

"Wow, that's great news," Riley said. "How are you?"

"I'm…I'm doing okay," she said.

"I know that," Riley said, "but do you *need* anything?"

"It's good to hear your voice," Olivia said softly. She didn't add *And that was just what I needed.*

There was a long moment of silence. "Yeah, same here. I was worried. I hate these fucking phones. Feels like you're a million miles away."

Olivia laughed. "Not a million, but I know what you mean. How is your leg?"

"It doesn't bother me at all."

"Are you taking it easy?"

"Of course."

The exaggerated way Riley answered made Olivia laugh. She wouldn't have believed anything could have right then. "Let me clarify. *Will* you take care of it? For me?"

"I'd do anything for you." The intensity in Riley's voice made Olivia quiver inside. "I'll take care of it. Promise."

"Thank you."

"Call me again when you can?" Another long silence and then, "I miss you."

Olivia bit her lip. She was not going to cry. "I miss you, too. I'll call."

"Go rest, then. It's late there."

Riley didn't ask her when she would be back, and Olivia was grateful for that. She didn't know how to say *I don't know*, or worse, *I'm not sure I'm coming back.*

"Good night," Olivia said.

In the guest room, she lay awake, watching shadows flicker on the ceiling. Her mind raced with fragments of the day—her mother's fear, her father's too-quiet form, her longing when she heard Riley's voice. So many things to do—she'd need to call the tenant who'd sublet her condo to see if she could stop by the next day and pack some clothes and other things she had stored there. She'd literally left Arizona with nothing but a change of underwear and a clean shirt for the next day. And her computer, of course. She wouldn't be staying in her condo, though. For the foreseeable future, she would be with her parents, where she was needed.

CHAPTER THIRTY-THREE

Riley's lungs screamed at her to stop, but she couldn't. Mile after mile, her feet hit the hard packed dirt, while she ran as if she could escape the reality that Olivia was gone. Five miles turned into seven, her thighs burning and her heart aching for what Olivia was going through. In the week since Olivia had been gone, they'd texted a few times and managed to connect by phone once. Olivia had sounded stressed and worried but in control—as she always was. Strong, capable, and always ready to take care of what everyone needed. Riley wished she could do more for her now.

She'd witnessed how close Olivia was to her parents, and how much they obviously loved her. Olivia called her parents often, and she'd been honest with Riley about her feelings of responsibility to them. Not out of obligation but of love. She couldn't ask Olivia to endanger her relationship with them, especially now. She couldn't ask when—*if*—Olivia would be returning. She couldn't ask her to make choices. She couldn't do a damned thing.

Helplessness was not an emotion she tolerated well. She was angry at herself, for falling for Olivia when she hadn't planned to, and at the Fates, for bringing Olivia back into her life when she was finally ready and it was too late. When her phone signaled a call from the station when she wasn't on call, she welcomed it.

"Hey, Had."

"How's your leg?"

Riley slowed to a walk and grunted. "It's fine. Stitches came out, no problem. What's up?"

"Big burn in Colorado. They could use you."

Colorado. She hadn't been back there since the accident. Finally, something she could do something about. "I'm in."

"Flight's in two hours."

"Thanks. I'll be there."

Hadley didn't answer for a second. "Be careful out there."

"Always am," Riley said, meaning it.

She packed the rest of her go bag on autopilot. Nothing to think about. A fire to fight. A crew to protect. That was what she did—what she was meant for. But in the half hour waiting for the chopper to arrive, she couldn't help thinking of Olivia. She needed to let her know she'd be out of touch. Olivia would want to know, wouldn't she? Riley mentally kicked herself. Of course she had to call her. And of course Olivia would want to know. This was now, this was them. They *had* something real between them, even if she couldn't see the shape of it. Yet.

She called Olivia's number, expecting voicemail, but that would be okay. She'd hear Olivia's voice on the message at least.

"Riley? Hi!" Olivia sounded more like her usual self for the first time since she'd left.

"Hi. How are you?"

"Great—my dad was transferred to a regular patient floor, and he's doing well."

"That's terrific!"

"How are you?" Olivia asked.

"I'm good. Listen, I'm heading out of state, so I might not be available right away if you try to reach me."

"A wildfire?" Olivia asked, suddenly subdued.

"Yes."

"What about your leg?"

"It's okay—I'm clear to work." Riley hesitated. "Don't worry, okay? I'll be careful."

"I'll still worry. You matter to me," Olivia said.

Riley's heart did a little dance even as it ached. "I'll text when I can. I'm glad your dad is better."

"Thanks. Be careful. I...I need you to come home safe."

"I will." Riley disconnected and grabbed her gear to board the chopper. *You matter to me, too.*

When they landed at the base camp below the ridge where smoke and flames billowed, she, Sven, and Travis joined the other hotshots milling around a ranger holding a sign with the Forest Service logo. Riley didn't know any of the waiting firefighters, but when introductions were made and assignments handed out, one guy gave her a long look.

As they stood waiting for the trucks to carry them and their gear to the front, he walked over and held out his hand.

"Name's Dave Chan. Just wanted to say all respect to you and your crew."

Riley's throat tightened. After the fire, she had never been able to see sympathy as anything but pity and had kept apart, remained outside the circle that had once been her family. Today what she saw in his eyes was compassion and fellowship. He and the other first responders knew that at any time, any one of them could be standing in her boots. The camaraderie they shared was one of trust, and with a nod of thanks, Riley stepped back into their circle.

The fire burned for another week, a week during which Riley slept little and, when she stopped to eat or drink, thought of Olivia. When they finally got word that the fire was contained, all she wanted to do was get to someplace with cell service to text her.

"You married?" Dave asked conversationally as they hoisted their gear into the back of a truck for the ride down the mountain.

"Nope," Riley said.

"Got a girl?"

Riley grinned. "Good guess. And, yes, well, sort of."

Dave's brows rose. "Does that mean she's not sure, or you aren't?"

"I'm sure," Riley said. And maybe it was time to do something about that.

CHAPTER THIRTY-FOUR

For Olivia, the last three weeks of constant stress, sleepless nights, and long days filled with worry and anxiety had passed in a blur. At least her father had been home for over a week, and his medical reports were all encouraging. He needed assistance getting to the bathroom and getting out of bed or to a chair, which he hated and tried to resist, but she and her mother prevailed. Now that the minute by minute, life or death worries over her father had subsided, she struggled with a restless sense of being in a world where she didn't belong. She'd never felt trapped before, but she thought she knew what that felt like now. She loved her parents and didn't resent her father's illness or her mother's need, but part of her wondered at what cost. For the first time since she was fifteen, she didn't have a job, didn't have somewhere to be, a schedule to keep, a problem to solve, or some major crisis to avert. She had no life here—everything that mattered, everyone other than her parents who mattered was thousands of miles away.

She hadn't heard from Riley since that one phone call. She thought of her constantly, sick dread filling her days and nights. She'd lost her appetite along with her ability to push aside the uncertainty and worry, and all that combined to set her nerves on a razor's edge. She stood out on the balcony watching the dawn after another long, nearly sleepless night and checked her messages, as she did constantly throughout the day. Only one from Elizabeth, who texted her daily. Nothing from Riley.

She missed her, ached for her, on top of the fear and longing. As she'd taken to doing at night when she couldn't sleep, she skimmed the many images of them she kept on her phone. Selfies of them the time Riley had taken her out on the motorcycle to see the Joshua trees, by the fireside when they'd been glamping, and with the kids the day they'd all worked at Horizon House. Olivia's heart hurt. She'd known she would eventually have to leave but hadn't expected it to be this soon. And she'd never let herself think about how she would feel when she did. Elizabeth had said she wasn't a coward, but, oh, she was.

With a sigh, she put her phone away, went inside to start coffee and, for her father, the herbal tea he complained about every day. The doctor had issued a moratorium on caffeine for the time being.

Her mother was already in the kitchen and asked, "Couldn't sleep?"

"Oh, just an early riser," Olivia said, mustering a smile.

Her mother gave her a long look.

"Is Papa awake?" Olivia asked.

"Yes, he's shaving."

"Of course he is." Olivia gave her mother a squeeze. "He really is doing so much better."

"The doctors say three months before he can resume full activity."

"Yes," Olivia said, "but he's going to be fine, Mama."

"Not if he goes back to that job," her mother said solemnly.

"A bridge to cross when we get there."

"Get where?" her father said from behind them in the doorway of the kitchen.

"To breakfast," Olivia said brightly, and took his arm and walked with him to the breakfast nook.

"Any special requests?" she asked him.

"In a minute, Ollie," he said, using the childhood nickname he hadn't used in years, and gestured to the chair opposite him.

Obediently, Olivia sat. "Do you need something? Are you not feeling well?"

"It's been a month," he said, touching his chest. "I'm sore, but I'm not an invalid."

"I know that."

He waved a hand in the air. "Enough about me. What's troubling you?"

Startled, Olivia straightened. "I don't know what you mean."

"Of course you do. And you never have been able to pretend with me."

"It's nothing, Papa. I'm fine." Olivia shrugged. "I didn't sleep well last night, that's all."

"*Mija*." Her father sighed, the way he had when she'd been a teenager and hadn't wanted to talk about whatever thing she'd been angsting about at the time. "I know this has been hard for you—looking after your mother and me."

"No," she said instantly. "No. You and Mama are not a burden to me. I love you, and I want to be here for you when you need me. I will always be here for whatever you need."

"We know that," he said, watching her carefully, "but you have your own life to think about, yes?"

Her own life. Olivia took a breath. When was she going to have that life? How would she have the life she wanted if she never admitted to herself what she wanted? Her father's gaze never left hers. She sensed her mother coming to stand behind her, felt the slight brush of her hand on her hair.

"I've met someone," Olivia said. "In Arizona. I…" Suddenly she wasn't uncertain any longer. Her parents loved her, and if they didn't understand or couldn't accept her for who she was, she'd give them time and hope that someday they would. But she owed them, and most of all, herself and Riley, the truth. "You've met her, too. Riley Mitchell."

Her mother drew a sharp breath. Her father glanced up at her mother, and Olivia saw the strength they'd always shared pass between them. "The firefighter. It's serious?"

"Yes."

"Does she feel the same?"

"I think so—we haven't talked about the future. It's complicated."

"Why?"

Olivia laughed, feeling like she'd fallen into an alternate reality. Was she really having this conversation now, sitting in her parents' home, the place where they held Bible study every week when she was growing up, where wedding arrangements were made for cousins, and baby pictures from friends and family adorned the walls? "Well, the twenty-five hundred miles between Wickenburg and here, for starters."

"There are airplanes for that." Her father continued to regard her steadily, with no judgment in his eyes.

Olivia's frustration at still having no solution that didn't hurt someone she loved boiled to the surface. "I don't want to break up our family—is that so wrong?"

"It is if it comes at the cost of your happiness."

"I'm not…" Olivia couldn't sit there and lie to them. She *was* unhappy, but at least she was dealing with one cause of that long-buried fear now. "I needed you to know about…us. About how I feel about her."

"Always, Olivia?" her mother asked quietly.

"Yes," Olivia said, knowing her mother was asking how long she'd kept this from them. "Always. But never like this. There's never been anyone like Riley for me."

"Are you finished with the work for Elizabeth?" her father asked.

"What?" Olivia frowned, trying to follow his direction. "No, but then Elizabeth always has another project she wants me to work on."

"Then you'll need to go back," her father said, "to finish what you started for Elizabeth and to decide what it is you want with Riley."

Olivia fell silent. Decide what she wanted with Riley? But she already knew, didn't she? Had known for so long but hadn't let herself admit it. She wanted… Her phone vibrated, and she pulled it from her pocket, catching her breath when she saw the caller ID. "I'm sorry. It's Riley. I need to take this—she's in the field somewhere." She answered and said quickly, "Hi. Are you all right?"

"I'm good. I'm fine. I'm at the Marriott."

Olivia's mind blanked.

"Olivia?"

"The Marriott where?"

"Times Square, I think?"

The relief was so intense, tears filled her eyes. She brushed them away impatiently. Her mother and father sat just a few feet away, but she didn't care. She had nothing to hide any longer. All that mattered was Riley, and that she was safe. "You're here? You're all right? You're sure?"

"Yes, at least I am now. Just a little tired. I flew straight here. I…I had to see you."

Olivia bit her lip. "You should get some sleep. I'll see you later today."

"Yeah? You're not upset I showed up unannounced?"

Riley sounded so surprised and so relieved, Olivia couldn't help but laugh. "Of course I'm not angry. I want to see you, too."

"I know you're busy—how's your dad?"

Olivia glanced at her father, who watched her with a thoughtful expression. "He's good. Better every day. I…I'll call you later when I'm free."

"Okay, of course. I'll be here. Any time. I'm a light sleeper."

"I remember." Olivia knew she was blushing. At least her parents couldn't hear the way her heart pounded or the buzz of happy anticipation zinging through her. Riley was here. "I'll see you soon."

When she disconnected, she faced her parents, who now sat side by side at the small table.

"She came here?" her mother asked, her hands folded tightly on the table. Like Olivia's father had done, she studied Olivia's face as she spoke.

"Yes—she's been on the line—um, fighting a forest fire—in Colorado for the last two weeks. They—the firefighting crews—aren't able to connect with people at home when they're out there."

"That's why you haven't been sleeping?"

"I…yes, mostly. It's dangerous work. It frightens me, but I'm working on that."

"She has burns on her arms," her mother said.

Olivia swallowed hard. "Yes. A bad accident a few years ago. She was nearly killed. Many of her friends were."

Her mother rose. "I have things to do in the kitchen."

Olivia's stomach sank. "Mama—"

Her mother said without slowing, "Call her back now before she goes to sleep and tell her dinner is at five."

Olivia turned to her father. "Papa?"

He shrugged. "Best do as your mother wants. Good things are worth fighting for."

"What?" Riley said, certain she had heard incorrectly. "With your parents?"

Olivia laughed. Just the sound sizzled Riley's brain. "They live here, so yes, dinner with my parents."

"Where are they now?" Riley asked.

"In the apartment. I'm in the guest room where I've been staying, why?"

"Can they hear you?"

"Not unless they have their ears pressed to the door. But if you're thinking phone sex—"

"Jesus, no!" Riley paced around her too-small hotel room, running one hand through her hair. "I mean—yeah, I haven't thought of much else for the last eighteen hours, but not over the phone and not with you *there*."

"I've missed you," Olivia said. "And I'm thinking about a lot of things right now, sex being high on the list."

"Stop. Not fair." Riley rubbed her middle as if that would calm the storm brewing inside her. She'd slept some on the plane, and a good thing, because she sure as hell wasn't getting any sleep today. "What's going on? Are you okay?"

"I am. Better than I have been in a long time. I'm sorry to spring this on you, but I hope you'll come to dinner." Olivia paused. "I told them about us."

Riley sat down abruptly on the side of the bed. "Us? As in you and me and sex—that us?"

Again Olivia laughed. "I told them I'd met someone who mattered and that someone was you. We didn't actually discuss the sex part, but I'm quite sure they got the idea."

Riley heard all the words unsaid—Olivia hadn't told her parents anything about being with women for nearly twenty years, and now she had. Olivia had taken a huge step as well as a risk, and Riley would do no less. "I don't have anything to wear. I only have a clean polo shirt and pants in my duffel."

"That would be perfect," Olivia said softly. "You'll come?"

"I'll be there. Because you matter to me."

Riley showered, paced, clock-watched, and finally decided to walk through Central Park to the address Olivia had given her. The apartment building was one of the tall stone buildings facing the park with lots of terraces adorning the front. When she walked into the spacious lobby, a doorman asked if he could help her.

"The Martinezes, uh, 1101?"

"Yes, of course. Take the elevator on the left."

"Thanks." When she reached the apartment, she didn't hesitate. She'd known before she'd finished talking to Olivia what she had to do.

Olivia answered the door so quickly, Riley grinned. "Were you waiting right inside?"

Olivia stepped into the hall, holding the door partially closed with one arm, and kissed her. "Maybe."

A simple kiss had never been so sweet and so soul-satisfying. Riley's exhaustion melted away. "That's exactly what I needed."

"Me, too. Come inside."

CHAPTER THIRTY-FIVE

Y ou look great," Olivia murmured as she walked her through the apartment, and she did. Riley looked every inch herself in a navy-blue polo shirt with the emblem of the WFD on the chest, her khaki pants, and her hair just a little bit windblown. She also looked tired, but without the sadness that had often lingered in her eyes. Olivia lightly touched her arm. "I'm so glad you're here."

"Me, too."

Her parents waited in the living room, her father seated in the chair that was *his* chair, and her mother on the couch. Her father had put on a shirt and slacks for the first time since he'd come home from the hospital. He was a fastidious man and always dressed in what he termed proper for guests. Her mother wore an orange and white print shirt, tan pants with plain brown flats, and just a little bit of light makeup. They both looked casual, but had obviously dressed for company.

Olivia gestured to the facing sofa and said to Riley, "Sit down, please."

She wasn't entirely certain what was about to happen, but she wanted to be close to Riley for whatever it was. Were her parents going to be accusatory, questioning, or, hopefully, welcoming?

"Mama, Papa, you remember Riley," she said as she sat next to Riley.

Her mother smiled. "Of course."

Her father said, "I understand you just come back from a few difficult weeks."

Riley nodded. "It's good to see you both. And I think the last few weeks have been tougher for you than for me, Mr. Martinez."

He chuckled softly. "Everything is relative, no?"

Her mother said, "It's good of you to come."

Olivia wasn't entirely certain what she meant by *good*. Good for who? For her, certainly. From the moment she'd heard Riley's voice, her anxiety and uncertainty had disappeared. Now that Riley was actually here, she felt calm and in control for the first time since she'd gotten the call that her father was in the hospital. She still worried for her father's health, but he was improving. She'd been there for her parents when they'd needed her, and she'd finally allowed them to know her.

Riley said, "I wish I could've come sooner," and glanced at Olivia. "I know it must've been difficult for all of you, and I'm sorry that I wasn't here."

She spoke directly to Olivia, and no one in the room could've missed it.

Olivia squeezed her arm. "I know you would have been, but you were needed somewhere else more."

Her father said, "Olivia and I were talking earlier about her going back to Arizona. Unfinished business there, yes?"

Olivia hurriedly put in, "Elizabeth has been telling them about the land purchase and the plans for the Sunset Vista development."

"That's quite a project," her father said.

"Elizabeth and Olivia," Riley said, "are a formidable team. They get things done a lot faster than most." She laughed. "Olivia probably didn't tell you, but I am also the county fire inspector. Somehow, Olivia gets those permits done and certificates of occupancy in place about ten times faster than anyone I've ever worked with."

Olivia's father chuckled. "Olivia has always known what she wanted."

That sentence hung in the air for a few seconds. Olivia took a deep breath. "Not always. Or at least, not what I was willing to admit, I guess."

"When I got on the plane last night," Riley said, directing her words to Olivia's parents, "I didn't have much of a plan. I just wanted to get here and see Olivia. But, like Olivia, I realized there were things I didn't let myself think about until just recently."

When Riley shifted to look at Olivia, Olivia's heart beat faster. She waited silently, barely breathing. This was for Riley to say and for her to listen.

"I'm a firefighter, and I can do that anywhere, even Manhattan. So if this is where you want to be, then that's where I want to be."

Olivia frowned. "What? You would hate Manhattan."

Her father cut in. "Why would you want to move to Manhattan? Isn't Wickenburg your home?"

"This is Olivia's home," Riley said. "And Olivia is more important to me than anything else."

Olivia drew a deep breath. "No. You're not moving to Manhattan, where I know damn well you'll be miserable."

Riley laughed. "I can get used to anything, as long as I'm with you."

Olivia shook her head. "You're not going to move here. We'll work something else out."

Olivia's father clapped his hands on his thighs. "Well, it seems the answer is clear."

Olivia and Riley both looked at him.

He shook his head, a soft smile on his face. "Olivia's work is with Elizabeth, where Riley already lives. The two of you belong in Arizona."

"But—" Olivia began.

Her mother, who'd been silent until this moment, said, "I have something to say to all of you."

Olivia reached for Riley's hand. Riley squeezed hers.

"I'm still catching up from discovering that my daughter has been afraid to tell me for her entire life that she preferred women to men, but that's inconsequential right now. What matters is the two of you, and what you plan to do about that."

"Mama—"

Olivia's mother gave her a look and she quieted.

"And you," she looked to her husband, "I have something to ask of you that I've never asked before."

Olivia's father frowned. "What is it?"

"All our lives we've worked for the life that we wanted for our family. I was happy to do it and wouldn't change anything. Now I want you to do something for me and, I hope, for you."

He moved to the sofa next to his wife and said gently, "What are you saying?"

Her mother glanced at Olivia and then clasped her husband's hands. "Elizabeth and I have been talking about this new development that she and Olivia are working on. I want you to retire, and I want us to move to Arizona and buy one of these houses. I want *our* life to be what matters now. This I want you to do for me."

Olivia's head was buzzing. Riley had said she wanted to be with her. Out loud and in front of her parents. She'd told her the same. Her parents moving to Arizona? To Sunset Vista?

"Hey," Riley whispered.

Olivia turned to Riley as her parents spoke in low urgent tones, having apparently forgotten all about them.

"I love you," Riley said.

Olivia smiled. Of course the answer was clear. It always had been. "I love you, too."

CHAPTER THIRTY-SIX

The sound of someone knocking on the trailer door woke Riley a little after ten. She'd taken to sleeping at home since she'd gotten back from New York, and she was actually sleeping five or six hours straight most nights. She pulled on sweatpants and a tank top and walked through the dimly lit trailer to the door.

"Who is it?"

"Special delivery."

Riley's pulse shot through the roof. Her hands shook as she yanked the door open. "What are you doing here?"

"Coming home." Olivia pushed a small suitcase into the room and threw herself into Riley's arms. "I need you right now."

Riley staggered back a few steps, barely managing to shove the door closed, as Olivia kissed her. Catching her balance, she pressed Olivia against the door while Olivia plundered her mouth with hot, fevered kisses. Her head spun as Olivia's lips found her favorite spot, just under her ear. Her legs trembled when Olivia pulled her shirt up. Riley clasped her hands, stopping her.

"Bedroom, baby, where I can take my time," Riley said, sounding much calmer than she felt. Between Olivia's unexpected arrival and her too-sexy-for words demands, Riley's arousal was at an all-time high already. If she didn't keep her focus, any second she'd be begging Olivia to make her come.

"Riley, please." Olivia struggled to free her hands. "I need to feel you. I need you to make everything go away except you and me, together. I promise, we'll talk later, but right now I just need you inside me."

"Anything you want." Lifting Olivia so Olivia could wrap her legs around her waist, Riley carried her to the bedroom. The weeks apart floated away when Olivia stripped, lay on her bed, and beckoned Riley to her.

"You are so beautiful." Riley pushed off her sweats and pulled off the T-shirt. "I've missed you so damn much."

"Show me how much," Olivia said, pulling Riley down on top of her. "Show me everywhere."

Riley knew what Olivia wanted. Hot, fast, and hard. She could do that, would do that, but first she needed to show Olivia what she felt for her. She leaned back, kneeling between Olivia's thighs. "Look at me. I'll show you."

Olivia, eyes glassy with desire, looked into her eyes. Into her heart.

Riley slid one hand down Olivia's stomach and stopped just short of entering her. Slowly, she stroked her clit, then lower, ever so gently teasing the warm, slick folds between her fingers.

"Touch me again. Just like that," Olivia whispered. "Touch me again. God, please touch me."

"Here?" Riley asked, teasing her clit. "Here?" Now stroking lower, gliding through the silky heat. "Here?" She slipped inside her, filled her. "Here?"

"Yes, just like that. Faster."

Riley increased her tempo, and Olivia matched her stroke for stroke. Riley wrapped her arm around Olivia's hips, pulling her closer to brush her thumb over Olivia's clit with every thrust.

"I'm going to come," Olivia gasped. "God, God, so hard."

"Keep your eyes open. I want to watch you when you come."

Olivia groaned and pressed her hips into Riley's fingers. Her whole body tightened, and she cried out, the sound piercing Riley's soul.

"You okay?" Riley asked, her mouth close to Olivia's ear.

"If I said yes, would you do that again?" Olivia said in barely a whisper. Her breath came in short gasps as she clung to Riley.

Riley laughed. "Absolutely."

"Good, I'll remember that." With surprising strength, Olivia wrapped her arms around Riley's shoulders and rolled her onto her back. "But first, I want what's mine."

When her hand slid between Riley's legs, Riley's vision blurred. She was so close another stroke would push her over. "Always."

"Always," Olivia echoed, and took Riley over the edge.

❖

Riley woke with the first rays of the morning sun. She lay still, absorbing the warmth of Olivia curled against her, the beat of her heart and the soft waft of her breath against her neck. Olivia had finally come home, and so had she. She stroked her hair and kissed her forehead.

"'Morning," Olivia murmured, wrapping one arm more tightly around Riley's midsection, as if she might go anywhere now.

"Hi," Riley said. "Nice surprise."

Olivia kissed her lightly. "I love you. I couldn't wait to get here."

Riley's chest tightened, gratitude and wonder and need filling her. "You're staying, right?"

She had to ask, a little embarrassed by the small kernel of fear that this was just a dream.

"Of course." Olivia pressed her hand between Riley's breasts. "You're mine now."

"I've been yours from the beginning."

"There's something you need to know, though," Olivia said.

Riley took a long slow breath. Whatever it was, she would deal with it, but she wasn't letting her go, no matter what it took. "What?"

"I'm not living in a trailer for the rest of my life."

The rest of her life. The rest of *their* lives. Riley laughed. "Okay, where would you like to live?"

"With you, just about anywhere, but I'd prefer that we stay around here because, you know, my job, your job, and my parents. And I love the desert, so not right in town."

"That's for sure about your parents?" Riley asked. "They're coming?"

"Oh, yes. My mother very gently told me it was time for me to go home…" Olivia kissed Riley's throat. "Meaning back to you, and I'm just getting my mind wrapped around all of that, but anyhow, they're much too busy internet conferencing with Elizabeth and architects and everyone else planning their new home to need me around anymore."

"If it's all the same to you," Riley said carefully, "I'd just as soon not live in Sunset Vista."

"God, no. I'll see my parents plenty with them living there. We need our own place with our own space. I'd like a dog. Maybe two."

"Puppies do better raised together," Riley said. "Two sounds good."

"I'm worried about Artie, though," Olivia said. "Who will look after her?"

"Artie will fend for herself, but you know, I can sell the trailer. I know a couple of people at work who would want it who Artie might allow to feed her."

"And you're okay with that?" Olivia sounded a little uncertain.

Riley pushed up on the bed and pulled Olivia up into her arms, refusing to let her go. "Of course. We need a bigger place. You know, dogs and...maybe kids?"

"Riley, sweetie, I'm not opposed to children as long as you know they're not coming out of me."

"I think if the time comes, and we're ready, there'll be plenty of kids who need homes."

"We've got all summer to decide where to move," Olivia said. "Elizabeth and I will be up to our necks getting work started on Sunset Vista for the next few months. Adelle will be here next month, and she wants two solid months to train her staff while Josie and the wranglers get the horses acclimated. The new equestrian program will be up and running by September in time for our busy season at the ranch."

"There's plenty of land out here," Riley said. "We'll find the perfect place."

"Well, I've got you, so things are already pretty perfect. I love you."

"I love you, too," Riley murmured, leaning above her on one elbow. "And before Elizabeth discovers that you're back, I want a few more hours to show you just how perfect things can get."

Olivia laughed and pulled Riley down into her arms. "You'll have a lifetime for that, but you can start right now by kissing me."

About the Authors

In addition to editing over twenty LGBTQIA+ anthologies, **Radclyffe** has written over sixty-five romance and romantic intrigue novels, including a paranormal romance series, The Midnight Hunters, as L.L. Raand.

She is a three-time Lambda Literary Award winner in romance and erotica and received the Dr. James Duggins Outstanding Mid-Career Novelist Award from the Lambda Literary Foundation. A member of the Saints and Sinners Literary Hall of Fame, she is also an RWA/FF&P Prism Award winner for *Secrets in the Stone*, an RWA FTHRW Lories and RWA HODRW winner for *Firestorm*, an RWA Bean Pot winner for *Crossroads*, an RWA Laurel Wreath winner for *Blood Hunt*, a Book Buyers Best award winner for *Price of Honor* and *Secret Hearts*, and a 2023 Golden Crown Literary Award winner for *Perfect Rivalry*. The first book in the Red Sky Ranch romance series, *Fire in the Sky*, is a 2024 GCLS romance award winner. She is also a featured author in the 2015 documentary film *Love Between the Covers*, from Blueberry Hill Productions. In 2019 she was recognized as a "Trailblazer of Romance" by the Romance Writers of America.

In 2004 she founded Bold Strokes Books, one of the world's largest independent LGBTQ publishing companies, and is the current president and publisher.

Find her at facebook.com/Radclyffe.BSB, follow her on Twitter @RadclyffeBSB, and visit her website at Radfic.com.

Julie Cannon has published twenty-three novels and numerous short stories with Bold Strokes Books. *Rescue Me* and *Wishing on a Dream* were finalists for the Lambda Literary Award Best Lesbian Romance, and *I Remember* and *Fire In The Sky* (with co-author Radclyffe) have won Best Lesbian Romance from the Golden Crown Literary Society. Visit her website at JulieCannon.com.

Books Available From Bold Strokes Books

The First Kiss by Patricia Evans. As the intrigue surrounding her latest case spins dangerously out of control, military police detective Parker Haven must choose between her career and the woman she's falling in love with. (978-1-63679-775-5)

Language Lessons by Sage Donnell. Grace and Lenka never expected to fall in love. Is home really where the heart is if it means giving up your dreams? (978-1-63679-725-0)

New Horizons by Shia Woods. When Quinn Collins meets Alex Anders, Horizon Theater's enigmatic managing director, a passionate connection ignites, but amidst the complex backdrop of theater politics, their budding romance faces a formidable challenge. (978-1-63679-683-3)

Scrambled: A Tuesday Night Book Club Mystery by Jaime Maddox. Avery Hutchins makes a discovery about her father's death that will force her to face an impossible choice between doing what is right and finally finding a way to regain a part of herself she had lost. (978-1-63679-703-8)

Stolen Hearts by Michele Castleman. Finding the thief who stole a precious heirloom will become Ella's first move in a dangerous game of wits that exposes family secrets and could lead to her family's financial ruin. (978-1-63679-733-5)

Synchronicity by J.J. Hale. Dance, destiny, and undeniable passion collide at a summer camp as Haley and Cal navigate a love story that intertwines past scars with present desires. (978-1-63679-677-2)

Wild Fire by Radclyffe & Julie Cannon. When Olivia returns to the Red Sky Ranch, Riley's carefully crafted safe world goes up in flames. Can they take a risk and cross the fire line to find love? (978-1-63679-727-4)

Writ of Love by Cassidy Crane. Kelly and Jillian struggle to navigate the ruthless battleground of Big Law, grappling with desire, ambition, and the thin line between success and surrender. (978-1-63679-738-0)

Back to Belfast by Emma L. McGeown. Two colleagues are asked to trade jobs. Claire moves to Vancouver and Stacie moves to Belfast, and though they've never met in person, they can't seem to escape a growing attraction from afar. (978-1-63679-731-1)

The Breakdown by Ronica Black. Vaughn and Natalie have chemistry, but the outside world keeps knocking at the door, threatening more trouble, making the love and the life they want together impossible. (978-1-63679-675-8)

The Curse by Alexandra Riley. Can Diana Dillon and her daughter, Ryder, survive the cursed farm with the help of Deputy Mel Defoe? Or will the land choose them to be the next victims? (978-1-63679-611-6)

Exposure by Nicole Disney & Kimberly Cooper Griffin. For photographer Jax Bailey and delivery driver Trace Logan, keeping it casual is a matter of perspective. (978-1-63679-697-0)

Hunt of Her Own by Elena Abbott. Finding forever won't be easy, but together Danaan's and Ashly's paths lead back to the supernatural sanctuary of Terabend. (978-1-63679-685-7)

Perfect by Kris Bryant. They say opposites attract, but Alix and Marianna have totally different dreams. No Hollywood love story is perfect, right? (978-1-63679-601-7)

Royal Expectations by Jenny Frame. When childhood sweethearts Princess Teddy Buckingham and Summer Fisher reunite, their feelings resurface and so does the public scrutiny that tore them apart. (978-1-63679-591-1)

Shadow Rider by Gina L. Dartt. In the Shadows, one can easily find death, but can Shay and Keagan find love as they fight to save the Five Nations? (978-1-63679-691-8)

Tribute by L.M. Rose. To save her people, Fiona will be the tribute in a treaty marriage to the Tipruii princess, Simaala, and spend the rest of her days on the other side of the wall between their races. (978-1-63679-693-2)

Wild Wales by Patricia Evans. When Finn and Aisling fall in love, they must decide whether to return to the safety of the lives they had, or take a chance on wild love in windswept Wales. (978-1-63679-771-7)

Can't Buy Me Love by Georgia Beers. London and Kayla are perfect for one another, but if London reveals she's in a fake relationship with Kayla's ex, she risks not only the opportunity of her career, but Kayla's trust as well. (978-1-63679-665-9)

Chance Encounter by Renee Roman. Little did Sky Roberts know when she bought the raffle ticket for charity that she would also be taking a chance on love with the egotistical Drew Mitchell. (978-1-63679-619-2)

Comes in Waves by Ana Hartnett. For Tanya Brees, love in small-town Coral Bay comes in waves, but can she make it stay for good this time? (978-1-63679-597-3)

Dancing With Dahlia by Julia Underwood. How is Piper Fernley supposed to survive six weeks with the most controlling, uptight boss on earth? Because sometimes when you stop looking, your heart finds exactly what it needs. (978-1-63679-663-5)

The Heart Wants by Krystina Rivers. Fifteen years after they first meet, Army Major Reagan Jennings realizes she has one last chance to win the heart of the woman she's always loved. If only she can make Sydney see she's worth risking everything for. (978-1-63679-595-9)

Skyscraper by Gun Brooke. Attempting to save the life of an injured boy brings Rayne and Kaelyn together. As they strive for justice against corrupt Celestial authorities, they're unable to foresee how intertwined their fates will become. (978-1-63679-657-4)

Untethered by Shelley Thrasher. Helen Rogers, in her eighties, meets much younger Grace on a lengthy cruise to Bali, and their intense relationship yields surprising insights and unexpected growth. (978-1-63679-636-9)

You Can't Go Home Again by Jeanette Bears. After their military career ends abruptly, Raegan Holcolm is forced back to their hometown to confront their past and discover where the road to recovery will lead them, or if it already led them home. (978-1-636790644-4)

A Wolf in Stone by Jane Fletcher. Though Cassilania is an experienced player in the dirty, dangerous game of imperial Kavillian politics, even she is caught out when a murderer raises the stakes. (978-1-63679-640-6)

The Devil You Know by Ali Vali. As threats come at the Casey family from both the feds and enemies set to destroy them, Cain Casey does whatever is necessary with Emma at her side to bury every single one. (978-1-63679-471-6)

The Meaning of Liberty by Sage Donnell. When TJ and Bailey get caught in the political crossfire of the ultraconservative Crusade of the Redeemer Church, escape is the only plan. On the run and fighting for their lives is not the time to be falling for each other. (978-1-63679-624-6)

One Last Summer by Kristin Keppler. Emerson Fields didn't think anything could keep her from her dream of interning at Bardot Design Studio in Paris, until an unexpected choice at a North Carolina beach has her questioning what it is she really wants. (978-1-63679-638-3)

StreamLine by Lauren Melissa Ellzey. When Lune crosses paths with the legendary girl gamer Nocht, she may have found the key that will boost her to the upper echelon of streamers and unravel all Lune thought she knew about gaming, friendship, and love. (978-1-63679-655-0)

Undercurrent by Patricia Evans. Can Tala and Wilder catch a serial killer in Salem before another body washes up on the shore? (978-1-636790669-7)